D1010594

All The
Good Little Girls
Keep Quiet

K. Kibbee

All The Good Little Girls Keep Quiet

This book is a work of fiction. The characters, places, incidents, and dialogue are the product of the author's imagination and are not to be construed as real, or if real, are used fictitiously. Unless other intended, any resemblance to actual events, locales, or persons, either living or dead, is purely coincidental.

Copyright © 2020 by Kristine Kibbee

All rights reserved. No part of this book may be used or reproduced in any manner whatsoever without the prior written permission of the publisher, except in the case of brief quotations embodied in critical articles and reviews.

For more information, to inquire about rights to this or other works, or to purchase copies for special educational, business, or sales promotional uses please write to:

publishing press

Incorgnito Publishing Press. LLC
1651 Devonshire Lane
Sarasota, FL 34236

contact@incorgnitobooks.com

FIRST EDITION

Printed in the United States of America

ISBN: 978-1-944589-72-1

10 9 8 7 6 5 4 3 2 1

For Mama

CONTENTS

CHAPTER ONE

My life is over. Come sun-up, every soul west of the Mississippi is gonna know just how redneck the Abernathy clan is. I'm gonna lose my last spitball of dignity, my sack lunches to bullies for all eternity, and worst of all, my best friend, Henry. His momma's already threatenin' to get herself some big-city lawyer, and even though I figure she'll drink any lawyerin' money down before it hits the bank, I know damn well that she's gonna crow about it all over town anyhow. I can already hear folks at the Piggly Wiggly whisperin' about us in the aisles... stuffin' fat bundles of okra in their shiny shoppin' baskets and sayin', "Oh, you know those Abernathys, they'd bare-knuckle box a gator for bait worms and most likely win. They probably pick their teeth with possum bones."

And I don't have it in me to cuss 'em no more. Maybe they're right. Maybe my family is just a bunch of stupid, loud-mouth hicks with nothin' better to do than hol' up in this crappy little town forever... never seein' a blue ox, or a buildin' as tall as an Ozark mountain, or the never-endin' ocean spillin' right off the edge of the map. Maybe they're just sick of the Abernathys with their little pea brains and their big, flyin' fists. And maybe I am too.

I lay in bed after the sun went down, wishin' on every single star up in the moody blue sky that I weren't born an Abernathy. I probably wish on a couple of the little ones twice, figurin' it's best to cover all my bases. A few times I even squeeze my eyes closed real tight and then pop 'em back open, hopin' to see a different room, in a different house, in a different town. But I never do. I just kept tossin' and turnin' and cursin' my fate. I must'a made a good bit of racket doin' that too, because Mama comes peekin' her head into my room. She asks, "You up?" but I don't answer back. I just roll over onto my side and leave her with only a huff and my back end for company. Of course, she's an Abernathy, so she's accustomed to the company of asses. She just waltzes right in and perches at my bedside. Then she reaches out and starts featherin' my hair. I pull away.

"You know, Olive; it ain't the end the world," she tells me.

I've got a strong hankerin' to swing 'round and give her back what she gave Henry's momma, but instead I just whisper, "Yeah, it *is*," real mean-like.

I can still feel her hand lyin' near my spill of hair. Her fingers are inchin' towards it again, like a Daddy Long-legs creepin' across my bed, as she reckons, "It'll be better tomorrow. You'll see."

"I'll see?!" shoots outta me as I flip over to face her. I can feel my cheeks flushin' good enough to light up all those inky dark corners of my bedroom as I keep on, "Only thing I'm gonna see tomorrow is a buncha kids chuckin' tater tots at me, and callin' me redneck trash.

And you know what I ain't gonna see? I ain't gonna see my best friend, 'cuz you done socked him outta my life forever. From now on, my life's gonna be a lonely, never-endin' shitstorm!"

Mama sucks in a breath. I can see her chest heave. I'm half expectin' her to clock me too, but she comes back quiet, and says, "honey, *life's* a damn shitstorm. But love's the eye."

I can't help it. I snort. I snort like a pig whose dinner bell got rung when there ain't nothin' in the trough. I'm fixin' to tell her that I'm only wallowin' in the shitstorm that *she* stirred up, when Papa breaks in wonderin', "Just what are you two on about?" and quick as a wink, Mama's up on her feet and scootin' right outta my room. I think maybe I hear her snifflin', but I don't care. Papa though, he follows her out and returns a spell later, waggin' his finger through the pitch.

"You mind yourself Olive," he spits. "Your Mama was defendin' *you*."

Pfft. "She's just bein' her ornery, redneck self," I says. Then I size up his shadow, thinkin' about how he still looks ten feet tall... same way he did when I was a little girl and he'd hoist me up on his shoulders so high that my pigtails brushed the heavens. "Why you love her anyways?" I ask him.

The shadow stays still, but somehow gets bigger, as it whispers, "Child, that woman's got a heart the size of an Ark. You ain't got no clue how many sacrifices she's made for you." Then the shadow peels itself right up off

11

the floor and lets my creaky door fill its empty spot in with darkness. The room gets real col' right then, and I pull my covers up tight to my chin, but it don't help. I ain't got a life, I ain't got Henry, and now I ain't got Papa either. All I got's that scrapbook tucked up under my mattress that's fulla adventures I ain't never gonna have. I sneak my arm outta the covers and fish down deep in the bedframe until I feel its cover brush my finger. I've about got a good grip on it when a butt-puckerin' ring sings through the rafters and spooks me up outta bed. The phone don't never ring before the rooster crows. Never with good news, anyhow.

I hear footsteps kick up downstairs and imagine Papa chasin' down that ringer in his stockin' feet. Right at that same time—*poof*—my little devil friend pops up to say hello and goads me into chasin' it too. He's bouncin' good on my shoulder as I tiptoe from my room, fast as I can manage, and scoop up the hallway phone just as the third ring trails off. It's one of those stupid clam-lookin' phones and I've gotta cup it like a bruised butt-cheek in one hand while I cover up the mouthpiece with my other. Me and the devil lean in as a sorta familiar-soundin' voice trickles outta the headset and says, "Hello? Missus Abernathy?"

My eyes bug out. My heart pitter-patters. The devil's whisperin' some rotten nonsense about fakin' like I'm Mama, but a click and Papa's voice sayin', "Hello?" save the day.

"Oh, yes, hello," says the other voice, soundin' good and befuddled. "Is this… Mister Abernathy?"

Papa says, "Yes, this is Jim," like he ain't sure that's his name at all.

Then somebody coughs. I couldn't tell ya who. But the man talkin' to Papa sounds quieter when he starts up again. He says he's Doctor Cummin's, from Saint Vincent's. He says he spoke with Mama earlier, and Papa does a slow *Mmmm hmmm*, that tells me he knows all about it. I realize just then that this is the same shrimpy, unibrow Doc who read me the riot act in Gramps' room earlier today. My shoulder devil says I oughta pipe in with some sorta fart noise, or call him *Doctor Cumquat*, but I hush him as the Doc starts fumblin' and stumblin' over his words. He's sputterin' fierce as Gramps' Olds as he goes on, "Well, your wife, Missus Abernathy, and I, we spoke…, and I told her about the blood clot we found. . . the one set off by your father-in-law's accident. And the… umm… need for surgery?"

Papa does another *Mmmm hmmm*. Sounds like he's garglin' gravel.

"Well, we… we can't. There won't be a need to do the surgery. I'm afraid… I'm afraid that the clot migrated quicker than we'd expected, and Mister Barton… well, he passed during the night."

There's a sound just then. And it don't come from the phone. It pops right outta my chest. I know it for sure, because I feel it there too. It feels like some grizzly fella with fists as big as boxin' gloves and nails in his knuckles punchin' me square in the ribs. And that sound… that crackin' sound, I expect it's the sound of my heart breakin' in two. I guess Mama's right. That little split at the top of everybody's heart means it was already half-way broken when God put it in there. But Lord, how it hurt when the job got finished off. I can barely get that phone back in its cradle without cryin' out loud, and then I just fall back against the wall and slide into a little puddle on the floorboards. Them tears come hot and heavy, and I get to cryin' so that I can't breathe. My ears, and my eyes, and my nose get all gummed up and I feel near passin' out, so I come up for air and blow my nose on my PJ sleeve. Right then I hear it... a sad sorta holler like a far-off cry from the loneliest critter on earth. But it ain't no critter. It's Mama.

I creep down the hall, snifflin' my way past the twins' door on tippy-toes, and inch into the light streamin' up through the banister spindles from downstairs. It falls across my feet like prison bars as I hunker down and press my face to the railin'. From there I can see Papa cradlin' Mama on the couch. She's rockin' and yowlin', and he's holdin' her body tight. Part of me wants to race down the stairs and hug her up in my arms. Part of me's scared to. So I just set there with my cheeks scissored between the musty oak bars, and watch. For a long time she just rocks, and cries, and cries, and rocks, while Papa pets her real gentle. Then, about the time my face is gettin' numb, she peers up at Papa with veiny eyes and says, "Dammit. Damn that girl," and it feels like the grizzly boxer fella come back for round two.

I didn't think there was any heart left to break, but

then again, I'm just a stupid Abernathy. Just a stupid Abernathy with no friends, no life, no Papa, and now no Gramps. But hell, I got a Mama. A Mama who hates me... more than ever.

I pull myself up on those spindles and scoot out of their shadow. I clomp past the boys' door, never mindin' the tippy-toes, and pass over my bedroom's threshold for the last time. I don't want no part of bein' an Abernathy no more. I don't wanna live in this damn museum. I don't wanna stay a little kid forever. Aunt Rosemary was right—Mama just wanted some good little girl who never fussed or spoke her mind or grew a level inch—and that ain't me.

I wrestle on my bluejeans, pack my knapsack to the gills with everythin' that a hobo on the lam is gonna need, and I don't take one single, solitary thing that reminds me I'd ever been an Abernathy in the first place; save my scrapbook. I wedge it deep down in the bottom of my pack, and tell it that we're orphans now... orphans who are gonna eat up the world and leave nothin' but shit behind 'em. Then I crack my window, creep on out to the porch roof, and shimmy down Mama's wisteria trellis. I squish all them little violet buds on my way down. I squish each and every one. And I don't give a good goddamn. I race off into the night and never even look back to see the bent petals. I don't wanna cry no more. I just want to leave this life in the rearview.

* * *

Somethin' about cuttin' through the dark makes a body feel free. I walk smack-dab down the middle of our cruddy ole road like I'm the cock of the walk. Weren't no headlights for miles, and no folks to tell me I'm a damn fool for goin' outside the lines. Matter of fact, the crickets cheer me on at a dull thunder, probably glad for some excitin' new stories to tell. I'm feelin' pretty fine, driftin' along to that cricket song and the crunch of my sneaker heels on the road to my new life... right up until the point where I realize I don't know where the heck I'm headed. My stomach starts percolatin', which Mama always said was either the flu, love, or nerves. Bullheaded women of adventure never get the flu, and my heart's too broke to go lovin' much of anythin', so it has to be nerves. My crunchy steps stop and my moxie dribbles right out there onto the ground. Suddenly the dark wants to swallow me up. Suddenly I hear little scritches, and screeches, and rustlin' critters kickin' up all around me. I think about Papa's Bayou Devil stories... think of all of the nasty monsters he's shooed out from under my bed and sent off to live in the swamp. I think about turnin' around, but only for a second. Powerful upset as my gut is, I decide that half of it come from them nasty brussels sprouts Mama's always crammin' down my throat. She's piled me up with mountains of 'em over the years, and I expect they've all bedded down in my belly, tryin' to sour my insides. Wouldn't surprise me if they were poison.

I spit at the ground, thinkin' I could taste brussels, or sprout, or whichever part was the nastiest. Then I peer out at the night with whittled-down eyes, half-darin' any critter to cross my path. The man in the moon is hung way up in the sky like a silvery dime simperin' down at me, and I flare my nostrils at him. He's had it in for me ever since me and Henry convinced my dumbass twin brothers, Pete and Wyatt, that NASA wouldn't hire astronauts with a lactose intolerance because the moon was made outta cheese. Just thinkin' about that makes me laugh out loud, and I'm pretty sure that I catch him glarin' back at me. But then all of a sudden what's left of my hard little heart starts fussin' about Henry. I conjure up a teeny-weeny Henry in my brain, probably no bigger than a trouser button, and watch him ridin' that ole yellow coffin of a school bus with no one to sit by, no one to tell him that his ugly ole suspenders look nice; no one to give his Twinkies to. Damn his black-eyed momma. I've gotta say goodbye.

I don't wanna see it; don't even wanna ever hear its name again, but Saint Vincent's Hospital rises from the grave as I slink into town. I try not to look over there. I try to take the side streets and the alleys to Henry's house, but it's like a spook standin' in the corner, moanin' at me, and I can't help myself from peekin' over. I've never seen it at night before, all lit up like it is, all monstrous and stuck with burnt orange bulbs that make it look like it's on fire. I imagine Gramps' col' body layin' in there, maybe burnin' in one of those orangey fires until he ain't nothin' but a little Tupperware container fulla ashes and dentures. I think I've cried myself dry of tears already that night, but my shriveled little eyeballs squeeze out a few more for Gramps and then drop them all along Buckeye Street, and halfway down 14th avenue. The last few trickle out on the Wormwood's back patio, where I stand tossin' pebbles at Henry's bedroom window. I'm on my third handful when I see his fat fingers poke through the blinds and make a part no bigger than a stick of Juicy Fruit. One of his squinty little eyes peeks through the hole he's made, and I start wavin' up a storm and jumpin' all around, half-wonderin' what kinda nincompoop I look like, and half wonderin' if he can see me at all in the dark. Once he pulls up the blinds and slaps his cheaters on, he lights like the fourth of July, and I feel warm inside for the first time in a long time.

Now Henry's house is ole as the hills. He swore he once found cave drawin's and Spam that predated Christ down in the basement. I don't know about all that malarkey, but I *do* know that the ole shack's been painted, and repainted, and painted over top of that. It's probably seen more brush-strokes than all the houses on his block put together, and the window jambs are sealed tighter than Audy Kaufman's coveralls. But lucky for me, Henry took a chisel to his bedroom window two summers back and pried it open so that he could shimmy outta there when his momma was on a bender and lookin' to cuddle him to death. It opens smooth as butter now, and in no time at all his mussed-up head is peeked out over the sill with cowlicks stickin' every which-way.

He's smilin' bigger than I think I ever seen him smile

and I can see his retainer wire strung around his teeth like Saturn's ring. He crows, "Hey! Olive!" louder than he probably oughta, but I don't have it in me to shush him. I just gallop over to his window, probably lightin' up the whole town with my pearly grin, and shine on as he asks me what I'm doin' there.

"I'm runnin' away," I tells him, bustin' my buttons. His cheesy grin melts. "What'chya mean, runnin' away? To where?"

I ain't thought on it much, but the word, "Everywhere," comes right outta me, and feels good on the tongue. Then I fess up that his momma hates me and my whole family now, and that I ain't never gonna see him again anyway. I come to say goodbye.

"Goodbye?" sounds lonely comin' outta him, and all the sudden he looks the same way he did when he was standin' beside his Daddy's coffin in a suit that was five times too big for him and holdin' his momma up like she was a piece of cut timber about to topple over. Then he says it again, "Goodbye," and somehow it sounds even lonelier this time.

I can't think what to say, so I tell him, "I'll send you postcards," even though we both know it ain't worth a damn.

He echoes, "Postcards," back and I reckon every solo word that comes outta his mouth sounds lonesome tonight. Then he just stares out into the yonder, maybe wishin' he could think up some friends to go with that word, and lets his jaw hang open. He's got a nice crop of grasshoppers millin' in the fissures of moonlight beneath his window and they chirp us a little ditty to fill in the silence.

I wish he'd smile again. I don't wanna remember him this way. I turn and watch the skyline too, hopin' for a fallin' star, and when I wind my head back to face him, he gives me this look like a whole mess of stars just landed right in his shirt pocket. He ducks outta the window frame and starts dashin' all over his room. It's clean as a whistle, so he ain't trippin' over clothes and overdue library books like I was, but I can recognize it plain as day. He's packin' to run away.

I probably should've stopped him. I probably should've hollered, "Henry, no! You gotta stay here. It's safer here," but I didn't. I just watched him pack his little blue gingham suitcase fulla stuff like toothpaste and trousers and underwear and thought how stinky my single pair of drawers was gonna be a week from now. I expect he fit half his room in that case, all puzzle-pieced together in neat little sections, and then he zips it up tight, tromps over to his window, and says, "I'm comin' with you!"

"Well, duh," probably ain't the most gracious reply, but it's honest. I scooch back a step or two from his window and watch him climb out like he was crawlin' off the back of a Clydesdale. He hits the burnt ryegrass under the sill with a huff and I find myself wonderin' how long a pasty townie boy who thinks macramé is an acceptable hobby can survive in the wild. Still, Henry's dodged rabid muskrats and limey bayou snakes aplenty and always made it out alive. Hell, one time me and him even slapped on a couple of Gramps' scratchy tweed suits, reasoned we could out-detectify Sherlock Holmes, and set out in search of the Bayou Devil. And when the sun sunk like a broke yolk into the swamp and we got all turned around, it was Henry who led us to safety. So as he stands before me, straightenin' his fussy tweed vest and his teensy glasses, I reckon that Papa was right... sometimes the bestest and strongest things are hidin' in the smallest packages. I don't tell Henry that though. I figure that if his head gets big, he'll just have more to carry. And the way he's schleppin' along with that fat suitcase, a fat head's the last thing we need. We're only a block or two from his house before I wonder, "Why'd you bring that big thing anyhow?"

He shrugs under the fuzzy moonbeam from a streetlamp so that it looks like he's bein' sucked up into a spaceship or somethin'. Soon as he scuttles outta that tractor-beam, he fesses up, "It's all I got," and then barks, "besides, it's not like I knew what to pack for. You ain't said word one about where we're headed."

I trail off, "Yeah, well..." kickin' on down the sidewalk, "I s'pect that's 'cuz I ain't quite sure. I didn't have much time to think about it with my Aunt Rosemary turnin' up outta the blue, my Mama deckin' your momma, and Gramps dyin' and all."

Henry's heels click to a stop and the sound of that ole slug of a suitcase trailin' behind him dries up on the spot. "Your Gramps died?"

I don't stop. I don't look back. I just keep walkin'. I mutter, "Yeah," so soft that I think it might get carried away on the night wind, but Henry snags it. Then he just drops his bag where he stands and comes runnin' up on me. He don't even wait for me to turn around. He just hits my backside with every bit of his eighty-six pounds and wraps his fat, freckled arms over mine. I can smell Vic's Vapo-Rub and spearmint toothpaste waftin' up off him as he squeezes me with all his might. Truth told, it felt like he could crumple a car like a tin can just then. His arms ring the tears right outta me and as I drain into a little puddle beside 'em on the sidewalk, he holds on tight to keep me from trailin' down into the gutter. Then he sets there, squeezin' still, as I bawl my fool head off, and he don't say a word. He just holds tight through all my waterworks and thunderin', until the storm's passed. And then wouldn't ya know it... it starts rainin'.

I tell you what. there ain't nothin' quite like a southern summer storm. It's like an ice cube got drug down your swampy-hot spine. The air gets soupy, your shorthairs stand on end, and you feel like a flea on a dog, watchin' God beat the heavens black and blue. It's fierce, and it's nasty, and it don't give a shit if you got every bit of your life packed into some hand-me-down, paper-thin knapsack and no roof to cover your head. But it's also short. Mama says southern storms are like teenaged girls—moody as all get-out and never content to stay in one place for more than five minutes. I think about Mama for long enough to get cross and for the storm to pass, all the while perched under the fat lip of Henry's suitcase. After the good Lord finishes throwin' a tantrum and cryin' himself dry, I get a good look at my stuff. A pair of Papa's hand-me-down tube-socks and my favorite sweatshirt look like a giant's used 'em as snot rags, but praise Jesus, my scrapbook's dry as a bone. I haul it out after a wary peek at the heavens, and crack it open to page one.

"Where you wanna go first?" I ask Henry.

He's wringin' out a shirt cuff and just says, "Huh?" as I'm makin' googly-eyes at a lighthouse off the coast of Maine. My postcard says it's got an ornery ghost livin' in it, but that's probably a load of hooey. Still, I feel like Henry oughta be more excited, so I tug at the drier of his two shirt cuffs and pull him down so that he can see all the wonders waitin' for us out on the open road.

"We gotta decide where to go first," I tells him, pettin' that lighthouse. Then I point to a card on the opposite page, from Kansas. It's got a bus-sized ball of twine on the front that looks like it could topple our farmhouse, slick as a bowlin' pin. "Think how many hay bales you could string with that," I say.

Henry starts blatherin' some borin'-ass business about transportation, and *stratergizin'*, and "gettin' our ducks in a row," so I make like I'm yawnin', and flip to the next page. This one's chock-fulla cards peppered with steam engines and slick-lookin' fellas in shiny-billed conductor hats. I flick my finger at a card from Albuquerque with an open boxcar on its front. It's got oceans of red clay spillin' across it and I imagine me and Henry swingin' our bare legs just above the rail while the sun's bakin' 'em like chicken drumsticks.

"We're gonna ride the rails," I cluck, thinkin' about my meaty parts stuck on New Mexico's rotisserie. "Just like Gran and Gramps did."

"Hmph," is all I get outta Henry. It's the same *hmph* he makes every time I try to get him to eat raw crawdads, climb a prickly monkey tree, or even leave his house without his sneaker laces in perfect bunny-ear knots. He always gives me some flim-flam about thinkin', "this is a bad idea," or "you're gonna get us whooped," or, "I'm pretty sure that's illegal," but I ain't got him killed yet. A little beat up, maybe, a broken bone or two... but nothin' that couldn't be mended. Hell, Mama'd fixed up bigger messes with her ole mint-green Singer.

So, I give Henry a good slap on the back, stow my scrapbook, and rise up, feelin' tough as a pearly possum claw. Mama might'a aimed to turn me into some sorta wax creature in her museum, but to my eye, that lily-white hand tuggin' Henry up and onto tomorrow was fierce as they come; wild as the wide-open, and ready to tear up the world.

"Let's get!" I says, but even in the pale light of the silvery moon I can see his face screwin' up. I figure he's either about to call me a loon, or ask for a potty break. But he don't do neither. He just does another *huff* and takes hold of my fearsome hand. I lead the way from there; dodgin' sidewalk cracks and potholes that get bigger, the closer we get to the poor part of town. All them purdy little picket-fenced dollhouses start fadin' to grey. We cross over to Bleaker Street, and they shrink down to boot. Their porches get saggy and their yards fill up with broken toys. One house, a shotgun with a crooked roof that looks like it's been sat on by a giant, has a big ole 4x4 pickup parked right in the middle of the front lawn. I peer over at that jacked-up beast, with its mud flaps big as screen doors, and think about ridin' through town in Mee-maw's jalopy Studebaker wagon two summers ago. We got stuck behind some fellah in a truck just like that one and she was cursin' up a storm. She told me to plug Wyatt's ears and then she sass-wagged her head and whispered, "Guaran-damn-tee-ya any man with a truck that big's got a pecker the size of a pig's tail."

I think I might'a told Henry the story already, but I tell it again, and he makes the same kinda nervous laugh he does when Papa jokes about castratin' the cattle. But I shush him up right quick, because we're creepin' up on the Calhoon's house. It's a big whopper of a thing, with fake Roman columns and an astroturf yard like the one the Brady Bunch folks've got. It looks plum out of place down here among the shacks, but everybody stops to look at it, and I expect that's what Missus Calhoon likes. She's got the yard decked out with them creepy little statues of kids playin', 'cept these ones are all down on their knees, prayin' under a big cross that looks about to fall on 'em. A couple of plaster girls, froze on the sidelines, have fingers pulled to their lips like they're forever hushin' everybody who looks 'em over. I guess God and Missus Calhoon like their little angels quiet. I guess if they can't talk, they won't fuss about everythin' there bein' fake.

I make eyes at that purple Firebird sittin' in the driveway and elbow Henry in the rib. "We sure could use a cool ride like that. You think Mayor Rowdy's got any filin' he needs done?"

Henry ain't got nothin' but a snort to give back to me. I'm sure he's busy figurin' which of us he'd less like to see shovin' everythin' from A-Z in Rowdy's drawers. Then he gets kinda squirmy, so I kick up the pace and leave the Calhoon's angels to keep watch over the fake grass. Before I know it, we're comin' up on the rail yard, and I spy a ruby red boxcar, prime for the hoppin'.

"That one," I croon, levelin' my finger at it. It's got a wide-open door promisin' sweet, sweet freedom, and I feel Gramps' hobo blood bubblin' up in my veins as I duck under a hole in the fence and start gallopin' towards it. Henry's hot on my heels, sputterin' my name quieter than the gravel crunch. I manage to pretend I can't hear him as I hopscotch over two sets of iron tracks, but he starts gettin' louder with every stride, so I glance back to find him shakin' like a fig leaf in a twister.

"This is a *baaaad* idea, Olive," rattles outta him. Extra emphasis on the *baaaad*. He's still trailin' along behind me though, so I just pull a finger up to my mouth slick as the library lady and keep on keepin' on. He makes a few more fusses along the way, but they float up into the night sky and get gobbled up by the darkness. Ain't nothin' but silence left as I lay hands on my steely ruby jewel. She's cool, and hard, and splattered stem to stern with rail grit and oil stank, but I love her in an instant. Henry kicks up with his yammerin' about how we's, "gonna get caught and end up in jail," but I couldn't give two shits.

I promise Henry, "It's gonna be fine. Ruby wants to show us the world, and I mean to let her." And I say it so certain, that even I believe it. Then I take up Ruby's wrought-iron handle and hoist myself inside her belly. It smells like fresh-cut timothy hay in there, and I can even see a few straw reeds left scattered about. "This was a hay car!" I tell Henry. He makes a grunt, and then a grumble at my backside as he joins me in Ruby's gut.

"I guess I'd sooner be in the car fulla what cows eat than the stuff that comes out after they do."

My eyes bug, thinkin' of Papa's big ole spring-time truckloads of manure that Mama said smelled like "money and politicians." That stank used to creep into my room at night, worm inside my nostrils, and give me nightmares about piles of poop big as the Pyramids of Giza. "Yup, hay's much better," I reckon, clompin' off to explore Ruby's dark corners. I can see somethin' big lurkin' on the north edge, and a little quiver works up my spine as my footsteps echo all around the hollow hull. Henry sees it too, and comes creepin' up behind me just about the time I make out the four furry corners of a hay bale. "Hey look, we got somewhere to sleep," I say.

Slap, zip, bam, whip, and Henry's fished a pocketknife outta the nethers of his suitcase. He flips it open to what's

Gotta be the teeniest blade ever forged and stomps on over to our hay bale. A couple'a clips of twine later and we got ourselves a fine bed of straw, fit to rival the manger. I don't realize how beat I am until I lay back on that amber blanket and feel myself meltin' into it. I probably coulda slipped off to Nod right then and there, if Henry hadn't started cluckin' about, "What we gonna do Olive? What's the plan?"

Hell, I got plans. I always got plans. I got plans on top of plans. I got plans when I don't need plans, and plans in case those plans fall through. But tonight, I don't got much of nothin' besides a bunch of weary bones and a body rung out to nothin'. Still, I've dreamt myself inside this boxcar bound for everywhere so many times that I don't need any schemin', or calculatin', or brain juice left to reason, "We sleep 'til dawn, when the trainmen come, and wait for 'em to tug us into tomorrow."

CHAPTER TWO

Mama named me Olive on account of some peculiar cravin' she had when I was in her belly for them little green olives with the red thing that sticks out the top like a lizard tongue. In all my life I ain't never seen her eat one of those olives, and sometimes I think she made the whole story up just as an excuse to give me this God-awful name. Other kids at school had Christian names like Adam, or Abel, or Mary. Some kids even had smarmy pirate names or movie character names. A girl in my seventh-grade biology class was named Sloan, which is without doubt the coolest name ever. But not one, not a single damn one, was named after some stupid food that people only ate at fancy dinner parties or put in their potato salads.

Times when I was hole up in my room, hatin' hard on Mama, I'd picture me poppin' right out of some ginger lady's coochie with a twist of red, lizard-tongue hair on my fat little head. Then I'd imagine a nurse who was too busy makin' googly-eyes at some handsome doctor gettin' me switched with Mama's real baby. I could see that nurse haulin' me in, all swaddled up and lookin' cute, and Mama forgettin' all about her own baby and just tellin' Papa that I looked like an Olive. They'd go on grinnin', none the wiser, as their real daughter was handed off to some freckle-faced lady who probably turned red as a beet whenever it sunned outside. But fact of the matter was, I didn't have any pretty red hair, or any pull with leprechauns, or any luck to speak of. And Mama's buck-wheat mop was always hangin' over to my soggy brown eyes to prove that I was hers. So I s'pose she named me Olive just to be contrary.

My brothers had normal enough names, but the story of how Mama picked 'em tickled her so that she retold it over and over again, which somehow made those names seem just as dreadful. By the time the boys were a year old, I could recite that stupid story down to the letter. I could even see Mama's baby blues swellin' up like fat Junebugs whenever she started up, "Oh, I tell you what, I was plum exhausted, havin' pushed out not one but two babies with heads the size of watermelons!"

Then she'd pat her brow, like she was fixin' to faint, and get all swoony as she crowed on, "And here, up shows this nurse, askin' for the babies names. Well, heavens to Betsy, I ain't even thought about namin' one lil' boy, let alone two! But there them little babies were, lookin' up at me, God, and all creation, and waitin' for their names. So I says to the nurse, 'I s'pose we oughta name 'em Pete and Wyatt, 'cuz that's as close to peace and quiet as I'm likely to get for the next eighteen years!'"

Boy-oh-boy, how Mama'd laugh, and laugh, and laugh her fool head off every time she told that story. Some-times I thought I could hear far-off coyotes howlin' along like they thought one of their kin was lost and callin' out for help. Sometimes I thought Mama heard them too. But Papa, he thought Mama's laugh was angel-song. Every soul in town with half a wit gave Mama the stink-eye whenever she sounded out her screechy-laugh, but Papa'd just smile on, big and wide. And whenever he laid eyes on her, it was like watchin' some fool who was watchin' some other fool about to do a magic trick. On soggy Sundays, when the rain boxed him indoors, he'd get that same goofy look in his eye and put on Glenn Miller records just so's he could waltz Mama across the floor like she was Ginger Rogers. She'd laugh her big ole laugh, and he'd say that his heart'd gone all wild in his chest like he'd "done swallowed a bullfrog." Then he'd chase her 'round the house like she was a chicken that flew the coop. She'd cluck, and flap, and make a big show of things like she didn't wanna be caught, even though everyone on God's green earth knew full well that she did.

Nights like those I'd just wander off and sit on the stoop, soakin' in the cricket song and the soft Southern twilight as the sun sank like a big ole biscuit into the bayou. Some nights I'd curse that godforsaken swamp with all its chiggers, and muskrats, and bitey skeeters, but other times I'd call it beautiful under my breath; just quiet enough so that no one else could hear.

Mind you, I grew up in the bayou. Ain't ever known nothin' but the bayou. While other kids were huggin' fistfuls of greasy quarters at the arcade and sneakin' out to watch that creepy-ass Michael Meyers tear people's faces off at Halloween, I was way out in bumfuck nowhere, shootin' gators with a slingshot just because Mama told me not to. Only escape I got from buggy, muggy Lafayette Proper is by way of all the stories folks told me on the Greyhound bus. Papa had to talk *real* sweet to the driver for a good month to get me a lift to school on that bus. He'd beat feet out to the end of the driveway any time he seen the steely beast rollin' down Indian River Highway and wave his arms like a scarecrow caught up in a twister. One time, Mama even sent him out there with one of her famous huckleberry pies, which she swore "sealed the deal."

Never made a lick of difference to me though. I'd just as soon avoid every dumb-bunny cheerleader and meat-head jock at that pit-stain of a school anyhow. I was over the moon when Principal Dunders said the bus wouldn't come way out to the sticks to pick me up no more. I near threw myself a damn party. But not Mama. No, never Mama. She got her panties in a twist and marched right down to General Lee Junior High, yowlin' loud as you could stand. She didn't get fierce with folks in town much at all—unless it had to do with me. And since most her wardrobe was made up of housecoats, she was quite a sight bustin' through those double doors in her Sunday dress. That thing was as green as a fresh corn stalk, and with her measly muscles pushin' out the fabric, she coulda passed for the Hulk's little sister. And I guess it did the trick 'cuz she got uppity ole Mister Dunders to bend the rules. I ain't never seen our principal so much as bend to pick up a tack off the floor, much less bend a rule. But somehow Mama done it. She got that big yellow behemoth steered twenty miles out of its way just to pick up lil' ole me. She'd beam every time it come rollin' down the road like she'd just parted the Red Sea and was watchin' the Israelites roll through. But them Egyptian folks musta thrown down some of the tacks that Mister Dunders never picked up because Mama's bus ended up with two flat tires not a week into makin' the caravan out to get me, and it never came out our way again.

Turns out, them tacks were the best thing that ever happened to me. Once Papa's month of pleadin' earned me a seat on the Greyhound bus that went past our farm on the I-90 bypass, I went from one borin' ole life to a thousand amazin' ones. At first, the huckleberry-pie-lovin' driver made me sit right up front with him, right behind his seat like some little baby gettin' a piggyback ride. I fussed and fretted about how I was nearly grown, but he'd just look up into that big rearview mirror of his and give me a fierce glare until I shut my maw. A day or two of that frustratin' business had me mutterin' some nasty names I'd heard my Uncle Ern use on occasion, which near got me kicked off the bus. Needless to say, I came the next mornin' totin' another of Mama's pies, this one stole fresh off the windowsill, which got me forgiveness from Huckleberry and a whoopin' from Mama.

Mama was right about one thing though, that "sweet pies make for sweet conversation" and sure enough, once Huckleberry had a few forkfuls in him, he loosened the reins along with his tongue and began tellin' me all about his travels across the country. He'd been as far west of the Mississippi as California and then back up to the lighthouse-dotted shores of Maine, all behind the wheel of a seventeen-ton passenger bus. Two weeks into my eighth-grade school year, he welcomed me on the bus with a smile wider than Mee-maw's backside and arched his Brillo-pad brows at my normal spot just behind the driver's seat.

* * *

"Ya don't gotta sit there today," he tells me, lookin' like the cat that ate the canary, "but I got a mighty fine tale I'll tell ya if ya do."

Boy, did Huckleberry have my number!

I plant my fanny on that bench seat before you can say *boo* and perch so far forward on the edge that any sudden stop for a varmint crossin' the road could splatter me right across the inside of his windshield. He seems plain tickled about it too. He eases back onto the main road real slow-like, peekin' at me in his sled of a rearview all the while. Then he makes like he's checkin' all his gauges and what-not, tappin' this and grumblin' at that, 'til I'm just about to crawl right outta my skin. I see his smile gettin' wider and wider in that mirror. His whole face is 99.9% smile by the time he finally croaks, "So you wanna hear this story or not?"

"I ain't sittin' up here for my health," I bark back, feelin' every bit as ornery as I sound. He sniggers. "Well, I was layin' up last night, listenin' to some ole Miles Davis records I got down there at the pawnshop, and I thinks, *hey... I bet that kid'd like to hear about the time I met ole Miles in that juke joint down on Bourbon Street back in the day.*"

"*You* met Miles Davis?"

"Sho 'nuf did. The very man himself. I tell you what... that was one cool cat. All slicked up, topped out, and lookin' like a million bucks. Fella coulda froze the Devil in a heatwave—he was *that* cool."

I moon into the yonder beyond the bus' windshield, imaginin' Miles Davis, cheeks all puffed up like a nut-packed chipmunk, tootin' away on his little brass trumpet. Good thing Mama and Papa were too damn cheap to buy a cassette player. I'd seen big, glossy albums with Mister Davis sweatin' his ebony ass across all their covers. There was somethin' about him... somethin' in his eyes that made me feel like he knew stuff. Stuff I wanted to know.

"*Wow*, Miles Davis. That's aces." I trail as rows of tall pines with tops fit to scrape the heavens bristle at us passin' by.

"Yup, *Miles Davis*. Even chatted him up too. Seemed like a real nice fella."

"Really?! You talked to him?"

Huckleberry nods, but his fat smile grows a little slimmer. He looks down at his lap like he's checkin' to see if he remembered to buckle his safety belt.

"Well," I says. "What'd he say?" Huckleberry peeks up again, this time with a snort. "Asked me to bring him a drink!"

"A drink?"

"A drink."

I puzzle for a moment and get real quiet, 'til Huck starts snortin' again. "Seems I was dressed like one of the help. He asked me for a Harvey Wallbanger, and I was fixin' to tell him my name weren't Harvey when I pieced it all together."

Now, I ain't never heard of no drink named Harvey, but apparently Huckleberry had, and he thought that was about the funniest thing anyone ever said in the history of the world. He just laughed his fool head off, all down Willow Road, past the general store and ole man Bixby's peach grove... all the way up to the I-90 turnoff where the farthest little crap-shack of a bus stop that the school would service stood waitin' for me. I could still hear his belly-rollin' laughter bouncin' around inside the bus as I waved goodbye from the side of the road. I ain't even sure he saw me, bellowin' like he was. But it was a nice sight watchin' his great, goofy face meltin' into the distance 'cuz the school bus driver who showed up next looked at me like she'd just smelled a dog turd.

This disagreeable ole mammy had been drivin' me to and from the primary school out near our farm since I was big enough to make a paper airplane, and yet she always looked me over like some stranger tryin' to hitch a ride. Maybe she was ticked that they changed her route.

Maybe she was tired of seein' my ugly mug. Maybe she just hated my family like everyone else in this town did and didn't want my likes on her bus.

"Mornin'," I says in my nice Sunday church voice.

She just grumbles, so I clomp down the aisle dodgin' gum wads, and textbooks, and Roger Hinkley's foot—which is plainly stickin' out there just to trip me.

Roger gives me a dirty sneer as I double-dutch past his size-6 Reebok. I decide not to turn around after I pass him 'cuz I know he's givin' my backside the evil eye. Meanwhile, the entire eighth-grade cheerleadin' squad is camped across two bench seats near the emergency side exit, gigglin' like magpies. One of the quieter ones looks up as I pass and turns up her perfect little nose. Apparently, she smells dog poo too.

It's all the same to me. I don't wanna sit with those chatterboxes anyhow. I make my way back to the ass-end of the bus, where all the kids with acne, and Dungeons and Dragons t-shirts, and wonky suspenders sit.

"Hey, Henry. New suspenders?"

"They were Dad's" pops outta Henry's mouth quiet as a church mouse, and I all the sudden feel like horseshit for askin'. His dad croaked about a year back, and if Henry Wormwood dressed and acted like a 70-year-ole crab apple before his ole man took a dirt nap, he was 90 now. We'd been thick as thieves since kindergarten, and in all that time he hadn't gone a single damn day without ironin' his drawers. Thinkin' back, I've gotta wonder if his momma bought him one of those teeny ironin' boards that they make for dumb little girls who wanna be house-wives. I glance at his white-bread hands as I slide into the seat beside him and imagine them all pudgy with baby fat and tryin' to grip the handle of some girly pink iron.

I manage to squeeze out, "They're nice," while makin' side-eyes at his dad's mousy brown suspenders, but the words stick in my throat like a burr. He just smiles his polite smile, the kind I seen him give folks at his pop's memorial, and his freckled nose tents up at the edges. Then we both get real quiet. Quiet enough that I can hear Roberta Higgins, two seats up from us, whisperin' to Becky Blevins about how she got felt up last night. My guts start to get real twisty, and the more Roberta goes on about "heavy pettin'" and the "tricky clasp" on her trainin' bra, the twistier they get. Meanwhile, poor Henry is grippin' his *Biology 110* book like a life raft, and his knuckles are turnin' pasty. Finally, I can't stand it no more.

"Hey, you ever heard of a drink called Harvey?" "A what?" Henry asks, not turnin' to look at me. "A drink," I says again. "A drink named Harvey."

Henry's grip on the book goes soft. "I... I don't think so," he stutters.

I laugh, but it comes out like what Mama calls "a tickled pig snort," and that near squishes Roberta's X-rated whisperin's. With her hushed up, I retell Huckleberry's story, makin' sure to be extra loud durin' all the best parts, which saves us both from squirmin' in our seats the whole ride to school. Henry laughs big belly laughs, probably on purpose too. I laugh louder still—a forced, awkward kind of laugh—as I get to thinkin' that Henry's drunk of a momma probably has every drink in creation memorized and all the ingredients tattooed across her eye-lids so that she can dream about booze even when she's sleepin'. We both keep on laughin' our canned laughs, and the bus driver looks us over like we're a couple of kooks when we finally thunder down the stairs and out the bus door. But like usual, we're the last ones off, so what do we care?

Henry cinches up his ole man bookbag tight on his shoulder as we fiddle-fart around in front of the school for another minute or two, waitin' for the stampede to die down. He glances at his papa's big ole wristwatch where it's hangin' off his spindly arm as the last of the kids skitter through the glass double doors at the front of the school. I think how puny his little bird-bones look under that big band as he fusses about bein' late even though we got a good ten minutes before the bell rings. But I can see his amber eyes wellin' up like sap-bubbles as they zing back and forth between me and those big doors like the Rapture might be comin', so I follow him in.

I smell burnt hot dogs and tapioca puddin' bleedin' in from the cafeteria as Henry toddles off to his first-period history class, wavin' goodbye all rushed-like. For a hot second, I think how he looks just like my kid brother Wyatt when the dumb little shit waits too long to take a piss and can't find a bathroom.

I call out, "See ya at lunch!" to Henry's backside, but he don't even turn to look at me. He just toddles down the echoey hallway, that big bookbag swayin' at his side like it means to knock him over.

I get out a little giggle, but it ain't even had a chance to stir the air when I hear, "You'd best get yourself to class, Olive Abernathy" barked at my backside. I don't even need to turn around. I know Missus Udd's voice sure as I'd know the Wicked Witch tryin' to sell me on a flyin' monkey. I'm pretty sure I can hear wings flappin' as she says my name a second time like I got cauliflower in my ears.

"Yes ma'am, I was just gettin' there," I promise, turnin' to face her. I draw my mouth up into a fakey grin as her bony white arms come into view. She's got them shiny, lacquered fingernails that some of the uppity ladies at our church got, and she's drummin' them on her folded forearms. They're about as blood-red as red gets, and I expect she could slice a kid's jugular with 'em if she had a mind to. No doubt she'd come for me first too. But she ain't got no time for me. Nobody around these parts does. That's what it means, bein' an Abernathy.

Missus Udd curls up her lip, and I feel like she might be about to do a pretty convincin' Elvis impression, but she just tells me, "Well, get to it then," and shoos me in the direction of Miss Beasley's English class, which I manage to scoot into just before the first-period bell rings. Miss Beasley's a nice enough lady, but she still gives me the eye as I take my seat, and I feel like a grade-A jerk as I settle into place. So, I listen to her extra intent as she goes on about Emily Dickinson, and Walt Whitman, and Robert Frost. She reads us a poem that Miss Dickinson wrote about flies buzzin' all around her dead self, and I think about a bloated possum carcass at the end of our driveway that Pete and Wyatt keep pokin' with a stick. I imagine all them flies swillin' around in the hot Southern sun, and my stupid brothers pokin' it, and pokin' it, and pokin' it. Then I imagine them harpoonin' it like a big ole blowfish and it poppin' open and splattin' them with its innards. I snigger out loud, and Miss Beasley gives me the eye again. I shut up.

I feel a little tug on my shoulder, like maybe the fat, sassy devil that sometimes sits there's got himself another urge, but when I crane my neck to tell him to hush up, I find Marcy Gibbons glarin' back at me. "Why you such a weirdo?" she hisses, squintin' her eyes like she's pushin' out a turd. "What's your problem?"

"Ain't got no problem," I say, tossin' my best constipated glare back.

She snaps her gum and pushes her eyes down to slivers. I wanna ask her if she just shit her drawers, but I just copy her until I can't barely see the bright red letterin' on her cheerleader uniform. Now I feel like a mole strainin' through the sunlight, but I don't give an inch. I keep my eyelids parted just enough to watch her passion-pink lips curl up as she says, "'S'not what I hear. I hear that you and your whole weird family have lice and eat chitlins all day long 'cuz you can't afford nothin' but pig guts." "WHAT. DID. YOU. JUST. SAY?"

"You heard me," she hisses, nice and quiet. "Lice 'n' chitlins."

Oh lordy, I was on my feet faster than a jackrabbit in June. Before Miss Beasley could even yowl out my name, I laid down a good right hook and clocked Marcy Gibbons smack in the jaw. I could feel each one of my knuckles notch up into her chin bone. I could hear her big head crack back. I could see the look of shock on her fat, stupid face as her bubblegum went flyin' into the air. And it was glorious.

Even as Miss Beasley marched me down the hall to Principal Dunders' office, I couldn't wipe the shit-eatin' grin off'a my face. She told me I'd "best stop that smilin' business," but the more I tried, the bigger my grin got. And I tell you what...after she plopped me down in the waitin' room, read off my rap sheet, and scooted on out of there, I seen her reflection backlit in the glass front of the office. Dammit if she wasn't smilin' too.

But I'll tell you who *wasn't* smilin'—Principal Dunders. He called me "a derelict," "a troublemaker," and a "ne'er-do-well," all in the same sentence. The way he come off, I was headed down a short dirt road with a manure pile waitin' at the end of it. His mealy mole-eyes fixed hard on me as he yammered on about my family "always caus-ing trouble" and "shaming this town." He says, "Olive," in this great, big voice that don't seem to fit him and his teeny hamster balls, "Olive, I know what you come from. I know what you and yours do. They instigate. They an-tagonize. They bring out the worst in folks. But you've gotta see your way clear of that. You've gotta push back all that blackness in your veins and try to be something better. Try to be somebody who's gonna make somethig' of themselves."

I beaver-bite my nails for a minute or two as his words are sinkin' down into me. I think up ten sassy things to say. I decide that nine of 'em aren't sassy enough. Then I tell him, "I *am* tryin' to make somethin' of myself. Can't ya see that I'm trainin' to be the next George Foreman? Just whiter and with lady bits."

He snorts. And not a good snort. "Have it your way, Miss Abernathy," he says. Then he starts grumblin' about my future workin' the street or, worse yet, at McDonald's as he rings Mama on the phone. I feel my guts percolatin' as he cups the receiver to his ear, and with every trill of that ringer, they bubble a little more. He keeps me pinned with his eyes all the while, but I can see the little flicks of fire in them growin' weaker and weaker as the seconds tick by with his call unanswered.

Before I know it, "Please don't answer, please don't answer" come burpin' up outta of my mouth like word vomit, and ole Dunders' fire kicks up again.

"You shush up!" spooks me straight as he slams the receiver down. "Don't you think for one second that you aren't gonna get your comeuppance for slugging that poor little Gibbons girl!"

Then he whips out this fat file, plops it down on his desk, and starts thumbin' through all manner of chicken-scratched reports with my name peppered through 'em. He taps one of the sheets like it's an X on a damn treasure map, hoots, "Uh-huh!" and then dances his fingers across that keypad on his phone again. This time it's answered on the first ring. I praise Jesus right then and there when I hear a familiar lady's voice come creepin' out of the receiver, followed right thereafter by Gramps'. And not twenty minutes later, I'm lookin' at the ole scallywag himself, rollin' right up to the school steps in his big ole boat of an Oldsmobile. The thing looks fresh waxed, shinin' like a new dime, and as the driver's side door yawns open, a creak comes spillin' out that coulda deafened folks five towns over.

"Well, what's that lil' shit done this time?" Gramps barks as he climbs outta the Olds with an unlit stogie clamped between his lips. Principal Dunders just stares, mouth hangin' open, so Gramps adds in, "Larceny? Malicious mischief? Homicide?" and then does a downright miserable job of hidin' the chuckle that comes afterwards. Dumb Dunders screws his face up into a scowl, which

I expect is the same kinda look he gives sugary cakes, muddy knees, and Mrs. Dunders any time she asks him for a smooch. And he keeps on scowlin' as he tells Gramps, "Nothing quite so off-sides as that, but she did stir up a scuffle in Miss Beasley's class. Punched one of our star cheerleaders right in the face!"

"Did she now?"

Mister Dunders clamps a hand on my shoulder and testifies, "She did!" back at Gramps, with his eyes all swollen up like fat ticks. I can feel his clammy palm through the back of my t-shirt. It feels like creepy, crawly, mealy worms inchin' across my skin, and I get a powerful itch to swat at his fingers. I think Gramps can tell too, 'cuz he marches on over, snatches my arm, and tugs at me until Dunders' hand slides off like a wet noodle. Then he looks me over real good, twirlin' his fat cigar back and forth under his woolly mustache.

"She don't look beat up," he finally reckons, and when he does, I let a little snigger fly right up into his ear. I remember that just last week he'd told me, "Gettin' ole's mostly about findin' hair in your ears and forgettin' where you left everythin' else," so I wonder if he heard it until he gives me that look like when he's hidin' a fishin' magazine in his hymn book at church. But then he turns real stern and glances back at fat, dumb Dunders, who looks to be chewin' up his words before he spits them out. "I think she's the one who did all the hitting," he says.

Gramps grumbles low, like a beastie. Then he says, "Well, we'll get her on home to her mama and see what come of it," which seems to tickle Principal Dunders right down to his doughy marrow. He still sees fit to tell Gramps that I'm suspended from school for the rest of the week though, which is almost as big a treat as watchin' Marcy Gibbons' gum fly. And dammit if I don't tell Gramps exactly that, along with every other chitlin'-charged, lice-laced jab that prissy ole Marcy Gibbons hurled at me before I socked her. All the way home I replay my mean right hook and her frizzy head poppin' back over and over again. And Gramps... Gramps just laughs. He laughs until big, fat crocodile tears roll down his cheeks and he can't see proper enough to steer. For the first time in a zillion years, I'm tickled pink that the Olds tops out at all of 25 miles per hour. Every ten minutes or so the cars back up behind us, and Gramps flips 'em the bird in his rearview, but he keeps on laughin' all the while. And in the heat of my slow-burnin' spotlight, I near forget where we are headed. About the time we come rollin' up Indian River Highway—that's when the panic sets in.

Before I know it, I'm beggin', "C'mon Gramps, can't I go on over to Hubbard's with you?" But Gramps only sputters along with the Olds.

He says, "No way, kid, you'll cramp my style," and he's probably right. Ever since Gran passed and Gramps checked himself into Hubbard's Retirement Palace, he's like catnip for the ole biddies. I once saw him swan into that joint wearin' a fedora along with freshly-shined penny loafers, and I swear one of them horny ole bats threw her drawers at him. But he said he didn't have no time for "wrinkly ole ladies with five-o'clock shadows and 6-o'clock bedtimes," so he spent a fair amount of time shooin' them off. Matter of fact, much as he flapped his trap about what an ole gigolo he was, I never did once see him with a gal on his arm. I suspect he missed Gran more than he let on. I know I did. She was always scuttlin' around our kitchen, sneakin' nips of cookin' sherry and stealin' me cookies from Mama's Fort Knox of a cookie jar. Sometimes we'd cook together, and she'd cuss up a storm, callin' Betty Crocker all manner of foul names for puttin' purdy pictures beside recipes that looked nothin' like what came out of our oven. Once, she even caught Mama's ugly ole orange kitchen curtains on fire with some hushpuppy grease and took her sweet time dousin' 'em with faucet water. I'd fussed to her more than once about how they looked like baby poo, and even as Mama stomped in and shook the rafters with her wailin', Gran shot me a little wink on the sly. Not sure if Mama saw it. Not sure if it mattered. She coulda put the fear of God into an atheist the way she caterwauled about them curtains. Damn, those were ugly things.

* * *

"Gramps, you think Mama's gonna kill me?" Gramps snorts. "Maybe."

I rustle in my seat and make one more plea to join the geriatric league at Hubbard's, but Gramps ain't havin' it. Still, I reckon a girl oughta get a dyin' wish, so I conjure up my best doe eyes and lay 'em down hard. I think he can feel 'em pressin' up on the side of his wrinkly ole mug because he looks at me sideways and croaks, "Waddaya want, girl?"

"Tell me a story," I press, scootin' towards him across the buttery leather. "Tell me one'a your train stories from back in the day."

He sniffs back at me. "Why you always wantin' to hear those fool stories? Don't nobody wanna hear about a pisspoor hobo ridin' the rails unless their marbles done rolled away."

"I like 'em," I says. "Best shot I got to see any country that ain't covered in chickenshit and skeeters... even if I gotta look through your eyes to see it."

Gramps shoots me a chuckle. "These eyes can't see much of anythin' nowadays without a decent pair of cheaters."

He's stallin'. I can tell. And our farm's comin' up fast. Too fast.

I give it one last coyote-howl of a "C'mon," but that damn Olds is already rockin' like a tipsy boat, makin' the hard right into my driveway.

"I'll owe ya one," Gramps promises, whippin' his liver-spotted hands around that steerin' wheel so fast that I go dizzy.

I don't say nothin'. I just plant my back against that stupid passenger seat, fold my arms over my chest, and look straight ahead as the Olds lurches to the left and tries to slide me back over Gramps' way. But I'm cross. I'd rather scooch closer to a hot cow pie. And so I clench my little butt up, thinkin' I can grip the seat that way. I musta looked a fool, slidin' back and forth on that seat with my bottom lip all stuck out and my face screwed up like I had to make. And apparently, Mama thinks so too. I spy her stompin' the porch from a football field away, and soon as she catches sight of Gramps' car, she gives me this look like I just farted in the middle of Blooming-dale's. I think even Gramps and his big ole beastly Olds are afraid to creep down the drive. He gulps. "Oh lordy, she looks hot."

I gulp too. I'm in for it. She's swingin' that redwood paddle good as Babe Ruth in the ninth innin' and I'm a teensy little baseball hurtlin' right at her. Gramps sags to a stop, tells me, "Out ya get, kid," but then gives me this look like he's leavin' a dog at the vet to have its balls cut off. Even the Olds creaks out a final goodbye as I let its passenger-side door fall closed behind me. I ain't even got one dusty Converse up on the porch steps before Mama snags me by the ear and gives a powerful tug. She hauls me across the porch, through the creaky screen door, and all through the livin' room yammerin' about Principal Dunders' phone call and me bein' dumb as a box of rocks, but I only hear half of it on account of my scrunched ear and her God-awful yowlin'.

I sputter up some business about Marcy Gibbons bein' a prim prima donna who was "askin' for it," but that just gets Mama all the hotter.

She tells me, "Mind your tongue, girl. Attitude's like a cheap wig. It's irritatin' as hell, and it don't look good on nobody," and then she pins me so good with her eyes that I can feel 'em cuttin'. That's when the paddle comes back out. That thing was twenty-four inches of oiled hardwood with whiffle-ball holes the size of buttermilk biscuits. Accordin' to Papa, Mama got it handed down to her by Gran, who got it from Great-Granny Aggie, whose daddy, Great-Great-Grandpappy Silas, cut it right from the trunk of a sweetgum tree whose roots went all the way down to Hades. As Mama levels it at me, I picture her all painted up red and sproutin' devil horns through her hair. She says it's gonna hurt her more than it does me. She always says that. Every kid on planet earth knows that's a load of shit, and this time, I told her so.

"You got a smart mouth, girl," she spits back. "And that smart mouth's gonna get you in a whole heap of trouble one day."

I make a smug snort. I'd mastered those shortly after turnin' thirteen. It was the best gift I got for my birthday that year. "At least I got a bit of smarts in me," I tell her as the snort's still swillin' around and poisonin' the air between us. "That's more than I can say for everyone else in this stupid family. If it weren't for y'all, I probably wouldn't even'a got in trouble today. Whole damn town and everyone in it's got me pinned for a big, stupid loser 'cuz I come from big, stupid loser stock."

Mama don't say nothin' back. Some of that redness I'd painted across her face with my imaginary brush drains away. She lets go of my ear. Then she goes over and sits herself down in one of the extra dining chairs with a creak. She pats her lap. "Come on, girl. Let's get this over with" is probably her way of fessin' up that I was right about each and every thing I just said. So I take my licks. I take my licks just to show her how right I am. Then I march straight to bed with only a "Sweet Baby Jesus" muttered under her breath for dinner.

I'm knee-deep in a fine fantasy involvin' Mama's death at the steely hands of a hay turbine and have near-cried myself to sleep when Papa comes rappin' at my bedroom door. I bolt up, fixin' for another fight, but when I see his rumpled head pokin' through the jamb, I fall back again and bury my face in my pillowcase.

"You still up, Sprout?"

Half of me wants to answer him. The other half don't. Both halves get together and give a little sniffle.

Papa cracks the door wider, so light spills in from the hallway and spreads his great big shadow across the floorboards. It's ten foot at least, with shoulders like boxcars and the chest of a ship's hull. Somehow, Papa always looked that big to me. When I was still in pigtails, I used to tell folks that he once beat Paul Bunyan in a bar fight... and funny thing was, it never felt like lyin'. But his voice is small and soft as a dove coo as he comes up on my bed. "Hey" is all he says. Then he lays his big, calloused-up rancher hand on my shoulder real gentle, like he's grippin' a hen egg, and asks if I wanna hear a story. Of course I do. Papa's got a silver tongue. Sometimes, when's he's up at my bedside tellin' stories, I reason he musta pulled the moon right down from the sky and licked it like a lollypop. Them nights, I could hear the beetle bugs and the garden slugs lined up outside my bedroom window, just waitin' on his yarns. Hell, even the monsters under my bed came out to listen. But tonight was different. Tonight he told about a sweet girl with baby blues and buckwheat curls—a girl who could work a dance floor like Ginger Rogers, a pick-axe like Casey Jones, and still make the world go all soft around the edges whenever she walked in a room. About the time his eyes light up like he's swallowed a belly fulla stars, I know damn well who he's talkin' about.

"Mama?"

"Mama."

I grumble deep down in my gut, feelin' there's a nasty monster in there tryin' to climb out. But I don't have it in me to get ornery, not with Papa... so I just roll off onto my side and push the monster back where he come from. Papa sits there in the stillness for a time, rubbin' his hands together. I can hear the scuff of his palms passin' their sandpaper skin back and forth. About the time that I imagine a little puddle of dust must be piled up beneath 'em, he whispers, "She's doin' the best she can, ya know. She's just tryin' to do what's best for you."

I snort my best 13-year-ole snort. Damn, I'm gettin' good at this.

"It's true. Your Mama... she's been tryin' to do right by you since the day God put you in her belly. She'd do anythin'—. Give up anythin'—." His voice sort of trickles off into the darkness before the warmth returns and carries up to the ceilin'. I shift in my sheets to watch it float up there, and a little sting shudders through my freshly-paddled backside. Then Mama's face appears next to them words and starts scowlin' at me, right alongside Marcy Gibbons', and Missus Udd's, and Mister Dunders' too. They're all lookin' me over like I'm some stupid, hick loser who's only good for laughin' at and shuckin' corn like a numbskull. Even after Papa leaves, I keep on grousin' about Marcy, and Principal Dunders, and most of all—Mama. I slip off into dreamland makin' little voo-doo dolls with their faces on 'em, and when I wake the next mornin' and see Mama standin' over me with her hair in rollers, I reckon one of them climbed right outta my insides with some innards still stuck to its head.

Mama gives me a fiery glare—the kind so hot that it could make dough rise—and I can't help but wonder if she felt me stickin' pins in her all night long. "I hope your smart ass is ready for some work," she clucks, holdin' her fly swatter like a scepter. "This ain't a damn vacation."

I give nothin' but my new-and-improved snort back, which earns me a second helpin' of "Sweet Baby Jesus!" who, up until age five, I thought was just a belligerent kid who lived in our attic and kept ignorin' Mama's naggin' calls. That's followed by an order of, "Christ on a cracker" and a promise that "if that Louisiana sun don't tan your backside, I will!"

I pull on my blue jeans and low-mutter a few nasty words that probably would've made the Devil blush eight shades of crimson, but Mama gives me *the Eye*, so I follow her to the kitchen rollin' both of mine at her backside all the way. Then she stuffs me fulla grits, and hushpuppies, and huckleberry pancakes that I do my damndest not to swoon over, and sends me out to the fields to help Papa. He's spongin' his brow with his furry arm hair when I skulk up.

"Mama says I'm to help," I tells him, and his eyes go all squinty gazin' up at the sun behind me. "She does, does she?"

I nod, but slow, and stare at his leathery hands, all covered in soil. I swear, that man loves soil like normal folk love their ice cream. He'd scoop it up in big gobs and give it the same woo-woo eyes that he gave purdy girls. I s'pose that's why Mama always calls him dirty names whenever it follows him home. And I s'pose that's why he acts like he's handin' off some great, big treat when he passes me a rusty, busted rake that looks like it predated Christ. "Don't roll your eyes at me, girl" is probably his way of tellin' me that I'm tramplin' on somethin' he loves, so I snap up that iron relic and tromp on out to tend to the garden.

I ain't out there five minutes when Pete and Wyatt come screamin' outta the house like damn banshees. They make a beeline for Mama's buttercups like they mean to pulverize the entire lot and earn themselves an early grave in the process.

Now I ain't sayin' my brothers are dumb, but they once whizzed on every globe in Sunday school because they were convinced that Pastor Higgins was testifyin' about "Pees on Earth" durin' his Christmas Eve sermon. I think Mama probably should've taken my suggestion to check on the hospital's return policy after she brought them little heathens home because they'd made my life an ever-livin' nightmare every day since. Matter of fact, last summer I took up unicycle ridin' with a mind to either run off and join the circus or at least render myself infertile—so that no little Petes or Wyatts of my own ever came into bein'. As they bumble up, all crazy-eyed and lookin' like a couple of backwoods inbreeds, I consider addin' idiot wranglin' to my résumé of circus skills. Sure as shit, that'd get me on the payroll at Ringling Brothers. And I'd gladly scoop elephant poo with a dinner fork rather than have them racin' their circles around me, prattlin' on about, "Hey Sissy" this and "Whatcherdoin'" that.

I look up from my rakin' about ten minutes in with a plan to harpoon one of them little devils the next time he yowls, *"SISSY!"* when I see Mama peerin' out from the kitchen window with a big, fat grin on her face. May be a trick of the light, but I could swear I see some little devil horns peekin' out through her updo. It's the same look she got when that feller dressed like the man from the Monopoly box showed up on our lawn talkin' about how "simple folk need politicians," and she turned the sprinklers on him.

So, stubborn shit that I am, I just toss that look right back. And I hold it, long and hard, like we're havin' ourselves the first-ever Mexican standoff on Louisiana soil. I stretch my eyes all big and wide. I don't even blink. And that distracts me just good enough for Wyatt to lob a dirt clod that smacks me right upside the head. That shit's got good aim too because my eyes get good and gummed up with scratchy little chunks so it's near impossible to see him well enough to hunt him down and kill him.

I must'a looked frightful chasin' Wyatt up one side of the garden and down the other like a rabid wombat because when Papa shows up askin', "What y'all yellin' about?" Pete run right up to him, wailin' about how scared he is.

"Sissy's bein' mean!" is all it took. Papa herds them

boys out of the garden and into the house lickity-split before circlin' back to me. I'm still pickin' dirt and wiggle-worms out of my hair when he sidles up and gives me that knowin' smile—the one that makes me feel like he's got all the secrets of the universe tucked in his back pocket.

"I hear you're a nasty, mean, no-good sister," he tells me, grinnin'. I rub my eye and pull back brown knuckles. "Yeah, says the one who ain't covered in dirt," I spit, which gets him to smilin' all the wider. His sparkly ole emerald eyes pinch up at the edges like they wanna smile too. It takes all I've got not to grin along, and he can see me fightin', so he walks on over and takes up my hand in his. It's all rough and soft at the same time, tanned leather worn smooth by a thousand swings of the shovel. Then he leads me out past the house and through the fields, skimmin' the cotton with his fingertips like he's brushin' angel wings all the while. Then he sets me loose in the bayou.

I'm about to skitter off when I think better of it and turn myself around to see him beamin' wide as a possum with a sweet peach.

"Thanks, Papa."

"Don't thank me, Sprout. Thank your mama."

CHAPTER THREE

Accordin' to Papa, the bayou folk were powerful super-
stitious, but since they didn't have no money for proper
funerals, they'd float their dead little babies out into the
swamp like Moses down the Nile, with rusted pennies
stuck to their eyes as payment for the Boatman on the
River Styx. I'm pretty sure that him and Mama made
all that up, thinkin' they'd scare me out of explorin' the
swamp, but it only made me go all the deeper. Matter of
fact, I made myself a little ramshackle raft out of willow switches and bailin' twine, determined to float until I
found me some creepy petrified baby dolls or maybe even
crossed into Texas. I'd wash up under some pignut hick-
ory tree on a Texan sandbar and tell folks my name was
Sloan Fawcett, Farrah's kid sister—the one who never
got a fair shake on *Charlie's Angels*. I'd claim no kin west
of the Mississippi, and with the Abernathy stain clean
off my skin, I'd make a new life for myself, signin' auto-
graphs and makin' guest appearances at the Piggly Wiggly.

I knew better than to spill my plans though. Mama
had a tighter line on me than a croc tuggin' meat bait.
She wouldn't even let me play Atari. Forget crossin' the
state line. Besides, I had a zillion different lives to imag-

ine before I could settle on just one anyhow. Such as it were, I kept that raft of mine hid round about half a mile from our farmhouse—just beneath a sky-scrapin' syca-more holdin' up the coolest damn treehouse that any girl with a stolen hammer and a few broken hay pallets ever built. Every time I climbed on up into that thing, I felt like the Queen of Sheba, and today weren't no different. Me and Henry'd set it up like a genuine domicile, with real runnin' water, an icebox made outta an ole gym lock-er, and fancy gridded windows on every wall. Granted, the water only ran when you poured it from the pulley pail, and half the windows were just pictures painted by yours truly, but I thought it was the cat's meow all the same. I'd tacked up a souvenir store's worth of postcards on those four mismatched walls—each one either bought for a quarter at Woolworth's or given to me by Gramps, Huckleberry, or some poor schmuck who caught me big-eyed and turnin' out my pockets at the store register. I had postcards from California, Texas, Florida, Colorado, and a dozen other states that I was achin' to see. Pretty pin-up girls with cat's-eye sunglasses and waists no big-ger around than a rubber band beamed at me from up on that wall, all lookin' happy as clams to be anywhere but here. Most of them girls had sisters back at the house, where all my best cards were holed up in a scrapbook tucked under my mattress. I had 'em tacked up on the walls for ages, but Mama insisted that my room was startin' to look like "a tacky travel agency," so she fer-reted the whole megillah away and trapped 'em under plastic. It was just as well though. I'd lay up at nights now, pawin' through them under the covers with my flashlight and moonin' over all the places I could go, all the things I could do. Sometimes I'd call Henry up on our two-way walky-talky and tell him about how I was fixin' to leap the Grand Canyon on my Huffy like some kinda bullshit-powered Evil Knievel, or swim the Great Lakes and find Nessy's American cousin as a tadpole. He'd always call me a "first-rate nut job" and then give me some flimflam about pocket money and permission slips, and I'd remember that he was a 12-year-ole boy trapped in a 90-year-ole man's body, and remind him to take his teeth out before he went to bed.

But damn, I miss Henry. One piddly day without seein' his dumb ole, buckshot-freckled face and I feel like a puzzle piece fell outta my ribcage and got lost under the Frigidaire somewhere. One measly day without his fussy eyes lookin' me over like I'm about to do a magic trick and I'm broken. Damn, I hate that. Now I got Henry rattlin' round my brain pain, fussin' it all up and ruinin' my well-earned vacation.

I reckon the day ain't gonna wait around for me much longer, so I skitter on outta my treehouse and hit the hot Louisiana soil, runnin'. I check my crawdad traps and my coon snares, and get all my piss and vinegar drained out into the swamp so that I don't feel like everythin's closin' up around me like a curly tater bug. Then I haul out my raft and set it in the limey-green water. I lay out flat on it for a spell, feelin' the tug of the anchor and countin' clouds shaped like different states. I count nineteen of 'em before dusk settles in and the sun starts slidin' off the sky slick as a sloppy egg yolk. That's when Mama's copper supper bell sounds out and calls me on back to the house. She's standin' on the porch as I scamper up, with her salad tongs holstered on her apron like six guns, and all I can think about is how she picked up my dead gold-fish with those. Damn, I hope she washed 'em.

She clucks, "You get your sassy bled out?" as I'm climbin' the porch steps, and I've half a mind to ask her the same thing, but I remember what Papa said about her showin' me a kindness and just tell her, "Yes ma'am" before I head inside. She's got hush puppies and fry dough sizzlin' in the kitchen, so I breathe 'em in real deep until I feel myself growin' fat on the fumes and my gut growls like a son of a gun.

The house feels like a tin-topped chicken coop in July, and I find Papa layin' flat-backed in the front room with Pete and Wyatt runnin' circles around him. Apparently, the breeze from them fat little legs zingin' back and forth works like a half-broke fan, and I watch Papa's eyes go all swoony as the twins make a pass by his forehead. It's the same look he gets whenever the new *Farmers' Almanac* comes out or he sees a John Deere that just rolled off the line. He catches sight of me, perks up, and cricket-hops to his feet.

"If it ain't my little Sprout," he says, smirkin' like he's got himself a secret. Then he grabs me up in his big ole clompy paws and gives a squeeze that near makes my eyes pop out. Mama swans in about that time, so he drops me like a hot tater and beelines it over to her. Before I know it, he's waltzin' her across the creaky floorboards like he's Fred Astaire, and she's all giggles, swattin' at his hands and battin' her eyelashes. The twins jump in about that time, damn little heathens, and start turnin' figure eights between Mama and Papa 'til I'm about to go dizzy just watchin'. Meanwhile, Papa plants a wet one on Mama, and the sickenin' combination of the whole mess turns me as green as a fatback bullfrog. I let out a croak to suit my mood, and Mama gives me that head-to-toe scan like she's sizin' up my coffin, so I shut my maw.

It's just as well anyhow. I ain't had nothin' but some lint-fuzzified gummy worms from deep down in my back pocket and a few thistle heads for lunch today. I don't wanna conversate. I just wanna stuff myself full of hush puppies and gumbo, and leave these chuckleheads to all their tomfoolery. I skulk on over to the dinin' table like I mean it and plop down in front of my empty plate, but my butt ain't in that chair for five seconds before Mama starts her snipin'.

"What do you think this is, child?" she snipes, "Olive's roadside diner? I'll thank you not to sit your filthy behind down at my table without so much as a heifer's hose bath." Then she tugs my seat back so I near topple out and arches her prickly eyebrow at me while she's tappin' the chair-back.

"Yes ma'am" sees me off to the kitchen, where I grumble under my breath while runnin' one of Mama's precious Ivory soap bars all up and down my skinny arms. Mama thought Ivory soap could cure most anythin'— filthy mouths, cooties... probably even typhoid fever. Once, in fourth grade, Billy Calhoon called me a "redneck retard," and somehow or another, it got back to Mama. I remember I was sittin' in Missus Waldrop's third-period Social Studies class at the time, starin' out the window at two crows peckin' over somebody's half-eaten apple, when Mama roars into class and grabs little Billy up by his shirt collar. She don't say word one to me, or Missus Waldrop, or even dumb, mean little Billy. She just drags him out the door and slams it closed behind her.

Now, Mama's temper was the stuff of legends—rarely seen by normal folk and only spoken of at a whisper—so Missus Waldrop don't even get up from her desk. She just freezes there like a critter who's got a flashlight pinned on it, maybe thinkin' Mama won't see her if she don't move. But she starts to shake a little bit when Billy's wails come bleedin' up the hallway. She starts chewin' her lip too, and her big ole glasses get to rockin' across the bridge of her skinny nose. Billy's yowlin' gets louder and louder, and she starts rakin' that mousy brown hair of hers. I think she's about to have herself some sorta nervous breakdown when a few of the kids pop up outta their seats and skitter on over to the door. They're cranin' up to tippy-toes and climbin' all up on each other's backs like puppies in a big pile, tryin' to get a peek through the teensy window at the top of the door. One of 'em musta spied Mama huffin' back down the hall, though, because they all the sudden scatter back to their desks, zippi-ty-doo-dah. Their fannies ain't but hit the seats when the door swings open so hard that it slaps the wall behind it, and in waltzes Mama with Billy swingin' from her arm. He's got tears streamin' down his cheeks and a fat, square block of Ivory soap stickin' out of his mouth like a damn harmonica.

I think for a second that I see Missus Waldrop perk up like she's gonna say somethin', but Mama stares her down with eyes good as bent razor blades, and so she don't move a muscle. Not a single one. She and all the rest of the class just keep quiet as the grave while Mama marches Billy back to his desk, plops him down in his seat, and vanishes out the door again like she was never there in the first place.

I tell you what, Billy Calhoon never called me or any-one else on God's green earth a cross name after that day. And even though Mama and me never spoke of it, I know she'd say that Ivory soap was what got the job done. The Calhoon folks, on the other hand, didn't have as much faith in the all-healin' powers of a soap sand-wich. Mister Calhoon showed up on our porch stoop that very night, callin' Mama all sorta filth. She was off in the kitchen stewin' tomatoes and none-the-wiser as Papa stood across our threshold like one of them fuzzy-hat-wearin' Queen's Guardsmen who won't budge an inch no matter how loud you shout at 'em. He just stood there, never inchin' an inch, as Mister Calhoon said Mama was "trash," and "trouble," and had "no business teachin' morals with none of her own." Then ole Mister Calhoon yammered some business about bein' a "good, upstandin' citizen" and a "God-fearin' man" before Papa cut him short. I remember peekin' out from behind the radiator and watchin' how Papa's eyes drifted towards some dandelions growin' wild in the drive. Then his voice got real cool, and he told Mister Calhoon, "Fella, that woman's twice the man you'll ever be. Now get your ass offa my porch."

* * *

I make an extra pass with the trusty ole soap bar now, thinkin' Mister Calhoon coulda used a taste of it himself and wonderin' whether Billy Calhoon can even sniff the stuff without wantin' to upchuck. Then I find my way back to the dinner table, all spit-shined and ready to strap on the feed bag. By now, everyone's got piled plates, and so I wiggle into my seat and start squirrelin' up what's left like the last piglet to the trough. Sure enough, I end up with cold grits, a nub of a corn cob, and a chicken breast so puny that it looks like it was plucked straight offa Chicken Little. Wyatt smiles at my plate and stabs a nice, plump drumstick with his fork so that I can see the crackly glaze break and the meaty juices flow out. Then he takes the whole thing in his sticky little paw, raises it up, and bites. "Mmmm... good" is aimed straight at me, along with his twinkly eyes. I hate them little eyes— them wide, fresh-sky eyes that look like angels are about to fly through 'em. Folks get duped by those eyes every day—folks at the bakery who give him free cookies, folks at the Piggly Wiggly who sneak him quarters for the gumball machine. Hell, if the dumb folks around these parts didn't know that Pete and Wyatt were actually Abernathys, they'd give 'em the damn keys to the city!

I snarl at Wyatt and his fat drumstick, and his stupid baby-blue eyes, and his pocket fulla free quarters. He snarls back. He sticks his chubby little leg out across the table and punts me right in the chin.

"You little shit!" ain't but made it an inch from my lips before I'm on my feet and knockin' dishes every which way, tryin' to get my hands around that little devil's throat. I'm fixin' to send him right back to where he come from when Papa catches my arm and holds on just long enough for stupid Wyatt to whip up some fake tears for Mama. And oh lordy, did Mama ever soak 'em up. I s'pose it was because Pete and Wyatt looked so much like Papa, but Mama thought those boys farted rainbows. I, on the other hand, looked like her—just run over by the ugly truck. My farts smelled like... farts.

She screws her face up into an angry red beet and levels her hand at the steps.

"TO. YOUR. ROOM."

Mama sure as hell don't have to tell me twice. I don't wanna eat cold grits and wimpy hunks of chicken with these nitwits anyhow. I hit them creaky steps runnin' and make no bones about stompin' them good on my way up. I can feel hot tears wellin' in my eyes about halfway up, but I hold 'em tight 'til I hit the top step. Matter of fact, I near make it to my room before they let loose and start spillin' every which way. I soak my favorite t-shirt, two pillowcases, and the better part of Gran's ole nubby afghan by the time the sun goes down. Then I lay there in the dark, stewin' in my anger. I hate on Wyatt good and hard. I think about how I hate that he's too short to notice people lookin' down on him. I think about how I hate him trailin' after Mama when she's sidesteppin' through the parlor to Artie Shaw. I think about how I hate that time never moves in this house. And it's like Mama can feel me hatin' all the way down the hall because I hear her stir and then come tiptoein' towards my room. She cracks the door and sorta lingers in the jamb. Maybe she's waitin' to see if I'm communin' with the Devil or somethin'.

I blink at her through the darkness and see her arms cross over her chest. She blinks back like it's some kinda Morse code and then says in her plain voice, "Grudges are like BMs, ya know. You go holdin' one in for too long, and it's bound to sour your insides."

I swallow down a groan. Mama's Southern brand of wisdom is a lot like her spicy Creole cookin'—always over-portioned and aimin' to light a fire under your ass. She's been servin' it up to me on a platter since I was old enough to push it back, but I weren't in no mood for a second helpin' right about now, so I roll on over and give her my backside. I can feel her stewin' in the doorway, probably eyein' my fanny with a mind to smack it, but she putters off after a while, and I almost kinda wish she'd stayed. Now I'm good and woke up though, so I fish up under my mattress and pull out a flashlight and my postcard scrapbook.

If ever I loved somethin', it was that scrapbook. My heart gets all twitter-paited every time I see the cover, and even though Mama picked it out and it's got some kinda nancy-ass buttercups all splattered across the front, my gut still starts churnin' every time I see it. Straight away I get to thinkin' about all them exotic places waitin' for me on the other side, like an aeroplane primed for flight. I crack the cover, and it's liftoff. I can hear a clunky biplane engine fire up, and it rattles my insides. A frisky trade wind tousles my hair. Then I'm soarin' way up high, passin' ole fiddle-fart Louisiana by as if it's a shit-splat on the map. I'm watchin' all those weevil-rotted fields fray off like a big patchwork quilt comin' undone, and I'm leavin' 'em all in my dust.

I set eyes on a glossy, pepper-red card with a fat steak on the front that sets me down in Amarillo, Texas. Some sweet, wrinkled-up lady from the bus last fall says her kin live there. I remember her slippin' that card out of a flowery duffle bag and handin' it my way. "They got underground mountains there in Amarillo," she tells me. "They's all fulla natural gas."

Boy howdy, did I have me a laugh over that one... imaginin' all them upside-down mountains beneath the red Texan earth, all fulla farts. It weren't until I got on the school bus later that mornin' and Henry gimme a twenty-minute lecture about the difference between "natural gas and *natural* gas" that I got the giggles worked outta me. But then he started laughin' about what an ignoramus I was, and after I got my panties untwisted about bein' called out, it turned out I had a few more giggles left in me after all. That's the thing about Henry. He'll go on grousin' about this, or that, or any ole thing under the sun like he's been on the earth a zillion years, and then he'll up and surprise you by bein' a kid.

I pretend he's right here beside me, all tucked under the covers, big eyed, and gapin' at the book as I turn its page and fly us down to Kansas to visit Dodge City. There's a big Longhorn on that card, and I remember how the dumb cow caught my eye when it peeked at me from beside the register at Woolworth's. Longhorns are goofy-lookin' things. Gramps calls 'em "redneck unicorns" and swears that up until age ten, my dumb-shit Uncle Ern thought they had mystical powers. But then again, Uncle Ern thought he could do magic the first time he walked past one of those automatic slidin' doors, so believin' in "redneck unicorns" ain't no stretch.

I tell the imaginary Henry beside me the same thing, and he sniggers real good and then elbows me to turn the page, which flies us over to Wyoming. I want to stop off in Casper, seein' as how Huckleberry handed that card off to me with a promise that there was no ghosts hauntin' it. But Henry, he don't want nothin' to do with spirits on account of his Dad takin' a dirt nap and all, so we head down Montana way. I've got two whole pages worth of cards from Montana. A fair-haired fella shoppin' in the pharmacy at Woolworth's bought me one from Missoula last June. It's covered in Olympic rings, which he busted his buttons tellin' me was 'cuz all manner of famous, medal-winnin' athletes made their beds there. Sometimes I picture all them sweaty, skinny runners and gymnasts stuffed into one little bed with their naked feet danglin' off the edges, toes all wiggly like bald baby bird heads.

But make-believe Henry don't think much of my squawkin' birds or all those stinky sporty folks. He's always hated sports, hated them right down to his two left feet. He couldn't do a pullup to save his life, and Coach Biggs said, "He's taken more balls to the face than a Bangkok whore," whatever that meant. Naw, Henry likes all the tall, spooky-lookin' brick buildin's on the Butte card... all the ones that look like they're fixin' to either scrape a hole in the heavens or tumble down into a big, crumbly pile. He's weird. He likes ole stuff like that: ole, stinky fedoras that his grandpappy wore down to a thread and swoony black-and-white movies fulla ladies who're always clutchin' at their chests like they're about to have a damn heart attack. I never could figure out why he liked that ole-timey junk any more than I could figure out why Mama did. Aside from all the dusty crap he had holed up in his room, the ol'est thing in his house was a hill made of empty wine bottles that his momma was forever addin' to. Every time I went over there, it got bigger and bigger and bigger, like one of them volcanos that spits up on itself so much that it makes a whole other volcano on top of its spit hole. And Henry's momma was always passed out beside it in her stanky La-Z-Boy with another couple'a bottles wedged under her armpits. I always figured that when she came to, she'd lean her weight on 'em until they broke apart and got stuck up under her skin. Sometimes I thought that might be her aim. And other times I just thought that she'd buried her smile in a wine bottle and was forever drainin' them in search of it. Or maybe Henry's Daddy'd done took her smile up to Heaven with him when he left and just forgot to tell her. Maybe he took Henry's too.

So, if it makes Henry happy to go to Butte... to Butte we go.

Below them crumbly ole buildin's there's a map of all Montana's roadways lain out in a big, veiny snarl. I put my pointer finger on the little Missoula dot and slide it down Butte's way. Not even the length of one fat fingertip. Not far at all. I figure we'll take the train from here. Of course, we don't buy a ticket. No way, no how. We do it hobo-style—like Gramps and Gran, back in the day. We ride the rails, scarf up the open air, and live off Cheetos and gummy worms I got socked in my backpack. We dodge the rail coppers not once but twice, and make it all the way to Butte by sunup. But then somebody on the next train car over starts cookin' up eggs and fryin' bacon. I can hear the sizzlin' and the grease splatter. I can smell hotcakes bubblin' on the griddle. My mouth starts waterin'.

"OLIVE! BREAKFAST!"

I ain't slept a wink, but my gut don't care. Imaginary

Henry vanishes with a poof, probably to eat Fruit Loops that his fool momma done drown in Chardonnay, and I scamper on downstairs. Bein's it's day two in purgatory, I expect Mama to cram me fulla fuel for all manner of miserable chores that she's got lined up, and sure enough, she piles my plate up high with golden silver-dollar cakes and a pig's-ass worth of bacon. She even smiles when she's doin' it, but I know better. She always says, "Puttin' sprinkles on a mud pie don't make it good for ya, but it sure as hell makes the thing easier to swallow." I can see those sprinkles splattered all over my hotcakes, but I'm too damn famished to care. So, I scarf them up and try to ignore stupid Pete and Wyatt as they're zingin' bacon bits at each other every time Mama turns her back. Them boys are always up to mischief... always waitin' for Mama to put her guard down. I think she relaxed once, on a Tuesday afternoon in 1977. She unknotted her apron, and that very second my brothers started shavin' the cat. She's got eyes in the back of her head though, and all it takes is one piece of precious bacon hittin' the dirty floor for her to spin 'round. And then—*the look*.

The look is the stuff of legends. *The look* was handed down to Mama by Mee-maw Aggie and by Aggie's mama before that. Capable of stewin' tomatoes still green on the vine and boilin' a gator in his own swamp water, *the look* was feared throughout the great state of Louisiana and maybe the whole U. S. of A. If ya go off of Lafayette lore, *the look* was borrowed off the Devil himself, and after my kin got hold of it, he was too scared to ask for it back.

Mama laid *the look* down on me a sum total of five times that week I was suspended. Once, not ten minutes after breakfast, for tryin' to buy my way into the bayou with the last three strips of bacon and some big eyes at Papa. A second time just after that for feedin' that no-good, fink bacon to Papa's ole hound dog, Boomer. And then three more times for stuff that didn't even have a lick of anythin' to do with me.

Come Sunday, Mama's makin' the sign of the cross at me like I'm possessed and prattlin' on about how the church is probably gonna burst into flames when I waltz through the door for services. Lucky for me, Pete and Wyatt toddle down the stairs about that time wearin' dirty drawers and t-shirts smattered in dirt boogers and boy gunk. Mama's eyes about pop outta her head and she starts fussin' at them and forgets all about me. One thing about Mama, she'd stand stoic as a plaster saint while people splattered us Abernathys with every dirty word in creation, but she'd never let one of us step foot inside that church unless we were spit-shined from stem to stern.

She ferrets those nasty, stinky boys into the kitchen quick as you like, slathers 'em in Ivory and buckets of her own spittle, and makes angels of 'em before packin' the lot of us into Da Beast. Now I tell you what, Da Beast weren't just a car; Da Beast was a force to be reckoned with. It was the only 1960-somethin' Wagoneer west of the Mississippi that ran mostly on imagination and re-gurgitated corn fuel milked from Papa's rotten crops and

Mama's leftover fry grease. Da Beast had outlived three tractors, twenty head of cattle, and probably some lon-glost relatives that I didn't even know about. It has a muffler held on by bailin' twine and smokes more than the Marlboro Man. Every now and again, I'd see it lookin' at me real sinister with its steely headlamps like it was thinkin' about gobblin' me up if I stuck another wad of bubblegum up under its seats. I always climbed inside it wonderin' if I was gonna live to see tomorrow, but on Sundays, the good Lord always saw fit to make sure I got my ass to church, like it or not.

Church was the worst. Not only did I get stuck up in some dusty ole pew that was like sittin' on a bed of nails for three hours, I had to see every single one of my cheek-pinchin', loud-mouthed, cross-eyed relatives all at once. It was like Christmas 'cept there was no good food and I didn't get any presents. Aunt Agnes was always there before everybody, probably even Pastor Higgins. Maybe even before God. And today ain't no different.

* * *

She's standin' out front, right under the big cross hung over the church's front door, lookin' like a fat, stupid an-gel in her white frock and big bouffant. I s'pose she does her hair like that because she's tryin' to tickle at God's toes and let him know she showed up.

She does a little jig when she sees us pull in and starts clutchin' at her teensy handbag and wrigglin' while Papa herds us towards her. "Lands sakes, y'all made it!" she hollers, like we's anythin' but early. Mama says back, "Just barely," and scoops Agnes up in her thick arms, which turns Agnes all pink and smiley. Mama's got one of those sorta hugs that's big enough to drown out the whole world, and even though Agnes is probably twice Mama's size, she looks fragile with those arms wrapped around her. But she shakes Mama off after a minute and clomps on over to us with her fat pinchers all ready to squeeze at our cheeks. "There's my niece-y!" she crows, twistin' my face good enough to rip it off. Then she gives me a fussy look and says, "This one's growin' up too quick! Losin' all her baby fat!" which makes me feel like she had big plans to eat me up in a stew or somethin'. But my brothers are plenty pudgy, so she gets all her squeezes in deep on them. Mama gives 'em both *the look* as they're poked, prodded, and smothered in slimy kisses, which keeps the twins from headin' for the hills. I hear Pete tell Wyatt that those lips feel like dead slugs. Papa and Mama hear too. They both grin.

After that, Aunt Agnes starts tellin' Papa that she's gettin' one of those *Jesus Saves* signs to stake in her yard "like some kinda landin' strip for the rapture, 'cuz Jesus is a man, and you *know* he ain't gonna ask for directions." Papa just bobs his fresh head of pomade, probably thinkin' about turbine engines or canoodlin' with Mama. He looks Mama over just then, his eyes sad as you can get. She's sorta pawin' at the ground just outside the chapel threshold with the right toe of her good heels like Boomer does when he knows he ain't welcome in the kitchen.

I don't know why that dumb dog keeps himself perched there, just inches away from all them sausages and stew bones and buttered taters, knowin' full well that he ain't gonna get nuthin' but a scowl when he creeps inside. But there he sits, droolin' on the outskirts just the same. And here stands Mama, dressed for church in her green dress and Gran's pearl earrings, knowin' damn well that everybody's gonna look her over like a steamin' cow turd anyhow. Adults are weird. They sure do waste a lotta time on crap that don't matter. And so Mama wastes her Sunday mornin' good...tradin' cheek-kisses with Agnes and Uncle Ern in the parkin' lot and sweatin' her ass off in that wool dress while folks from town make wide sidesteps around her and pinch up their noses. She even wastes herself a good 'nother minute makin' a big, fakey smile up for Pastor Higgins when he pops his bald head outta the chapel doors. He sends it back, but it looks like he's smilin' for school pictures or somethin'. Everybody playin' nice for Jesus.

But Mee-maw, she ain't playin' nice, not even for the Man Upstairs. She lumbers up to Higgins just as we're makin' our way in and hangs her arms out like Christ on the cross. She's eyein' those big slabs of skin swingin' from her biceps with giant eyes. "These'd better be meant to fly ole ladies up ta Heaven!" she tells Pastor Higgins, who gets struck dumb silent and starts grippin' his Bible so hard that his fingernails sink into the cover. "See this here," she bellows, givin' that hangy flab a flick with her finger. "That's the start of some damn angel wings, that

is! Only goddamn explanation for it, wouldn't-chya say?"
I almost feel sorry for ole Higgins. If him and his weren't
shamin' Mama in the parkin' lot and makin' Papa have
sad eyes, I just might too. But I reckon he deserves what
he gets. And Mee-maw must figure the same because she
don't budge an inch. Not a'one. She presses her wrinkly,
fuzzed-up face up into his and just goes, "Hmmmmmm?"
Higgins rolls his eyes all around, lookin' at the Saint
Francis statue, at the ceilin', at the door. I think for a second he might bolt, but Papa pops in about that time, shinin' like a knight outta one of his storybooks, and grabs
up Mee-maw's arm. "You're lookin' classy today," he says
to her.

"Classy, my arse! I ain't a damn car!"

Papa smiles as good as he can manage and drags
Meemaw towards our pew with her arm flab wavin' goodbye to the bug-eyed Pastor while Mama, Pete, and Wyatt trail behind them. Agnes and Ern are gummin' up
the doorway with their chitter-chatter at Higgins, and I
hang back, watchin' folk watchin' us. They make like they
ain't lookin'. They check their watches, and squint at the
stained-glass windows, and bunch in big clumps down
the aisle-ways, whisperin'. Mostly they're women—the
kind of women who manage the church bake sales and
always got fresh lipstick on. They look at us like stains
that won't come out of their clothes. They look mostly at
Mama. I feel sad for a second, but then I remember all
of Mama's fierce talk about sadness bein' some mangy
critter scratchin' at the back door that only comes in

when you let it, so I buck up. That's about the time that Mee-maw gets loose of Papa and hooks me by the arm. She pins me by the little kids' pew that smells like piss and melted crayons, grumblin' on about how she used to be a "pretty young thing" like me. I try to say somethin' nice, somethin' about how she's still a foxy ole dame like Gramps says, but she spits, "Darlin', I'm ninety-three. My body's like an ole salad: half-wilted and looks way better with dressin' on it."

I get me a good chuckle outta that, but since Mee-maw moves slow as molasses, I'm still laughin' as everybody gets ahead of us and starts stealin' up all the good seats. Of course, folk in church don't let us get much beyond the nosebleeds anyhow. Every Sunday, this trio of prissy gals that Mama calls "The God Squad" make themselves a human blockade between us and any pew worth sittin' in. Billy's momma, Debbie Calhoon, is their undisputed leader. She looks sorta like Hawkeye from *M*A*S*H** but with hair and knockers like Dolly Parton. Henry lives spittin' distance from City Hall and swears she's boffin' Mayor Rowdy 'cuz she stays late nights secretaryin' for him when don't no one file jackshit at 10 p.m. He says Rowdy done bought her those tits and the purple Firebird she's always washin' in her front yard. But to look at her now, all decked out in her polyester blazer and chin-high turtleneck, you'd guess she was just as pious as Higgins' sermon is long. She's got her hooks deep in Cheryl Hinkley and Nettie Biggins, whose families have been around these parts for as long as the Abernathys. They both got deputies for husbands, and Stan Hinkley's makin' a race for sheriff this year that his good ole boys'll make sure he wins. I seen his big, fat face smilin' out from cardboard cutouts on every shop front and telephone pole in town like he's watchin' every move we make. Papa says folks do that when they got somethin' to hide. That leaves me thinkin' about Mama watchin' me with those eyes in the back of her head and all the things that she must be hidin'. Probably lots of Mallomars in the vegetable crisper.

The God Squad curls lips at me from the second-to-last pew as I'm tryin' to hurry Mee-maw along, but the ole ninny's like a great, big turd: If you rush her, you just get yourself a pain in the ass. So, sure as shit, I get stuck sittin' next to Uncle Ern. He's already fast asleep and snorin', with a big globber of drool tricklin' down his prickly chin. I glower at him good, and then at Aunt Agnes, who's latched herself to Mama like a swamp leech and don't wanna set down nowhere near her brain-dead husband. Mama's sittin' up good and tall, with eyes on the pulpit like she don't see Missus Calhoon and her nosy friends staring daggers. She's fingerin' the gold cross always danglin' from her neck, and I think how heavy it looks. I think how dumb she is for hangin' on to such a heavy thing. Then I look over at Uncle Ern, and Mama don't look so dumb. Last time I seen Uncle Ern was at the Walmart in Church Point. He was squirrelin' around the store like he'd just got called down for *The Price Is Right,* and he didn't even notice me wavin' hello. About twenty minutes later, me, Mama, and the twins caught up to him at the checkout register, where he was tryin' to get one of those price-scanner jobbers to take his blood pressure. Mama said somethin' like, "Lord love him, but that man's a few shits shy of a full outhouse," and then we all just stood there, watchin' him lean over the checkout with his trousers halfway down his ass. Tell you what, between his saggy drawers and that big ole Budweiser gut of his, Uncle Ern'd shone more full moons than the lunar calendar. And here I am, stuck sittin' right next to his stanky behind... as always. Between his snorin' and Mee-maw's chatterin', I don't hear one lick of Pastor Higgins' Sunday sermon, not that I care to. Aside from school, I get treated worse in church than I do anywhere else. Folks here look me over like boys do when I wander into the Comic Shop—like I don't belong. Every minute I set here drownin' in the pew dust and the righteous talk, those cold eyes just stack up like another stone on my sholder. Mama says I'm here to find the love of Jesus. He musta been hidin' it real good.

My bony butt's numb as a sack of taters by the time Pastor Higgins finally shuts his trap, and I don't realize until folks start gettin' up from their pews that Gramps snuck in while I was wedged in between Tweedle Dee and Tweedle Dumb. He gives me a cantankerous wink and pats the flask in his front pocket. Gran used to say that he nursed that thing like Mary nursin' the Baby Jesus, but any time I get to thinkin' about that, a picture comes to my mind that makes my guts crawl. So, I push it on out of my brain and shoot him a grin. Then I manage to peel myself offa Mee-maw's sweaty side-boob and make my way over. Once I get close enough, Gramps peeks around to make sure no one's listenin' in and peeps, "How goes it, kiddo?"

I ain't gonna lie. "Kids in those Chinese sweatshops got it better."

He snickers, and his ole baby blues light up 'til they twinkle. About then, Preacher Higgins happens by us, still thumpin' his Bible, and asks, "So, did you two enjoy the sermon?" like his Mama told him he had to ask.

My eyes start dartin' all around. Coulda been a tennis match goin' on in there. I try recallin' one single word outta his testifyin' mumbo-jumbo that weren't gummed up by Uncle Ern's snores or Mee-maw's jibber-jabber. I ain't got nothin'. But thank the good Lord up in Heaven, 'cuz about the time that Higgins looks ready to exorcize me, Gramps pipes up and says, "Yeah, sure enough. All that *reward beyond the Pearly Gates* stuff was really top drawer!"

That gets a good nod out of the good preacher, but he gives me an over-the-shoulder glare as he glides away, still palmin' his Bible. Once he's outta earshot, Gramps leans my way and goofs, "If ole Higgins is behind them Pearly Gates, I hope my reward's a ladder."

I ain't laughed so hard in church since the time I got Wyatt to pick his nose all through Leviticus 1:4 because I told him there were M&Ms stuck up in there. But all that tomfoolery catches the uppity nose of The God

Squad. They give us somethin' like *the look* (but loads less scary), so me and Gramps skitter towards the door and make us a clean getaway before Higgins, or God, or Debbie Calhoon and the Boobettes are any the wiser. The twins bullet by us and beat feet to Da Beast, pushin' and sluggin' each other every fifth step. I lean into Gramps and tell him, "Welp, I guess God's not watchin' anymore."

Right about then, I feel eyes burrowin' into my backside. They're like hot cinders off a bonfire that got stuck to my clothes and are burnin' their way through—*Mama.* She comes up alongside me and whispers real low, "Oh, God's always watchin'."

There's a quiet bit as Mama points back at Higgins and The God Squad where they're glarin' at us from the chapel threshold. Then she says, "Cuz God don't live in there" before dialin' a finger right down over my heart and addin', "He lives in *here."*

CHAPTER FOUR

I ain't never been so happy in all my livin' life to see that big, ugly Greyhound bus as I was come Monday. I let it roll on up close to me so that it kicked dusty gook from the dry earth up and into my nostrils. And I didn't even care. I just stood there, beamin' at Huckleberry's face through the windshield like he was cruisin' down Main Street in the Independence Day Parade. A few pebbles even kicked up over my sneakers and I just pretended they were candies.

The bus come to a standstill not but a few feet from mine and gave a powerful groan like it'd been runnin' all over creation lookin' for me. Then it yawned its side door open and Huck peered out from inside its belly. "Well, if it ain't the dead risen," he said, grinnin' real wide so I can see about every one of his teeth.

I'm sure there's a snappy comeback rattlin' around somewhere in my brain, but the dust gummed it up, so I just smile back and climb on in. I'm so fixed on grinnin' like a dumbshit that I all but sit right on top of this ole biddy who's got herself planted in my normal seat behind Huckleberry. She smells like Mentholatum and Cheese Whizz, and when I glance at the open space on the bench beside her, she gives me a little scowl and drops a rat's nest of crochet crap right in it.

I can see Huck watchin' our exchange in the rearview, and for a second I wonder if maybe he put my seat up for grabs 'cuz he really *did* think I was dead—or worse yet, homeschooled. But he shrugs at me like it don't matter either way, and so I dish the ole crone a little scowl back and then continue on down the aisle.

Now, I ain't had no civilized conversation for days, so I don't just jump at the first bench I get my eye on. I stroll through, real slow, studyin' each rider like one of those pictures with some other little picture hid inside it. The first couple of folks I pass look real stuffy, with newspapers pulled up over their faces and briefcases sittin' shotgun. They aren't good for conversatin', not on any day of the week. Then I come across another ole gammy-type. This one gives me a gummy smile and arches up her prickled white eyebrows. I could tell in five seconds flat that she means to prattle on about a bunch of fool nonsense, probably about her thousand-and-one grandbabies, each one cuter and smarter than the last. Nope. Not today, gammy.

Then I sees him—a feller with big, gnarly tattoos all up his arms and hair drippin' with enough grease to choke a chicken. He's got a pack of cigs poochin' out his shirt pocket, and I can see the word 'Marlboro' plain as day through the white cotton. This dude looks like trouble. I just found my copilot.

"Hey mister, mind if I sit here?" I asks in the deepest voice I can muster. His lip curls up. Hand to God, I spy a gold tooth. "Sure, kid."

Turns out his name is Miles. He says his momma named him for Miles Davis, but I reckon he's traveled enough to earn the name without the Davis. He tells me he's been all the way from New York to California and back again. He learned engines from his "jackass daddy" and pieced together some sorta Frankenhog outta junkyard bits and "sheer stubbornness" the summer he turned sixteen. Then he lit out. He told me about catchin' bugs in his teeth on the highway and ladies flashin' their busoms at him. He told me about chasin' the settin' sun until it dropped off the edge of the earth and about sellin' his soul to a devil outside Albuquerque for a bottle of scotch and a dime bag. And then he told me I wasn't gonna see any of it, not one single bit of it, because my roots were all stuck down deep in the grubby Louisiana soil. And dammit if he weren't right. I got off the Greyhound that day cussin' Mama and all her bullshit about stayin' where you were planted and keepin' close with your kin. Hell, nothin' in our shit-shack of a farmhouse had changed since Mama was sixteen, and if she had her way, I'd end up just like her... stuck there in 1950-somethin', polishin' ole silver with a baby diaper that'd seen more shit than all the dude ranches in Texas put together. Gramps was right: Don't nobody but a straight-up nincompoop wanna watch their folks get ole and wrinkled up and play Parcheesi all day long. Mama just wanted me stuck in borin' ole Lafayette with her so that I could wipe her fanny when she got too old to do it herself. But I didn't owe her nothin'. Not a damn thing.

I get to ruminatin' on that real good and let it sink deep down into my bones until it sticks there. By the time the school bus rolls along to pick me up from my ramshackle bus stop, the Mama in my head is a big, fat spider that has me wound all up in her web. She keeps huggin' on me and knittin' me into these silky cocoons. Her love is holdin' all my wobbly bits together but also makin' me feel like I'm bein' eaten by a python.

"What's your problem?" Henry says as I plop down on the bench beside him.

I just growl *"Her,"* which makes him peek up at the bus driver.

He asks, "What'd she do this time?" like I'd need a new reason to hate that ole bat, but I just tell him *nevermind* and flop my hand-me-down bookbag on the floorboard with a good thunk. Worst part is, all that hatin' on Mama stole away somethin' I'd been lookin' forward to for a week now—Henry. "You look different," he says to me. His eyeglasses slip down to the tip of his fat nose, and he pokes them back up to the bridge again.

"Yeah, I s'pose a week of house arrest with the meanest warden in all of Louisiana'll do that to ya."

He chuckles. He always chuckles. I couldn't even say if he thinks the stuff I say is funny or not. But he always chuckles anyway. Then he tells me, "Well, you didn't miss much," and whips out his mini-man briefcase. The thing's got more snaps and zips and pockets than sixty pair of blue jeans, and he starts pullin' papers out of it by the fistful. "I've got all your homework," he says, passin' over this fat stack of mess that I wanna see about as much as Marcy Gibbons on my porch swing.

"Gee, thanks," I say, not meanin' it one little bit.

Ain't a second goes by before my ole nemesis Billy Calhoon uproots himself and starts stalkin' down the aisle towards us. The wussy in me starts chantin' real quiet, *Don't sit by us, don't sit by us, don't sit by us,* but the ornery little devil nosin' around on my shoulder tells her to shut up and gets big-eyed as Billy throws his bookbag down on the seat in front of ours.

"Hey losers," he spits, curlin' up his mealy mug. He ain't called me a cross name in ages. His balls must be fixin' to drop. But my blood's already half-boiled from stewin' about Mama, so I clench up my fists. I'm about to lay down some choice names of my own when Henry pokes me in the rib and wags his head. His big hazelnut eyes are all shiny. He holds his eyelids open extra wide and then shutters them a few times like he's tellin' me *don't, don't, don't* in Morse code. All that fannin' of eyelashes cools me down a bit, and I find my fists unfurlin'. I swallow them names down too, but they leave a sourness in my guts that gets me to squirmin'. Still, I leave 'em there and tell 'em to stay put until the bus chugs off again and Billy whips around to face us.

"Heard ya got expelled," he hisses like a two-bit garter snake. "Heard you was s'posed to come back end of last week, but your Mama whooped you so good, you couldn't sit down in a desk 'til Monday."

Billy's grinnin' *real* good now. I can see half a Cocoa

Puff stuck between his two front teeth. I want to punch it out. And I'm fixin' to right about the time that Henry's little peep crops up beside me. "That ain't what happened," the peep says. "She got the whole week off on account of turnin' Marcy Gibbons' face into ground beef!"

I feel Henry scoot forward on our bench seat so that he's nose to nose with slimy Billy and his Cocoa Puff grin. "As I recall," Henry goes on, turnin' his peep into a crow, "last one to get a good whoopin' from Olive's Mama was you."

Oh lordy, that Cocoa Puff vanished in a wink. Billy give us that same look as when Mama dragged his ass outta Miss Waldrop's class by his collar—the look of a kid imaginin' his own death. I remember him givin' me the very same one when his team was playin' mine in the Lafayette peewee softball regionals. He'd been hecklin' me for about five innings when Mama scampered into the dugout and yowled, "Girl, you gotta teach that boy a lesson. You knock that ball so far into the heavens, that little shit's gonna have to pray to God to get it back." He'd locked eyes with me just as Mama was raisin' her fist up in the air, and I thought for sure he was gonna crap his uniform right then and there. Same look now—the very same one. But he whips around in his seat without another word, and the look's gone.

Henry arches his little eyebrows and relaxes back into the bench. I think I see a couple of the buttons on his blazer rise up like they mean to pop right off, but then they settle back down again, and all is right with the world. That day, when we get off the bus, Henry walks in front of me. He ain't never done that before. It's kinda nice. And I get to feelin' sorta happy, sorta safe, sorta okay with bein' back at this shithole kid prison. But I s'pose stuff like that ain't meant to last. Mama always says that "happiness is like a set of lost car keys. You ain't never gonna find it until you stop lookin'," so sure enough, soon as I got happiness all curled up in my paw, it decides to bite me. It probably got spooked the second it saw Marcy Gibbons. I can tell she's still nursin' a shiner because she's wearin' these big, ugly Jane Fonda sunglasses like I seen on the *Cosmo* mags at the Piggly Wiggly. She skitters off right quick when she sees me, but I should'a known she just run off for reinforcements because right about the time Henry beat feet to his first-period class, she shows back up with a half-dozen of her dipwad friends and they start circlin' me like stupid turkey vultures. I manage to get myself into class as they're closin' in, but I can feel them all cuttin' me with their razor-blade stares as Miss Beasley starts passin' out last week's graded homework. She does this funny sidestep when she passes me by, like I might be contagious or fixin' to bite her. I think I hear her voice quiver as she tells everybody, "Some nice writing, class," and then makes her way back up to her dinged-up desk, where she starts fishin' through the drawers. Judgin' by her mussed hair and her cattywampus glasses, I reckon that she might be lookin' for her marbles. But then she peeps, "Ah hah!" and plops a fat book on her desk as thick as Uncle Ern's entire *Hustler* collection. I can't help groanin'.

Miss Beasley flips the monster open and makes this moany sound like Mama does when she finds a good coupon. Then she tells us we're gonna write about our family trees. She goes on about grammies and grampies, and aunts and uncles, and branches with all kinda offshoots, and other ones all bare and shrively. Then she gets a sad sorta look and runs her fingers through that mop of hair. I'm a little surprised when she don't get her hand stuck but even more pickled when her eyes get shiny and she gives a little choke. "No babies for this gal," she says to no one in particular, and everybody gets quiet. So quiet. Quiet enough to hear her blowin' snot into one of them Kleenexes that ole ladies always carry around in their ole lady purses. She blows on as we all just stare, and I'm thinkin' to ask her if she's okay when she touches that book again. It's akin to Pastor Higgins layin' hands on a Bible.

"Well then, how about it?" she says. She takes up that book and smooshes it to her chest. She tells the whole mess of us that it's filled with her own Family Tree, her "Opus," and thirtysome-odd eyes go dartin' around the room in search of Opal Biggins, who wears fat braids and has a notebook with David Bowie's face plastered all over it. Opal ain't even in this class, but I can hear people whisperin' her name like she's about to pop out of the woodwork anyhow. This pains Miss Beasley, who flares her nostrils at us and barks, "not *Opal... Opus!*" and does a damn fine job of not addin' *you morons* at the end, even though I know she wants to.

"An *Opus* is like a master-level play... a symphony...

a writer's grand performance lain to paper," she blathers on as half the eyes in class continue on searchin' every nook and cranny like Opal Biggins might be hidin' in one of 'em. I watch her watch them. Her nostrils fan open wider. Her face gets pink. She looks up at the ceilin', eyes rollin' real good, and I think I see her whisper *God help me* to the man upstairs. He don't answer, and so she gets fed up with askin'. She flops her book back down on her desk, which gets them thirty eyes back on her right quick. Sounds like she's chokin' on dry grits as she gets on with it. "Let's just…. Why don't we…. Let's just…. Let's just get out a clean sheet of paper and draw ourselves a nice, big tree trunk on it."

There's a big scramble as everyone does as they're told, and for a minute it feels kinda like we're all back in kindergarten. Two rows over, Tim Allwine sticks his tongue out sideways as he's drawin' him a nice, fat sucker right down the middle of the page. One desk up from him, Alice Piven makes hers kinda crooked like maybe it got caught up by a storm a few years back and ain't never been the same. I make mine squatty and thick like the sweet gum tree in our front yard that always drops a shit-ton of leaves every year and makes Mama crazy. Miss Beasley gives it the once-over as she's traipsin' around class with her arms crossed. She tells me, "Well done, Olive," like she's givin' out gold stars to kids who can manage to breathe through their nose, since most of us are as dumb as a box of rocks. Then she hangs at my side long enough that my arm hairs start to prickle. Most teachers only fix on me for longer than the great state of Louisiana pays 'em to because I done somethin' wrong. I got all sorts of ole misdeeds tumblin' around my head when Miss Beasley leans in close. Close enough that I can smell the cat hair on her cardigan. "I know this might be a tough one for you, Olive," she whispers low.

I perk up. I count six different colored hairs on her sweater. *How many stinkin' cats does this lady have?* "Tough?" I say back. I know I ain't gonna win myself a million bucks on *Jeopardy* or anythin', but I can draw a damn tree!

"Well, on account of..." comes soft from her lips. Sounds like wind rustlin' the cottonwoods. It don't last long, though, as she gets quiet again and just presses me with her eyes. I feel like somethin's inside her that wants to get out but can't. It's like she's holdin' in sundown's woesome howl. Finally she spits up, "It's just... well, it's real nice, Olive. It can be tough gettin' that trunk just right." Then she wanders off, peculiar as she came, and I hear her say versions of the same thing a few more times as she makes her way back to the head of the classroom. She stops there and uncrosses her arms, leavin' her frumpy, ole-lady top all fulla wrinkles. "Alright, so now we're goin' to add the limbs," she tells us real slow. "These will be the *branches* of your family... the different people who make it up. Since everything springs from the trunk, these limbs illustrate what's grown from it."

She glances my way again just then. I get to puzzlin' over her puzzlin' over me. I start thinkin' about her whim-perin' and her shriveled-up lady parts. *Maybe she wants me to be her kid. Maybe she's thinkin' of scoopin' me out of my bed at night and goin' all 'Diff'rent Strokes' on my ass. I wonder if I'd have to share a room with sixty cats.*

Tim Allwine's hand shoots up. He's wearin' overalls, and I can hear the clickity-clack of metal buttons rubbin' their holsters as he worms all around in his seat, pleadin' for Miss Beasley to call on him. She forgets about me and says, "Yes, Tim?" since he looks like he's about to wet himself.

"But what if it ain't springtime? Won't nothin' grow outta the trunk then?"

There's a big ole *smack* that rings through the room as Miss Beasley plants her palm on her face. "*Springs* from the trunk doesn't have anything to do with springtime, Mr. Allwine," she groans. "Spring is also a verb, which means *to grow*."

Tim scratches his head good and hard. Either he's fixin' to get down to skull or he's got lice. "Ain't that what I was askin'?" is all he says before Miss Beasley tells him to *just hush up* and slugs up to her chalkboard. She draws a long, skinny trunk up there with a single branch on either side so that it looks like a half-starved Jesus holdin' his arms out or somethin'. "Here... just do like this," she tells us, turnin' back to face the class with a sour look like she's got gizzards on her dinner plate. "Just make a branch on either side. One for your mama, and one for your papa."

There's a big paper shuffle and a bunch of scritchity-scratchin' as everybody draws themselves a mama and a papa branch, and right about then, a soft little knock comes at the classroom door before Principal Dunders' secretary pops her head through it. She's got a round face and a smile that stretches from end to end, and her silly head could double for the Cheshire Cat's hangin' there in the jamb. She calls Miss Beasley out into the hallway in a voice no bigger than a squeak, and Miss Beasley tells us to "keep at it" as the door shuts behind her.

It ain't two seconds gone by before I feel a nasty ole snake hiss tickle my ear. I whip around and there's Marcy Gibbons and two other girls loomin' at my elbow like Lafayette's own Charlie's fallen angels. Marcy gives me the eye and says, "That's an awful fat tree you got there, Olive."

"Yeah, awful fat," says the second girl. She's called Vanessa Chatsworth. Her momma spit at my mama six years ago durin' Lent, when Mama was fool enough to try out for the part of Blessed Virgin Mary in the Easter play. Missus Chatworth said Mama didn't have no business layin' claim to such a saint and oughta sizzle in Hell for all she was. Of course Mama couldn't keep her fat trap shut. She gave snooty Missus Chatworth the business, sayin' how ignorant and blind and backwards her and everybody around these parts was. That got us kicked outta church until after Passover. Best couple months of my life. But Vanessa, she couldn't string a thought together with the toughest bailin' twine in Louisiana, so coversatin' with her ain't likely to get me a vacation from church or anythin' better than a blank stare. She just sass-wags her head 'til I hear her brain rattlin' around in there and stands still waitin' for Marcy to do the talkin'.

Oh, but Marcy, she's got talk enough for both of 'em. She adds on, "Yeah, awful fat for a redneck family who lives off'a gut worms and roadkill," which sets off a good snicker through the room.

Now them girls got an audience, so they mean to put on a show. Marcy gets herself up nice and close to me so that I can smell her bubblegum and that plastic stank that kids carry when they got brand new stuff on. Even though she's plenty near to hear, her voice gets real big as it booms, "Way I hear it, Olive's family's so poor, her Mama once fed the whole scabby bunch of 'em on free samples from Lubock's Mega Mart and government cheese so old that Mary Lincoln probably churned it herself!"

Good Lord, that done it. Every Tim, Alice, and imagined Opal in the room starts hootin' and hollerin' like they just heard the funniest words in all existence. They carry on so much that one of the puny kids who sits towards the front of the class even has to get out his inhaler. Tim Allwine falls right outta his desk. But I don't make a peep. I don't crack a smile. I just lock my eyes on Marcy's, half tryin' to put the fear of God into her and half tryin' to figure out if it's worth gettin' stuck at home for another week to beat her ass.

I can't say what Marcy's thinkin', but that girl don't bat an eyelash. Maybe she feels tough with them yahoos at her side. Maybe she thinks I have it comin'. Maybe she just wants a shiner to match her other one so that she won't have to paint on that God-awful purple eyeshadow of hers no more. She ain't tellin', and I ain't askin'. And Miss Beasley does all the talkin' for us when she flings the door open and yowls, "What's all this racket about?!" That sends Marcy slinkin' back to her desk. Okay, so maybe it's more of a middle-finger march than a slink, but that ain't how I tell it to Henry come lunchtime. He ain't got but one butt cheek planted on the cafeteria bench before I start in. I tell him all about Marcy and the turkey vultures, Miss Beasley sizin' me up for kidnappin', and that moldy ole cheese that even Mister Lincoln wouldn't take for free. He keeps his mouth sealed up tight 'cept towards the end, when it falls open a little bit.

"So did ya sock her?" he finally asks.

I poke my chin up in the air and shake my head. "Nope."

Now he's eyein' me. His little hazel peepers squish up 'til I can't see the whites no more. "Why not?"

A good half-dozen answers stew around in my brain for a minute and then come shootin' down the pipe all at once, so they get sorta jammed up in my throat and nothin' at all comes out. I'm fixin' to swallow five of 'em down when a tater tot goes whizzin' by my head and beans poor ole Henry right in the noggin. His eyes swell back up to their normal size. Maybe bigger. I'm already riled up just from retellin' my tale, so I whip around, ready to bare-knuckle box Muhammad Ali, but don't find a single soul standin' there. Off in the distance, I spy a gaggle of girls in miniskirts with hair teased up higher than Aunt Agnes' church doo yuckin' their fool faces off. Marcy Gibbons is dead center. She's smilin' her big, fakeass smile—the same one she does on school photo day and Parents Day... the same one her pretty momma, and her spit-shined governor papa, and all her blonde-headed, prissy little sisters have. I remember Mama seein' all those Gibbons folks at the Piggly Wiggly one Sunday and tellin' me, "the purdiest lookin' family trees are just the ones that got fertilized with the most bullshit."

Just thinkin' about that, I wanna haul Marcy Gibbons into the ladies by her pretty little pigtails, dunk her face in the toilet, and give some leftover turd a real family reunion. And Henry knows it.

"Don't do it, Olive" is all he says. Then he slides a fat, foamy, golden pack of Twinkies across the table. "These are for the fiercest, *smartest* girl west of the Mississippi," he says. He always says that. He always trades me some lukewarm, dry-ass, crappy sammich of mine for the most glorious snack food known to man. I don't even know if he likes Twinkies, but his momma sure do buy a lot of 'em. I know for sure that he don't like stinky ham sammiches that look like they ain't good enough for the trash, but he trades me every day anyway. So I take 'em. I always take 'em, and I let my boilin' blood get all cooled off by their poofy cream fillin' as I watch Henry pick tater tot bits out of the rims of his glasses. He's near got them all fished out by the time the fifth period warnin' bell rings, but when I catch him after school on the bus, I notice some ketchup goobers still hangin' on. It looks like he spent the last part of the day knockin' chicken heads off or somethin'. I tell him so, and we ruminate on chickens dashin' around well after their heads have been knocked off. Henry wonders if the Headless Horseman is part chicken. I reckon he is. But then Zach Tilston over-hears us, whips his weasely red head around, and gives me hateful eyes.

"You're so stupid, Olive Abernathy. Just 'cuz you and your whole redneck family got chicken blood runnin' through your veins don't mean everyone else does."

And that was it. That was goddamn it. I'd had it with family trees and government cheese, tater tot torpedoes and Aqua Net updos. Some loudmouth ginger slingin' shit and callin' me chicken was the final straw. I reeled back my right arm like Robin Hood stringin' a bow, and then I let 'er fly. My right hand was still scabbed over from mee-tin' Marcy's chin, and I about cried out as the crusty little bits grated off on Zach Tilston's cheekbone. Then there was a big lurch, and I thought for sure that God, or Fa-ther Time, or worse yet, Mama, had hit some ginormous pause button so they could haul me off for a whoopin'. It was nearly as bad. "OFFFFFFFFFFFFFFFFFFF!" come screamin' down the aisle-way right along with that big ole grump of a school bus driver. She's got a fire in her milky eyes that I ain't never seen before, and the way she's poundin' towards me, snortin' and steamin' like she is, I might as well be wearin' a red cape. But her big ass stops right next to Zach, who's palmin' his face and tryin' real hard to hide his teary eyes, and then she points a meaty finger at me. "YOU. OFF." That says it all, so I scoop up my bookbag and wiggle my way past her.

I can hear her pantin' real hard as we brush sides, and I peek over, thinkin' I might see one of those big rings swingin' from between her nostrils. I reckon it'd be an improvement. I'm tempted to tell her so, but I can hear her fumin' some business about "I don't get paid enough for this," so I just tell it to the little devil on my shoulder, and he chuckles. Me and him are havin' a nice, good laugh together as I make my way off the bus. Once I lay feet on the red dirt just outside the door, I find myself wonderin' if Hell's really as bad as Pastor Higgins makes it out to be. Maybe hellfire's kinda nice come wintertime. Maybe me and the Devil'd roast marshmallows. Maybe he'd tell me ghost stories. I bet he's got some good ones.

I'm feelin' pretty cocky about my new life as the Devil's girl Friday when the ole Bus Bull slides her door shut and clips me in the backside. I whip right around to see her beamin' from behind the glass and Henry standin' just shy of my elbow. "Hey," he says, wavin' a weak hand. "Hey," I says back, givin' my head a scratch. "Why'd ya get off?"

Now he's scuffin' at the ground with his clompy ole-man shoes and watchin' 'em like a yellow brick road might spring up under there if he clicks 'em together just right. His mussy hair falls over his eyes 'til I figure he can see about as good as Mee-maw's nasty ole Shih Tzu, and then he tells me, "Well, I wasn't gonna leave you out here all alone. And besides, someone's gotta keep you out of trouble."

The shoulder devil don't like that, but Henry's probably right. I'd got myself in a mess of hot water today, and it weren't even suppertime yet. I peer up at the fat, orange sun hangin' mid-way in the sky and figure I got a few hours left to get myself back in God's good graces. But when Henry says, "We oughta call your Mama to come pick us up," I decide that me and the Devil still got time to play a few rounds before I call the game.

"You crazy?" I say back. "My Mama's gonna whoop me six ways from Sunday if I call sayin' I got kicked off the bus again. And 'sides, I ain't got a quarter."

Damn Henry... He whips that Shih Tzu hair outta his eyes and fishes a bright, shiny quarter from the pocket of his trousers. I don't think I could hate those starchy, ole-man pants any more right now if he asked me to iron 'em. "Here," he says, handin' it over, but I just peer at the thing like it's got cooties. He keeps his hand held out though, and I'm watchin' a little piece of pocket fuzz stuck to the coin flutter around in the wind when my ole shoulder devil hangs over and whispers in my ear. Henry sets eyes on me right about then and says I'm "gettin' an evil grin," but I just let the corners of my mouth curl on up anyway, and then I snatch me that quarter.

The pay phone's a few hundred yards off, but I got long, strong legs that can climb any tree in the bayou, and Henry's always scudderin' around like he's pushin' an old-people walker, so I beat him there by a mile. I feed my quarter in the slot, dial up my favorite set of numbers shy of my birthday, and do a miserable job of bein' patient as the rings keep countin' up in my ear. Somewhere between five and six, I start gettin' antsy, which is right about when "Thank you for callin' Hubbard Retirement Villa, how can I help you?" pops outta the handset.

It's Dolores. I can tell. I'd know that chirpy, fake voice anywhere. It always seems sorta funny to me that this sweet little voice, this voice that sounds like a Tinker Bell fart or somethin', is trapped inside a big, ugly yeti with fake nails that look like turkey claws. I figure she knows my voice too, so I make like I got a frog in my throat and grumble, "Yes, I'd like to speak with Mister Arthur Barton."

I think I hear them turkey claws clickin' on a desktop. "You would, would you?"

I croak back, "I would," just as Henry rolls up, all flush-faced and lookin' ready to expire. I can tell he's fixin' to say somethin', and I bug eyes at him so he knows to hush up. But it's like Dolores can feel my nerves wormin' through the phone line. "This Olive?" she says, real snipey. Forget Tinker Bell, that was a Holstein fart.

The frog's still inched halfway up my throat, and I can feel him jerkin' around in there like he ain't sure if he's meant to talk or if I am. While me and him are muddlin' our predicament, I hear another ring come from Dolores' end of the phone. She tells us, "Hold on," and starts playin' some God-awful disco music that probably gets piped in from the elevator headed down to Hell. I listen to that until my ears are fixin' to bleed as Henry's burnin' a hole through me with his eyeballs. I can tell he's about to pop his lid if I don't say somethin' soon, so I cop to callin' Gramps just before the music cuts out.

Then there's a funny click in my ear, and "Hey kiddo" comes tootin' in to join it.

"Hey Gramps!" I say, way louder than I oughta. "Thought you was Dolores comin' back to screech at me." Gramps sniggers. He hates Dolores too. It's our thing.

Then he asks, "What's up?" but I can barely hear it over the sound of a couple ole biddies cacklin' it up on his end of the line. I hear one of 'em call him 'Albie' and then add some nonsense about strip shuffleboard, so I just talk all the louder. I give him the lowdown on me and Henry's pickle, so he tells them old turnips he "ain't got time for games right now" and pledges to come to my rescue. Ten minutes and four games of dirt tic-tac-toe later, I spy the Olds creepin' up on us like a stupid dog that don't know it's too big to be sneaky. Gramps steers the ole boat around about twenty feet off from the phone booth, parks, and climbs out wearin' a moth-bitten, three-piece corduroy suit and enough hair oil to fry up a family of pigs. Then he swaggers on over to us, tuggin' at his lapels and waggin' his head. I'm fixin' to call him slick when he beats me to it and starts in about "lookin' pretty smart for an ole fart."

Henry chuckles at that and smiles for the first time since we got off the bus. That makes me smile too, and Gramps joins in with a big, toothy grin fulla shiny dentures that probably coulda eclipsed the sun. So we's all smiles pilin' into the Olds. Me and Henry both call shotgun at the same second, so everybody squeezes in up front, and since Gramps says seatbelts are "codswallop," it don't matter a lick that there ain't enough to go around. But Henry gets to fussin' somethin' fierce about folks launchin' through windshields and havin' their fool heads popped off, so I scoot on closer to Gramps and tell Henry to strap himself in. Of course, he won't. He just folds his stubby arms over his chest and gives a good pout until I agree to share with him. Meanwhile, Gramps revs up the engine and lays a smooch on Gran's picture. He'd had that thing hangin' up in his visor since the day the angels called her home, and sometimes, when he was trollin' around town, folks'd say they heard him singin' "Brown Eyed Girl" so loud that Gran could probably hear him up in Heaven. Of course, if you pressed him, he'd tell you some nonsense about her havin' a "fanny the size of Texas" or "a temper like a shotgun—with a hair-trigger and the power to take a man's head off." Hell, at her funeral, he even stood up in front of Pastor Higgins and half the town talkin' about how he'd been hangin' his "hook in the waters of Louisiana for sixty-five years and never caught a colder fish" than Gran. But to this day, he loved her somethin' crazy, and he did a miserable job of hidin' it. I had a thought to tease him as he laid lips on that photo of hers for the zillionth time, but I weren't about to lose my free ride. Mama didn't raise no fool. But it seemed Henry's momma did. He made some dumb *woo-woo* noise, and Gramps clapped the visor shut.

"So what'd you little twists do this time?" Gramps barks, side-eyein' Henry through his dime-store cheaters.

Of course, everybody on God's green earth knows that Henry didn't never do nothin' naughty unless Olive had her fingers all stuck up in it, but Henry just shrugs anyhow. Gramps goes *humph*, and pretends like I'm not a big, fat elephant sittin' smack-dab between the two of them, and even though my little devil says not to, I fess up to sockin' Zach Tilston a good one. That gets me a growl from Gramps 'til I add in the bit about Zach callin' us all chicken-blooded rednecks, and then he comes back with a high-five and says, "How's about a malt?"

Like he needs to ask. Mee-maw says, "Sweets are like little children. Have too many and you'll find yourself dealin' with a fat ass and uncontrollable shits," but hell if I care. Mama and Papa don't never take us out for malts. They're way too cheap. But Gramps is livin' high on the hog on account of Uncle Sam, and so he pops his eyebrows and we head towards Mott's Diner. It's all full'a blue-hairs eatin' their supper around this time of day, but that's all the same to me. Those ole-timers usually got plenty of stories and hard candy to share. And Gramps starts us off with a whopper. He's crusin' us down Mulberry Drive, where it scoops under the interstate, braggin' about how him and Gran hopped this train west of Alabama that was goin' some fifty miles an hour, when I hear a screech that rattles my bones. Then it's like God jerks me up by the shorthairs, my seatbelt cuts into my guts, and the whole world turns upside down.

CHAPTER FIVE

In the summer of '79, Hell bubbled right up through the loamy Louisiana soil. The air got frightful heavy, and the sun swelled up into an angry tomato fixin' to sizzle us all like ants on the sidewalk. Mama said the Devil must'a come down to Georgia and taken a wrong turn. But every damn day, no matter how sticky and itchy my drawers got, and no matter how buggy and muggy that swampy air was, I walked the mile and a half from the school bus stop up to Saint Vincent's to visit Gramps. He said he had, "ole, crumbly bones" that were a helluva lot easier to break than ones "still green in the middle" like mine, but I reason it was him crackin' his dome on the windshield that landed him in the hospital and not us kids. Bein's that me and Henry came outta that accident clean as a pair of turtle doves, I ask him later on if he still thought seatbelts were a bunch of hogwash, but "Pfft, seatbelts," was all he said.

It was a fine time for me though, perched up beside his hospital bed with all the beepin', and boopin', and video-game-lookin' gadgetry lightin' up his crazy stories. Mama was fearsome cross with me since the accident anyhow, so even the hospital was a vacation from home. I s'pect she knew just as well as I did that had I not been booted off the school bus, Gramps'd never have come to get me and never got T-boned by a Chevy Nova with shit brakes and a cab fulla fresh-drained Budweiser cans. Of course, Henry's momma was plenty ticked too. Probably because she wanted all that Budweiser for herself. Still, she cursed me up one side and down the other, sayin' my name like it was Devil-speak… sayin' that I was the worst friend that any kid ever had in all the whole history of the world. And who knows, maybe she was right. So I just listened real heard to Gramps tell about gators in Kissimmee and starlit skies over Winnipeg until I forgot about what a shitty girl I was.

Most'a Gramps' stories were about as historically accurate as a *Flintstones* episode, but we liked our little lies, me and him. He even gave me glossy new postcards every day, sayin' they landed in his lap by way of some measle-ridden gypsy or bungled-up pilot who swooped in to have his knuckles cracked. Of course, we both knew damn well that they come from the gift shop. But neither of us said so. A week in, we'd been through the high plains of South Dakota, tucked up under Washington's evergreens, and on out to Minnesota to see Paul Bunyan and his big blue ox. Gramps said those ole roadside attractions were "about as useful as a fork in a soup kitchen" since they were always gummed up with tourists, but hell, I'd pay cash money to see a blue ox any day of the week. And I reckoned that any place plugged up with touristy folks was a place worth visitin'. I told Gramps so, but he just squinted at me like he was channelin'

Popeye's ghost and said, "Naw kid, all the best places are off the beaten path." Then he tells me about him and Gran hoboin' up the West Coast rails and seein' all manner of monstrous whales, and furry otters, and seals that'd sun themselves on flat rocks like fat ladies on the beach. He says them seals would eat up every goddamn salmon in sight until the fishermen spat at 'em and called 'em dirty names. Gramps figures the seals were pretty smart, though, because they were always plump and sassy, while most the fisherman were scrawny and looked flat miserable most the time. He reasoned them seals were even more clever than that pet possum he had five summers back... and to this day he swears that thing understood more words than most kids in the Louisiana school system. He was goin' on good about that ole possum durin' one of our afternoon visits when in walks this busty nurse whose clothes musta got shrunk in the dryer. "Hey there, Mister Barton,' she says, all smiley. "Got a visitor today, I see."

That nurse had some purdy blue eyes, but Gramps didn't notice. Seems he was more worried about her hot dryer and that dinky little top. He was talkin' all soft and sweet at her when a fussy little fella in a lab coat waddles in and asks if Gramps recognizes him.

Gramps just snarfles and says, "Fella, I'm 87, and I got glaucoma. You could be a coatrack for all I know."

That fussy man don't seem too impressed. He's got these thick, black eyebrows that coulda been squares of Papa's electrical tape. He pushes 'em together 'til they touch and makes a fierce unibrow that gives me the giggles. That don't seem to impress him either, so he shoos me outta the room to "talk grownup stuff." Funny, 'cuz he don't look grown to me. But I soldier on out into the hall anyway, stop just shy of the door jamb, and plant my back against the wall outside Gramps' room. From there, I can hear ole unibrow-ribbin' Gramps about his shoddy vision, and bathroom breaks, and everythin' in between. He starts fussin' about bruised this and broken that, and how all Gramps' bits oughta be mendin', but they aren't. "Well, I ain't no spring chicken, Doc," Gramps says back. "And that's just as well. They usually find their way to the dinner table anyhow."

That pops a laugh outta me that probably coulda passed for a burp were it not for the little snigger at the end. I hear a commotion just after my jaw stops waggin', and before ya know it, Doctor Unibrow is standin' in the open doorway and starin' his mean little dagger-eyes at me. I sorta bat my lashes, but folks are right... you gotta be pretty for that to work, so he just twists his daggers in all the deeper, backs up into the room, and then slams the door in my face. Yeesh, I must'a sat there on the floor beside Gramps' door for hours. Okay... so maybe not *hours*... but some of the longest minutes in the history of my young life. Sittin' there in a stinky hospital with sick folk draggin' by their tennis-ball-feeted walkers and rolly-coat-rack-IV-stands makes time slow down. I have it on good authority... that's a genuine fact. Meemaw's got stacks of those *Enquirer* magazines and once, when she was showin' me irrefutable evidence that Elvis is alive and livin' in a condominium in Mobile, Alabama, I saw a blurb talkin' about how the space-time continuum is all cattywampus in places where lots of dead or soon-to-be dead folks congregate. That got me to thinkin' and wonderin' which of these droopy-faced hobgoblins wheelin' past me is primin' up for the big dirt nap. Most of 'em got those breathin' straws stuck up their noses that Gramps says are for folks nearin' tits-up, so I reason that just about everybody passin' me is courtin' the Grim Reaper. Hell, one gal comes scootin' by who looks so close to croakin' out that I feel like tellin' her to waddle on down to the morgue. She just calls me "Kitty" and starts makin' a good go of tryin' to pet me when Gramps' door pops open and the Doc waddles out.

"You can go back in," he says, kinda quiet. He looks like someone just told him that his puppy died, and his little tape eyebrows have gone back to where they oughta be. I'm glad he ain't cross with me no more, but even gladder that I didn't become some half-dead lady's lap pet.

I beat feet back into Gramps' room before either one of 'em can snatch me, or needle me, or make me sit in that icky hallway one minute longer. When I come up on him, Gramps is lookin' just like the Doc, and so I ask him if his puppy got run over too.

Gramps sniffs out a laugh, but I can tell it ain't real. Then his eyes circle around the room like he's lookin' for the answer to my question, and when they roll back, he smiles extra big to make up for that fake-ass chuckle. "Naw," he drawls, "I'm just wonderin' where that nurse got to. There was talk of a sponge bath. Promises were made."

All I can say is "Eeeewwww" as I'm screwin' up my nose. I ruminate for a second with my face all puckered up, and then I reason, "That earned me another story."

Gramps says he "figured it did," but this time he calls me right up onto his bed with a pat. We get all stretched out side by side, like me and Mama used to do under the clotheslines on wash day, forever ago. I can near smell the sweet Ivory soap twistin' around on the same breeze that carried wispy clouds overhead. Mama always said it looked like "some lazy fool tried to whitewash the sky," and then she'd *snap, snap, snap* away with her clothespins as God and everyone in the great state of Louisiana got a good look at my underthings. I remember one time I was out there, starin' up at some fancy kerchiefs that Mama and Papa got on their weddin' day, and I told her, "I'm gonna grow up and marry me a man who's gonna treat me like a princess."

She peeped out from behind some sheet the size of Mexico right then and hooted, "Child, you believe that… I got some magic beans to sell ya!" And then she laughed and laughed… like she was the funniest gal ever to hang a clothesline. But that laugh cut off real quick. I remember wonderin' if she swallowed a bug or somethin', but I peeked up to find her starin' off into the yonder, where the road cuts in for our driveway and the mailbox post makes a big cross sproutin' from the earth. She stared there for a time, and came back at a hush, "I always thought I wanted me an older man. A fella who was sorta dark and mysterious. A fella with an accent. A fella who could dance."

I sniggered, "So you was gonna marry Gomez Addams?" but I didn't get nothin' but cricket-song in return. Mama just kept on lookin' at that mailbox cross and pinnin' her laundry. I decided right then and there that she didn't have no sense of humor and wouldn't never understand me. So I went off and did my own spot of daydreamin', but it wasn't nothin' compared to the tales that Gramps tells. And it's him I'm layin' beside now, not that Morticia wannabe.

I peer back and see his eyes all lit to the nines. I can tell he's cookin' up a hot story under that tongue of his, and sure enough, he starts in about waves of harlow-gold wheat toastin' under the ripe Kentucky sun. Then he tells me about the rail lines that took him and Gran through a ghost town out West Virginia way, where great big houses with saggy faces and hollow bellies had sat empty for a century 'cuz folks were too scared to live in 'em. He swears up one side and down the other that him and Gran camped in one of those drafty ole houses overnight and seen a bona-fide ghost traipsin' around, rattlin' its chains. He knows I ain't no rube though, so he pops in as I'm quirkin' my eyebrows and says, "I get ya, kid. I trust folks spoutin' all that ghost hogwash about as much as a fart after Mexican food, but I seen that thing with my own damn eyes! And I about soiled my drawers when it looked back!" I don't say nothin' in return, but I feel little goose pimples pop up on my arms as he keeps on talkin' about all the boo'in' and slammin' doors, and other ghosty noises that kept him and Gran up all that night. He says they hit the bricks come dawn and caught the first train outta Dodge. He says he ain't heard a rattlin' chain since without thinkin' of that spooky ole specter with its face slidin' off and its trap stretched open like the mouth of a grave. Then he goes, *"Boo!"* and needles me real good in the rib. I think I might'a soiled my drawers too.

It seems that after the ghost town, they made it out to the Great Lakes. Gramps' eyes turn twinkly as he trails on about him and Gran lookin' out over the moody blue, watchin' lily pads fulla fat bullfrogs and snags of cattails float on by. He says the nights out there were real clear and that when the train climbed over the hilly parts of Wisconsin, the stars got extra big and lit Gran's face up like a shiny apple dumplin'. He says that he figures way up there, they were closer to God, and so the angels just shone a little brighter. I think I see him tear up a bit.

"You cryin'?" I ask.

Gramps sniffs. Sure as shit he was cryin'. But he bucks up right quick and tells me, "Cryin's for ninnies" before ramblin' on about some fierce mulberry sky they seen after a Southern summer storm back in '54.

I can't help it. I cut in, "Why'd you do it, Gramps? Why'd you give up seein' all that beautiful countryside?" 'cuz I can't help but wonder.

He answers back with some yammer about havin' a family and makin' a home in Louisiana, but that don't sit right with me. "Why'd you want some yowly, no-good, spittin'-up babies to chase around when you coulda kept on chasin' fallin' stars and all that adventure with Gran?" That perks him on the spot. He hoists his saggy ole self up in bed to where I'm near nosin' his armpit, and then he says, "Child, I seen a beautiful thing or two, but your mama was the purdiest thing I ever seen in all my days. I gotta say, I never thought much of babies. Hell, they get born every day. But when your Gran laid that pink little thing in my lap and it scooped up my finger, I couldn't remember any day before that."

I wonder if Gramps has finally gone Looney Tunes. Every baby I ever seen was sticky, and wailin', and usually had its drawers fulla shit. I peek up at him, muddle what size straitjacket he's gonna need, and bite my tongue as he picks up talkin' about Gran sittin' with Mama on the porch in some hand-me-down rockin' chair that'd probably seen more ladies' fannies than Elvis Presley. His eyes turn misty again, thinkin' on Gran, and baby Mama, and that ole creaky porch. He says that back then, folks'd congregate on their screened stoops sippin' sweet tea and homemade huckleberry wine as the moon waxed like a wink from God's silvery eye. Then he sorta sputters like a dyin' engine and says, "But she's all grown now, and a fine mama herself."

"Fine mama?" shoots outta me like firewater. I jerk up and spin to face his moony mug, snarlin' nasty as I can.

He don't bat a salty ole eyelash. Just nods. "Yup. Only mama I ever met who could do magic." "Pfft, what magic's that?"

Gramps draws his horsehide arms over that hospital gown of his. I can see his knobby elbow bones pokin' out from under his skin. The right one's got two liver spots on it that are starin' me down as he muses, "As I recollect, she's the only mama in all of Louisiana who can turn olives into thimbles and monsters into dust bunnies."

I blink back. He grins. "A little girl named Olive told me that, way back when."

I blink again. Then I curl my lip. He's still grinnin'. That's about the time my brain puzzles all the pieces together. This sappy ole coot ain't my Gramps. My Gramps sent Pete and Wyatt out into his garden to pick up rabbit poop and told 'em it was Easter candy. My Gramps swore his greatest regret in life was never figurin' out how many licks it took to get to the center of a Tootsie Pop. My Gramps didn't go on about the moon and tear up over ole rockers fulla fat granny fannies. It was all the fault of that ever-lovin' rainbow splatter of pills and drippy IV bags that numbed his brain to mush. But I didn't wanna tell him so. Who wants to hear that they're swallowin' down fistfuls of crazy pills? So I just nod and throw back that fake smile he give me earlier. It's some Oscar-level stuff, so he slurps it up like hospital cafeteria tapioca.

The puddin' grin don't stick long though. I don't mean to, but I wonder out loud, "Why here, though? Why stick your roots down in shit soil, where everybody hates your guts and wants ya to rot?"

"Oh, it weren't always like that," Gramps fesses up. Then his eyes go off lookin' at somethin' far away like he's Columbo's noodlin' a murder mystery. They get a little wet around the edges too as he draws a knuckle past his nose and tells me, "Folks around here liked us just fine at first. In fact, your Gran had her a dress shop down on Main, and everyone in town stepped outta there feelin' like the cat's pajamas. Me too. I had good work back then. Steady pay."

"Yeah?"

"Yeah," Gramps says back. Then he gets quiet. He's still starin' off, maybe tryin' to figure whodunit. Was it Gran with a candlestick in the dress shop? Maybe dumb ole Uncle Ern with a wrench in his playpen?

Finally, I gotta ask, "So what happened?"

Crickets. Nothin' but crickets and that bee-bop-boo-beep of all those hospital thingamajiggers.

"Gramps?"

He spooks. But when he looks up, it's like only part of him comes back. I figure the other part's still back in 1950-somethin', big-eyein' Gran in her silk stockin's and swimmin' through the fatbacks in the land of milk and honey. "Welp," the here part of Gramps says, "There was a little trouble with your mama down there at the church and, well... after that... things were just... *different.*"

I'm already imaginin' little mini-Mama doggie-paddlin' through the holy water fountain and stickin' chewed-up bubblegum between Saint Mary's toes as I ask, "Different how?"

"Oh," Gramps drawls, "folks stopped comin' to your Gran's shop. I got me a pink slip at work. Had to sell the house in town."

Bee-bop-boo-beep. Bee-bop-boo-beep. All o' Gramps goes back to yesterday. None stays to talk to me. I watch his wrinkly ole lips break apart and then snap close like a rusty screen door. I think I hear them creakin'.

"So?" I whisper, cranin' towards him on the bed so we're just close enough to pass a secret without no one seein'. "What'd she do?"

His eyes wheel around and get bright. Every bit of him floods back. "Oh," he hoots, "don't you nevermind that. Ain't nothin' for a young thing like yourself to be thinkin' about. That was way back when. Hell, we were still writin' on stone tablets as I recollect!"

I grin. I can't help it. I know he's tryin' to throw me off the scent, but it's good to hear him sassin' again. Still, I can see the sad holdin' onto him, and I know who put it there. "Leave it to Mama," I growl. "Ruinin' ever'thing, like usual."

He shoots me whoopin' eyes. "Don't you act grown, girl. Don't you go thinkin' you know, 'cuz you don't."

Damn. I think I'd rather have crazy Gramps. I droop my lower lip, and he gets soft again. Then he spies the time, and says, "Besides, little miss, you'd better get your rear outta here if you mean to catch that Greyhound bus!" He's right. That clock pointin' its sour face at his hospital bed ain't givin' me but ten minutes to make the bus stop if I wanna catch a ride home with Huckleberry. "This story ain't over," I tell him, gatherin' up my book-bag and givin' him the business stare. It ain't *the look,* but I throw in a sassafrass grumble that makes it nearly good-as.

He swears, "Next time…" and shoos me off with all them IVs swingin' from his veins like cooked spaghetti noodles. It takes me six stanky hallways, a few flights of steps, and one slow-ass automatic slidin' door before I shake the thought of askin' Mama to make spaghetti and meatballs for dinner. My sneakers hit pavement. Now I only got seven minutes.

I did a season of track back in fourth grade. Never was keen on team sports, but the notion of lappin' some lily-white, namby-pamby jock who spent half his time flex-in' in front of a mirror had its appeal. Besides, I'd out-run Mama's paddle more than once, and if that didn't make a girl fleet on her feet, nothin' would. So, as I am chuggin' down 8th Street, pumpin' my arms and pantin' harder than a bulldog in a sauna, I just imagine Mama chasin' after me with her monster of a paddle, swingin' up a storm. In my mind's eye, I see that fearsome vein popped outta her forehead, same way it did the day I brought home my first and only-ever doctored-up report card. I can see her stompin' off to grab the paddle even now, yowlin', "Girl, you didn't get no B in Math! You can't even count the number of whoopins you're due!"

I sail over the asphalt, slick as croc snot. I even step

on a few cracks, just to spite Mama… and still make it to the bus stop in four minutes flat. Probably a new world record. Hell, I even have time enough to sit down and jiggle a few rocks outta my shoe before the ole Greyhound hisses to a stop beside me and kicks 'em right back in. "Hey there, Miss Olive" comes spillin' out as Huck opens the door wide as his smile. "How's Gramps today?"

I slip my sneaker back on. "Bonkers."

Huck's eyebrows curl up into smiles as I climb the steps. Then he says, "Ya don't say?" but he's peerin' up in his big ole rearview mirror at some folks in the way back of the bus, and I can tell he ain't got his mind on me. One of 'em, a young gal with a goofy hairdo, makes her way up the aisle and then plops down just across from my usual seat. I park it opposite her, half hopin' she'll talk to me and half hopin' she won't. I ain't there ten seconds before the bus sets off and she says, "Hey, kid."

I ain't no kid. You're the kid! comes inchin' up my throat, but I swallow it back down again even though it feels like a rock in my gut. Mama says you got a "better chance of ridin' a gator in the Macy's Day parade than makin' friends with a smart mouth," so I just say, "Hey" back. Now I really *do* feel like a kid. And now she's lookin' me over like she oughta ask where my mommy is or somethin'. But instead, she starts messin' with her funky, chunky hair, and tiltin' her head like a dumb dog that just heard a noise he ain't accustomed to.

"Where you headed?"

I answer back, "Home," but sorta wish I didn't. Now

she probably thinks I need a diapey change. She's interestin' enough though, so I twist her way and fix on them
fat braids of hers. I don't mean to say it, but, "What's
with your hair?" jumps right outta me. She laughs real
loud, and as her lips peel back, I spy a set of the nastiest brown teeth I ever laid eyes on. Them things could
be wood chips for all I know! She's barin' a picket fence-
worth right at me as she keeps on twistin' them ropes of
hair and callin' 'em "dreadlocks." She says you've gotta
go a good, long while without washin' your hair to get
'em all nice and clumpy like hers. She prattles on about
body oils and *nature's way* and all sort of other funny
business that seems like a bunch of hippy-dippy hooey to
me. She's got patchouli comin' off of her in great, big Pigpen waves, and I'm startin' to wish she didn't sit by me
when she up and drops some nugget about hitchhikin' all
across the country.

I cut her right off with a, "Say what now?"—not givin'
two shits how rude it sounds. And she don't seem to mind
either 'cuz she cuts them dreads off by the shorthairs and
starts in spillin' her adventures.

Damn, I wish I had my postcards on me, 'cuz I'd bet
dollars to donuts that she's been at every single stop in
the book, and then some. She says she's howled at the
Mississippi moon, slept in the well of a California redwood, and watched Manhattan's gunmetal sky cry buckets on all the sad folk who have to punch a time clock
every day. She and her beau'd hopped rail cars, just like
Gran and Gramps, crisscrossin' the nation and livin' off

wild goose eggs and sweet dandelion heads. She tells me they'd had their fill of civilized livin' and hit the wideopen road, playin' their fiddles for vittles and soakin' in the marmalade sunshine. About that time, her fella drifts on up to us and scooches in beside her. I can tell by the look in her eye that she's cross with him. It's the same look that Mama gets when Papa brings home another stray, or worse yet, another woman's cookin'. But this fella done just like Papa always done... he needles her in her soft parts and pecks her behind the ear, and all is forgiven. He tells me his name is Rob, and hers is some funky, made-up bullshit thing like Starshine, or Moonbeam, or some crap like that. It don't matter much to me. After Huckleberry plunks me down at the end of my driveway, I can't remember her name or even his name with any real certainty. All I recall is the way she said it felt, ridin' that open-air boxcar like God done slapped a pair of angel wings on her back and taught her how to fly. I amble down the driveway starry-eyed, holdin' my arms out and dreamin' like I'm flyin'. My bookbag's stuffed with all manner of heavy crap that I couldn't care less about, so when it starts throwin' off my flight path, I drop it right there in the dirt and just kept on soarin'. I fly past Papa's tomato vines, all plugged up with plump little numbers waitin' to hit the spit 'o Mama's fry pan, and acres of glossy cucumbers hangin' fat on the vine. A twisted ole mess of snapdragons is hangin' heavy heads into the strawberry patch, and I sail past 'em, thinkin' back on all those summers that me and Papa spent out in the fields, sucklin' on ruby-stained fingertips and gigglin' like grasshoppers. Mama used to come out too back when she made berry pies for the Farmer's Market. Them Saturdays spent sittin' in the hot sunshine with ladybugs crawlin' over my toes and sellin' Mama's pies was probably some of the best times any girl ever had in a church parkin' lot. Folks with sweet teeth and flat butts from sittin' in their cars all damn day used to come from states over to buy them pies. Ain't a one of them pies ever went to anyone who knew where they came from. Ain't a one passed the lips of anyone who ever spat the name Abernathy. But that weren't enough. All them folks in Lafeyette Proper who knew us enough to hate us didn't want no one knowin' our pies well enough to like 'em. They drew a big red X that looked more like a cross over the spot where Mama'd set up her little pie tent and told her she weren't welcome anymore. She stopped pickin' berries and gigglin' out in the fields after that. But beyond our farmhouse walls... lordy... her stubborn streak was as wide as the Mississippi and scattered with the bones of anyone who dared to cross it. I'm flat flabbergasted when she ain't sittin' on the porch waggin' her ladle at me as I fly up the steps. But inside, it ain't much better. She's talkin' in whispers to Papa in the livin' room and they both look up like spooked possums caught riflin' through the trash when I waltz in. Don't neither of 'em even say hello. Not even Papa. Of course, Pete and Wyatt rocket right over and nearly take me out at the knees. They got a jump rope strung between the two of 'em, and those boys get busy loopin' it around my ankles as a means to hogtie me. I swat at 'em, and call them "lil' shits," which don't sit right with Mama. She rises from the couch like a damn Amazon and threatens me with an Ivory soap bar, but I'm still blowin' bubbles from suckin' on one two days ago, so I give her a quick, "Sorry ma'am" and study my shoes as Papa cools her jets with a fanny pat and a soft peck. He's always kissin' on her rough edges to make 'em smooth, and that does the trick as well as you'd expect. She plops herself back down on the couch and waves me over. Her and Papa slide apart as I make my way, and before I know it I'm wedged in between the two of them. Mama asks how Gramps looked, and I just say, "Crazy," which tugs at the corners of her mouth. She don't have a stitch of makeup on, not that she ever did, and I think how plain she looks next to all those rougedup nurses and red-lipped receptionist ladies at the hospital. But Mama don't care. She don't envy no one, even though they all have loads better stuff than her. I remember she once caught me fussin' over some frilly little number in a shop window, and she just stared strong at her reflection and told me, "Fancy's for folks who don't know their own worth."

Lookin' at her now, she looks worth about a sad-sack fulla pennies, so I go on tellin' her about the dreadlock daredevil from the bus with stars in my eyes. I think I see her smirk when I start in about this mop-headed gal yippin' at the California moon like a fool coyote. And by the time I get to the part where she was fightin' hoot-owls for inchworms and drinkin' toilet-bowl hobo gin, Mama's grinnin' somethin' fierce. I wrap it up, gushin', "I wanna be her! She's my hero!" But that's when Mama's smile flattens like a board. She cups my chin up in her hand so I can smell that Ivory soap twistin' off her wrist bones. I feel my gut lurch a little and make a funny face, which sets Mama's crow's feet to crinklin'.

"Girl," she drawls, "the only hero you oughta be lookin' up to is the one in the mirror."

My funny face gets funnier, and I can feel Papa leanin' into my other side; I smell that earthy smell that's always hangin' onto him tight. I'm thinkin' how Mama ain't got it right at all—that I got oodles of heroes all tucked up in my scrapbook. I got postcards with Amelia Earhart wearin' big, goofy goggles and beamin' like the noonday sun, and I got ones with Gertrude Bell standin' out front of a pyramid that looks big enough to poke God right in His eye. I even got me one from Florida, Missouri of Samuel Clemens holdin' his *Huckleberry Finn* book with that fearless little raft-sailin' shit starin' right back from the cover. Who needs a mirror?

I tell Mama as much, but she ain't got no time for that. She spits back some nevermind business about "silliness" and tells me, "Well, you look a mess. You might wanna find yourself that mirror before Aunt Rosemary shows up for dinner."

"Aunt Rosemary?" ain't but made its way past my curled-up lips before Mama's mouth droops in the opposite direction.

"Rose's drivin' down to check on your Gramps," she tells me. I think I can smell the sour grapes on her breath even though she's leanin' away and into the couch cushions like she wants to disappear in there. Mama's kid sister ain't been out to visit us for a few years now, and I can tell by the twitch in Mama's veiny temple and the way her voice gets dry that absence ain't made her heart grow fonder. I, on the contrary, get to beamin' my fool face off in that very instant. I do as I'm told for perhaps the first time in Abernathy history and scoot off with a quiet smile to brush my tangle of buckwheat curls, and wipe the city soot off 'a my cheeks. Aunt Rosemary ain't like my other relatives. She's got class. She's got a big, fancy loft right there in downtown Chicago. Hell, she's even got all the Bee Gees albums—on cassette tape!

I'm makin' a third pass through my rat's nest of hair and wishin' that Mama'd let me get it blown out into feathers like Farrah Fawcett's when I hear a rare motor that ain't clunkin' growin' nearer to the house. A race to the nearest window shows me a midnight-blue Trans Am with a big, goofy bird painted right across the hood comin' down the drive. Pete and Wyatt slam into my calves as I'm oglin' it, and I kick 'em off as I crane over the sill to get a better look. Sure enough, it creeps up a few feet closer, and I spy Aunt Rosemary's big hair spillin' out the driver's side. She's got those fighter-pilot shades on, and her car's growlin' down to a stop like it's just come in for a landin'. Talk about cool.

I yowl out, "She's here!" and make it to the front door

in two seconds flat. I ain't for certain, but I might'a trampled one of the twins on takeoff. Who cares? Aunt Rosemary's here! She cracks her driver's side door, and there's this long yawn that I imagine is about what angels make when they wake up from a good night's sleep. And *critch-crunch,* down come the spiky ends of two fancy-ass heels settin' foot in our redneck gravel driveway. They got shimmery, gold, bell-bottom cuffs hangin' just over the top of 'em in halos, and I gotta figure those pants smell somethin' like honey and money.

"Well, look at you," are the first four words I've heard from Aunt Rosemary in as many years, and I reckon they've aged themselves to perfection. She gives me the full elevator scan with those emerald eyes of hers as her waves are bobbin' in the breeze. "Miss Olive Abernathy, all grown up," she purrs.

Damn right. It's about time that somebody noticed I was grown. I bullet past the threshold, off the porch, and down two steps before I get to thinkin' that grown folks don't act like Santa Claus done come to town every time their aunt shows up. Then my legs get stiff, not knowin' how fast or how slow ladies of a certain age oughta walk, and I sorta stick on the spot. So, I'm just left there, pawin' at the dirt with a little girl's sneaker and watchin' lightenin' bugs fill in the space between me and Aunt Rosemary.

She smiles. Her teeth are so dang white. *How'd they get that white? Do they have fancy places in the city where you get a massage while they paint your teeth with white-out and teensy little brushes?*

The crickets get to chirpin' extra loud just then, fillin' in every bit of air that ain't stuffed with lightenin' bugs. Then Aunt Rosemary smiles all the bigger. The lightenin' bugs probably think she's their queen or somethin'. "Well," she busts, "you just gonna stand there, or do I get a hug?"

I forget all about bein' a grownup. I run over. I plant myself smack-dab in her bosom just like I done when I was little. She's bony as hell, but she smells like the little perfume samples that fall outta magazines at the Piggy Wiggly. I feel her skinny arms wrap around me and give a squeeze. That kinda muscle couldn't get the last of my Crest toothpaste outta the tube, but it feels nice to have her holdin' me. It feels nice to have somebody as classy as her not touchin' me by accident. She lets go too soon, though, and I hear her big, hoopy earrin's clankin' against one another as she raises her head and says, "Hello Bess" in a voice that could freeze lava.

Mama's voice is far off—porch steps, maybe further. "Rose" is all she says.

I get shook off right after that, but Rosemary takes up my hand in hers as we follow the voice inside the house while Mama's apron strings vanish past the door jamb. Pete and Wyatt pop up on the porch right thereafter, lookin' shy and mischievous all at once. Them little monkeys bat their eyes and hang thumbs on their overall straps, and all the sudden I'm yesterday's news. Rose beats feet over their way with her heels leavin' holes in the raw earth behind her. She's shriekin', "Oh, you little dolls! Oh, you were just babies when I saw you last!" as if two snot-nosed boys who play marbles with rabbit turds and eat their own boogers are somethin' to get excited about. But it's enough to get Pete and Wyatt wound up and Papa out the door. He gives Rose a kind smile and ducks his head.

"Good to see you, Rosemary" seems like somethin' he'd say to a stranger.

"You too, Jim" seems like somethin' a stranger'd say back. So, we all stand there on the threshold, feelin' strange and passin' around the same strange smile until Pete and Wyatt ditch the innocent act and start playin' like Rose's shimmery pantsuit is a fireman's pole. Papa's gotta scold 'em like he does Boomer for humpin' folks' legs just so that we three can get ourselves inside and watch Rose peerin' around the house with her eyes laid wide. She gets herself a good gander before whistlin' Dixie and callin' our place "the land that time forgot."

"You haven't changed one thing" is what she tells Mama not a minute later. And standin' there, with a yam in one hand and a Mason jar fulla Gran's sweet tea in the other, Mama ain't got a spare finger to wag in protest. She just clips lips as Rose rattles on, "This place is the same as when you were sixteen," after which everybody gets real quiet. Mama and Rose toss around that same strange stare that me and Papa were tradin' with her on the porch, but this time I'm even less sure what it means. So Mama does the same thing she does whenever folks' mouths get quiet... she tries to stuff 'em with food. She starts haulin' out baskets spillin' over with hot cross buns and cornbread the color of Papa's wheat fields in high July until Rosemary's eyes get big as Mama's thighs. Mama always did live her life by the golden rule—butter makes everything better. And about the time I reason there's enough food here to feed half the folks on *The Love Boat* and the whole cast of *Hee Haw*, Rosemary looks out over the table and asks me, "So are you havin' some company over too, Olive?"

Now I know better than to ever invite company over to the house. One time, in second grade, I suckered three girls into comin' out to our place for a sleepover. Papa kept us up into the wee hours tellin' flash-lit tales of the Bayou Devil with its pearly eyeeteeth like possum claws and cackle like a gator crunchin' bone. That story was so damn scary that even the Man in the Moon hid under his cloudy covers, and them girls was so spooked shitless that their folks had to come and pick 'em all up before sunrise.

But Rosemary gives me the wise idea to call Henry for the 453rd time and see if he wants to come for dinner. Henry's different. Henry says we're all just lost buttons, searchin' for our mates. And given all the weird, ole-timey getups he's got hangin' in his closet, I s'pose my family fulla odd buttons fits him real good. Plus, he's funny, and smart as a whip, and good at talkin' to grownups. Last time we ate lunch together, he called this mean sixth grader with a pale face who wears nothin' but black and loves Mexican food "Taco Tuesday Addams," and the cafeteria lady shot a pea out of her nose. Sure as shit he can get Rosemary and Mama smilin' and talkin'. If he can't, no one can.

Only the promise of seein' Henry's goofy, freckled face could tear me off'a Rosemary's elbow, where the scent of Love's Baby Soft seemed to be coursin' through her veins and spillin' over into our house until it smelled like a fancy diaper factory. I can still feel it stickin' to my nose hairs as I skitter into the kitchen and plug the same seven numbers into our phone that I'd dialed so many times before, the paint was wearin' off the keys.

I cradle the receiver as its ringin', and ringin', and ringin', and I'm twistin' that green pigtail cord around, and around, and around my finger until the meaty parts start bulgin' through and turnin' purple. I'm about to give up the ghost when I hear a click, and a big breath, and then Missus Wormwood says a "Hello?" that sounds like it came from way, deep down in a tin can.

I squeak "Hello" back with all the moxie of a mouse, and ask to talk to Henry. Right away, I can hear a grumble risin' up through the receiver, nasty as an ole corpse crawlin' out of its grave.

"No, you may *not,* Miss Olive Abernathy. Just like you couldn't yesterday, and the day before, and the day before that!"

I clap my hand over my mouth, not knowin' if I'm tryin' to keep somethin' in or somethin' out. Most times I call, she's three sheets to the wind and don't even know my name. Either she's back on the wagon or the ole man's monthly liquor-buyin' pension check ain't come in yet. I think I prefer her drunk. And when she starts up talkin' again, I'm sure I do. "Now listen here, little miss Olive. Henry don't need no trouble-makin' friends like you. My little Henry's goin' places. He's gonna be a lawyer, or a doctor, or some kinda big-deal businessman. He don't need no heathen, car-crashin', bare-knuckle-fightin', sassafrass little twit like you draggin' him down."

My hand clamps a little tighter. No good. This shit's gettin' in. I think maybe somethin''s fixin' to come out too, but it just tastes like sick. Missus Wormwood don't care any which way though. I can hear her huffin' through the receiver so fierce that it's pipin' out the other end. She gives a good, final snort and tells me, "Don't you never call here again, Olive!" and then hits me with the *click*.

I don't know what to do with myself after that. I've still got that banana of a handset all pressed to my head and the curly phone cord so tight around my pointer finger that I can't feel it no more. I'm just listenin' to that dead tone ringin' in my ear and tryin' to breathe through the fingers still cupped over my mouth. *Never? Never, ever?*

I keep hearin' it, *Never,* like a far-off holler, tumblin' around in my brain, over and over. I keep seein' Henry's toothy grin bunchin' his freckled cheeks up so they look like dumplin's that got dropped in the dirt. Before I know it, I got hot tears tumblin' all over the kitchen floor, and Mama near slips on 'em as she makes her way in. Her voice ain't much more than the coo of a dove as she asks me what's wrong, and I'm too damn out of sorts to do anythin' but spill the beans. She don't say much. She just pulls me in with those thick arms of hers and says, "Girl, don't you never let no one tell you that you ain't worth a damn, 'cuz the second you believe 'em is the same one it comes true." Then she wicks away my salty, snotty, blubbery tears and gives me a steely eye. I ain't sure whether to hug her or run, but Aunt Rosemary bustin' into the kitchen means I don't gotta do either. She gives us a spooked look and then scuttles over.

"You okay, kiddo?" makes it out of her mouth, but I can't answer back with nothin' other than a bunch more blubberin', which is as close to *no* as you can get. So she scoots up on the opposite side of Mama and swings her soft, wispy arm around my free shoulder. It don't do nothin' to ground me like them meaty ones of Mama's, but it manages to squeeze out a few more sobs that are as good as hiccups.

Mama tells Rosemary that I'm "just havin' some trouble with a friend," which sets Rose's perfect little halfmoon eyebrows risin' on her face. I wonder how she gets 'em so neat like that with no wild hairs pricklin' up. Mama says that ladies draw 'em on with pencils. Despite my fussin', I make a mental note to use the big pencil sharpener in Missus Waldrop's class and get my #2 nice and pointy so that I can draw me on a neat pair like Rosemary's. They look even finer when she tents 'em in the middle and fixes 'em right on me.

"What kind of trouble?"

I burp up, "Henry trouble," but I wish right away that I hadn't 'cuz Rosemary gets all giggly.

"Ooooh… boy trouble" makes me feel like I done somethin' naughtier than what I really done, and all the sudden Rose is needlin' me in my rib and curlin' her hot-pink lips towards the rafters.

I spit back, "It ain't like that," and she gets a sour look, like she's mad that it ain't what she thought it was. I'm tryin' to think up a fib about some *other*, non-Henry boy who *is* like that when Mama breaks in.

"Olive don't chase boys around like that," she says. I can feel her hot eyes lightin' up the cowlick on the tippy-top of my head like a lantern wick as she's glarin' through it at Rosemary. Then I feel Rose glarin' back. It's got a cold lick to it.

"Of course she doesn't, Bess," Rosemary says while fingerin' the cuff of my best shirt. It looks like a genuine Indian's jersey if you squint at it just right. But pinchin' it tight, Rose says, "Just look at her! You've got her dressed like you did four years ago… like you did four years before that. You're tryin' to trap her here in this damn museum… just like you did me… just because you're afraid. You're afraid of…"

And then—crickets. Nothin' but crickets… bitin' through the coldness of that kitchen all the way from their thistle perches out on the back forty. Crickets that knew Mama's story, and knew my story, and probably knew Rose's story too. Crickets that sat under the violet sky, chitter-chattin' about us crazy Abernathys. Crickets with noisy lives like ours. And half of me wanted to follow their lead and start swappin' stories, because all of me felt like I was watchin' a movie I'd missed the first half of. But just as soon as I cracked my lips, it was like Mama knew what was comin'.

She sputters out a *pffft* that'd put Da Beast to shame, tells Rosemary she's "got no right" and "don't know a damn thing," and then loads me up with a shepherd's pie the size of a hubcap. If I weren't ready to chew my own leg off, I'd'a probably pressed her, but my gut gets the better of me, and so I skulk off to load the table with meaty curls of steam like dragon's breath leadin' my mind and self in the opposite direction. If the dinner table were a few feet further off, I'd have taken a whoppin' bite right outta the top before I made it. But I set it down nice and slow, right next to my plate, and think hard about lickin' the top so no one else will want any. Pete and Wyatt pop up about that time, though, and I can feel Wyatt lookin' me over with his squinty eyes. Either he can tell I been cryin' or he's wise to my lickin' idea. He licks his chops, and then him and Pete start circlin' the table like hungry hyenas. Them steam curls are callin' my brothers too, and so I hunker down over the shepherd's pie with my tongue half hung out, ready to lick away.

Papa gives me a goofy scrunch-face as he pops his head in the dinin' room, but then he catches sight of Rosemary swingin' in behind me and flattens out. He's studyin' her face and its look that tells the room she's been put upon. I can see confusion wormin' its way into his brow. But then Pete clamps his thigh and draws Papa's eyes down. Quick as a wink, he's a pussy willow again, pattin' Pete's doughy little mug gentle as can be. All that mushy shit's just for show though, 'cuz while Pete's meltin' into Papa, Wyatt swoops in and snakes my pie right out from under me.

This ain't my first rodeo. I snag that little turd by the back of his overalls before he can get a single step in, and all five pounds of that glorious, meaty pie takes flight and rockets down to earth... right at Mama's incomin' feet.

"Ooolllliiiivvvveee!" just officially became a curse word. Mama chases me up one end of that table and down the other. I ain't never seen that woman move so fast. I'd swear she has cheetah blood runnin' through her veins if I didn't know better. And the way she growls—boy howdy, she'd be the leader of the pack. She'd-a caught me too, were it not for a slimy carrot chunk that catches her heel and sends her to the floorboards near Rose's chair. But she ain't down a hot second before risin' up with a chicken giblet stuck to her forehead. I make a break for the front door, thinkin' I'm home free, but I don't get a step over the jamb before I catch sight of Henry's momma, marchin' up the drive. She's wearin' a powder-blue pantsuit with pleats like daggers and one of those I-wannatalk-to-your-manager looks that says she's all business. I ain't seen her this spiffied-up since before Henry's daddy died. And she sure sees me. She's barkin' my name with every click of her shiny heels up the porch steps, and I don't know whether to run back in the house or juke my way past her and head for the hills. Dumb-ass me, I just freeze.

All I hear is, "Where's your folks, Olive?!" before Mama's hot bull breath comes ticklin' at my ear and her big shadow spills over my shoulder onto the porch boards.

All the sudden, Mama's cool as a cucumber. She asks Miss Wormwood, "What's the problem, Ida?" but don't get another word in before that prim ole blueberry starts spittin' nails.

"Problem is your girl," Mrs. Wormwood hisses. "I done tol' her a hundred times if I tol' her once to *stop* callin' my house. I don't want my boy hangin' around her no more, and she can't seem to get that through her thick head!"

I feel Mama boilin' up beside me. It's like standin' next to Satan gettin' a suntan. But it seems that Missus Wormwood don't feel the heat inchin' her way. She just puffs her chest out all the bigger and goes on, "Ever since you and me were girls, Bess... ever since that mess down at the church... well, you and your kind've just been trouble. I didn't never want my little Henry hangin' around with your Olive anyway, but he... well... he ain't got many friends. And he don't know a good egg from a bad one."

Now Mama's tappin' her heel. Maybe she's fixin' to charge. Papa and Rosemary must hear it too, 'cuz I feel 'em flood in behind me before gettin' dammed up by Mama's anvil shoulders. Missus Wormwood hears it for sure, 'cuz she shuts her pie hole up, and somewhere between Mama's fumin' and her silent seethin', I get to thinkin' about Henry. That *"never, ever"* starts pingin' around my brain again, and I see Henry sittin' on our raft, floatin' down the bayou all alone, gettin' twisted up in the mossy vines and prickly pines until he's nothin' but a little wink on the horizon. It makes me wanna cry, and I can't stand it. So I do the only thing I can think to do. I beg, "Please Missus Wormwood, *please*. I know I messed up. I know I'm a half-rotted egg that stinks eight days a week. I know I don't deserve him... but Henry's my best friend in the whole, wide world, and I just can't lose him. I just can't. Please, please, *please* don't say I can't never talk to him again. He's all I got."

Then I just stood there. I just stood there with my eyes pinched closed, waitin' to get drown in Miss Wormwood's shitstorm. But she just peeped. She just peeped like a little baby chick cluckin' its first cluck. And when I opened my eyes up, she weren't starin' me down like I spit in her sandwich no more. The little pleats in her pantsuit sorta wilted and got softer. I could see her mouth pinch up like maybe she had a smile tucked inside her cheek just waitin' to get out. So I baited the hook. I talked sweet to that smile... I told it that Henry was "the best boy" and "the best friend any girl could ask for." I even said, "I'd be broke without him."

The smile started wormin' around, peekin' its little head out... tuggin' Missus Wormwood's lips up and up. But the thicker I laid it, the hotter Mama got. Her breath was fire on my neck as she come up behind me and whispered, "Girl, don't you say that. Fragile things get broken. Women like us—we do the breakin'." And sure enough, that spooked the smile back to where it come from. Henry's momma huffed her an ornery huff, drew her arms back over that blue blazer, and swallowed any forgiveness that was creepin' up her throat down deep. "You know what your problem is, Bess?" she says, like it's a question that ain't a question. I know it ain't a question because she don't even give Mama the time to answer back before she goes on. "Your problem is that you don't know how to keep that filthy mouth of yours shut. Never have. Never will." Then she stands there a minute, fumin' like a kettle that's got a stopped-up hole with nowhere for the steam to go, and gives Mama this look that ain't nothin' but pure evil.

"If you'd just done like you were tol' back then, Bess... you wouldn't have ruined everything. You wouldn't have ruined good folks' lives. Just like your filty, loudmouth little girl's ruinin' my sweet boy now."

Maybe Mama wanted to reply. Maybe she was waitin' for all those crickets to tell her what to say. Or maybe she was just listenin' to their stories break through the darkness—tryin' to remember way back when to figure what was worth fightin' for and what wasn't. But I guess Missus Wormwood and all that hate-speak was more than Mama and a zillion noisy crickets fulla Abernathy tales could abide because Mama pushed right past me and socked Ida Wormwood square in the face.

And thus was born the legend of Black-Eyed Ida.

CHAPTER SIX

Whenever my little Louisiana town felt like it was closin' up around me like a curly tater bug, I'd daydream of a life on the rails... with the rumble of boxcars and the light from scrollin' stars playin' like a lullaby in the big sky where anythin' was possible. But wakin' up on a steel floor colder than a witch's teat with hay nettles stuck in my drawers weren't quite how I'd pictured it.

* * *

I give a few blinks and pan around Ruby's rusted insides, hopin' she'll rosy up the picture for me, but all I catch is the wide back-end of a trainman passin' off in the distance beyond her open door. I give Henry a poke, and he makes a startled snort like a spooked pig. His momma says that he's got somethin' called "early-onset sleep apnea," which makes him sound like a barnyard animal watchin' *The Exorcist* when he's catchin' Z's. I give him a second poke to pull him outta the pigpen, and he shoots up in a wink sputterin', "What? What?! What's goin' on?!" all crazy-like. He's got a mess of hay stickin' out of his hair, and I figure that about any coyote on God's green earth'd mistake him for a porcupine right about now. Maybe I should tell him. Maybe I shouldn't. Maybe he'll keep predators off our tail.

"You got hay in your hair," I fess up without meanin' to.

Henry's big eyes shoot upwards and near cross themselves. Then he starts pawin' at his head like that time we raided a honey hive near Uncle Ern's house and got all stung to shit. I'm elbow-deep in rememberin' Uncle Ern tell us, *Honey don't come from hives, it comes from the Piggly Wiggly*, before I remember, "I saw a trainman."

Henry freezes mid-swat. His eyes uncross and then they shoot right out the door. "Where?"

I level my finger at Ruby's open mouth. "Out there," I says, "a few hundred yards off."

Henry Jiminy-crickets to his feet, and them last few hay straws fall into a little halo around him. "We gotta hide," he chirps. "We gotta hide, or they'll catch us. They'll beat us. They'll probably lock us up."

Pffft sputters outta me easy as air from a balloon butt. "They ain't gonna do nuthin' to us," I tell Henry, feelin' my Levis get a little tighter. Mama always said, "Girls who get too big for their britches are just fulla shit," and I snarl up my face just thinkin' about that. Then I hear a far-off crunchin' sound of footsteps stompin' through the gravel yard. They're gettin' louder, gettin' closer, and maybe my jeans loosen up a bit.

It feels like burpin' up hot lava, but I admit, "Maybe we *should* hide," and right that second Henry starts scurryin' around, rollin' up our stuff faster than some crazed dung beetle. He tosses me my bag about as good as he does a dodgeball, and I gotta make a catcher's dive to stop it from landin' on that grimy floor with a thud. My slide makes Ruby bellow though, and all the sudden them gravel crunches start gettin' a whole lot louder and whole lot closer together. Now my heart's thumpin', and me and Henry are jumpin' out the same way we came in. We both get a good pan around the yard and don't spot a soul, but I can still hear them footsteps comin' up from Ruby's other side, and they sound more fearsome than a grizzly crunchin' bone.

Henry whispers, "Over here" from beneath his clutched-up little hand, and I feel like we's Watson and Holmes, on the case again. We shoot on over to an up-turned tractor scoop the size of an outhouse and skitter underneath it. It's dark under there and stank-nasty. Smells like motor oil and gear grease, like Papa's workshop, or Gramps... when he'd spend a whole day hangin' out of the Olds' hood like it ate him.

There's a bit of light pokin' up through the scoop's teeth, and I can see that Henry's breathin' hard. For a long time, his momma made him wear an inhaler on a little shoelace strung around his neck. But then one day, we was out in the bayou and got ourselves spooked up a tree by a momma bear amblin' through with her cubs. He started suckin' in breath real fast like that, but his inhaler was plum outta juice. Meanwhile, Momma Bear was gettin' closer, and his breath started comin' faster and noisier. We both knew that he was gonna get us caught, so I grabbed him up and stared him hard right in the eye, the same way Mama done to me when I get myself overwound. I told him that "everything's gonna be okay." That "nothin' matters but you and me," and then I started breathin' like I was breathin' for him. Breathin' slow, and breathin' calm, and breathin' like the whole world weren't crashin' down around us. And then he started breathin' like *me*. And then he didn't need that stupid ole inhaler anymore.

"You okay?" I asks, watchin' his chest heavin'. His shiny eyes roll around in the darkness like wet river rocks and then fix on mine. I feel myself breathin' slow. Slower. Slower still. He hears it too. He starts breathin' slower too. And even though both of us can hear that crunchy gravel sprayin' all over Ruby's insides and those thick trainman boots rattlin' her floor in search of stowaways, it don't matter. The whole world ain't crashin' down around us. It's just me and him, holed up in a tractor scoop, playin' detective in the dark. We sit up in there for a spell even after the trainman's scuffle dies away, whisperin' about the time I ratted Roger Hinkley out for hidin' in a dirty towel hamper inside the girls' locker room. I expect that hamper was a quarter the size of this tractor scoop and Roger was twice as tall as Henry, so it had to get powerful stinky and stuffed inside there. But as I recollect, Roger stayed in there for hours on end... probably rubbin' himself against musty towels that smelled like Prell and nether regions. I remember gettin' red-faced when I told Coach Biggs what I saw while I was comin' in from Phys Ed. And I had to say it twice 'cuz he acted like he didn't hear me the first time. He said he'd rather I'd just kept quiet about the whole thing. *That's what good girls do.*

I'm just about to ask Henry if he thinks Roger might grow up to do shampoo commercials or sell towels at Sears and Roebuck when a sudden lurch outside sends us both ground-hoggin' our heads outta the scoop.

"Shit, the train's goin'!" I bust out, shimmyin' past the tractor teeth. Ruby's already creepin' slow along the track like she means to get away but also like she wants to get caught. Her red-apple hide's more dinged and battered in the daylight, and somehow I like her all the more. I chase her down lickety-split, with Henry right behind me, and get to feelin' like a real hobo as I sling my pack up onto her deck. It ain't much of a fight to board her from there, but once we get up, me and Henry trade looks like we just held up a Wells Fargo and got away scot-free. Then we watch miles of chain-link fence, and mountains of gravel, and ugly ole work trailers slide by at all of five miles an hour. I find myself peekin' up at the head engine, half wishin' I could shout out for the conductor to throw in some extra coal and get to the good stuff. Even with my head poked out like a damn dog lollin' from a car window, I can't get enough breeze to blow my hair back like I'd imagined.

"Why aren't they speedin' up?" I finally bark, kinda wishin' I *was* that dog rollin' down the interstate.

Henry hangs his head out into the dull breeze, but just a peck. He shoots the conductor a lip curl and tells me he "ain't sure" as another round of grey gravel cowpies and big lard-cube-lookin' trailers pass on by. I feel like I'm sittin' in history class, all geared up 'cuz there was talk of a movie, and now I'm watchin' little black-and-white fellas in stuffy uniforms march around philosophizin' about war, and diplomatic relations, and all other kinds of useless hogwash. I reckon I oughta curse Gramps up in Heaven for all his hobo romanticizin', but the thought of it gets me real sad. About then, the impossibly slow train slows up even more and coasts to a full stop. "Why we stoppin'?" is the first thing I think to say, but I follow it up with a few curse words just 'cuz that's the kinda thing that hobo girls do.

Henry don't give me any reply other than a shrug as he eases back into the shadow laid down by Ruby's corrugated canopy. Then he plops himself down cross-legged on her floor and tells me he's keepin' his "eyes out for that trainman." I join him and paw through a little pile of leftover straw as we listen to the big steam engine idlin'. I think to march on up and ask for a refund on my ride, and had I forked over a red penny, I just might've. Henry says he was gettin' motion sick anyhow, and I think about that time we rode a big octopus-lookin' contraption at the Lafayette County Fair and he turned green as a Granny Smith apple. He made me promise never to ask him to ride it again and then bought me four turns at the ring toss for my troubles. I won me a Kewpie doll and used its empty head to stow fishin' bait in. That thing could float and spook water moccasins like nobody's business.

A good ten minutes of me scowlin' and jibber-jabberin' about Gramps and all his bullshit stories goes by before Ruby gives us a little jolt and starts rollin' along again.

We both cheer like idiots, and I hang my head out the door again, waitin' to feel that sweet breeze of freedom tanglin' my hair up in knots. But we just plug along, slow as you go, for another quarter-mile or so before we slide to a second stop. "I think that snail beat us here," Henry says, pointin' down at the still gravelly ground.

"Wouldn't surprise me none," I snarl back. Then I peek up at our Sunday-drivin' conductor and hear his engine windin' down right about the time the trainman spies me. I don't even got time to finish my "Oh, Shiii..." before Henry hits the deck and yells for me to bail too.

All the sudden we're huffin', and puffin', and pockin' the gravel with our tennis shoes flyin' through that rail yard. It's like runnin' in damn quicksand, and I can't seem to find my feet. I ain't even got ground enough under me to catch up to Henry, and every time he glances backwards, his eyes are swellin' up fatter and fatter. I know why too. I can hear that trainman gainin' on us, and I'm just too scared to whip around and find out how near he is to nabbin' me. Henry peeks over his shoulder one final time, and his eyes stretch wider than his glasses. He starts fallin' back, yellin' "Olive! Olive!" right before a thick arm wrangles me around the waist like one of them big canes pullin' a crappy act off'a the stage. All the breath goes outta me, and I heave forward, near folded in half.

"Gotchya!" comes a growlin' in my ear right that minute, and I see Henry stop on a dime and come speedin' back to me as I'm hoisted off the ground.

"Hey, put her down!"

"What *her*?" the growly voice spits back. "All I see here is a dirty train hopper."

I'm still danglin' on this fella's meathooks as Henry stomps up. His doughy cheeks are all flushed, and his chest is flutterin' like a robin's breast. "She ain't no dirty train hopper," he roars. "She's my friend. Now put her down."

The trainman laughs. Sounds like he's tryin' to cough somethin' up. "Well, true as that may be, she *was* hoppin' off a train, and..." he sorta simpers, "she don't exactly look clean."

Henry's still eyein' us both, kinda foamin' at the mouth. If I didn't know better, I'd think he had rabies. He gives my hangman his gruffest look, the same one he gave Libby Jackson that time she threatened to put a flamin' dog turd on his Papa's grave, and then he says, *"Put her down."*

I feel the grip on my gut go soft, and then I feel myself slidin' down smooth as melty ice cream. The voice behind me comes back gentler this time. It says, "Okay, little man, you've got it," and then my soles set down with a crunch. Soon as I feel that lasso come free from my midriff, I shoot on over to Henry's side and finally face the trainman. He's a big, burly fella with shoulders just like them boxcars at his back, and his wide face is beaded up with sweat enough to sink a dinghy. I don't think he means to, but his mouth curls up at the ends like he's fightin' a smile. He says his name is Mack, and he ain't caught a train hopper young as me in all his eighteen years of railroadin'.

"Nobody much hops our trains," he drawls, wickin' away some of them fat sweat dollops with a handkerchief. "Nobody that wants to get anywhere, anyhow."

I gather up some'a that moxie that got me tattlin' to Coach Biggs and ask, "Why 'cuz?" as he spits up another laugh.

"See that," he says, pointin' to a gate off in the yonder. "That there's the end of our yard. We only run cars around here and back up to the paper mill. We ain't got but four miles of track, all told. Hell, I ain't never even seen our locomotive hit ten miles an hour."

Now I feel dumb. Redneck dumb. And I hate it. I hate the feelin' of that stupid Abernathy blood swillin' around inside me. My cheeks rosy up good, and I make like I'm gonna stomp off, but Mack pipes, "Hey, hey, you ain't goin' nowhere," and then comes up on me. "I gotta take you two in," he tells me, shootin' eyes at Henry too. Then he spouts some fancy talk about "federal regulations" and "felony charges," and other words that make my brain and my eyes swell up 'til they hurt. All the sudden, I can't think straight. All I can do is whittle together little pictures in my head, mostly of me and Henry all wrapped up in black-and-white stripes and trailin' little chains like horsetails behind us. Somewhere in the middle of that goofy cartoon playin' in my head, I hear Henry twistin' at the handle of his suitcase. Then I hear his size 7s scuffin' through the gravel as he walks near to Mack. "You ain't really gonna haul us in, are ya?" I hear him sputter.

I glance up as Henry's liftin' his chin and squintin' at

the sun perched on the trainman's shoulder. His little amber eyes are soft and sweet—the kind he gives his momma when she's clutchin' a bottle in one hand and his Daddy's photo in the other. He lays 'em hard on Mack as he keeps on: "I mean... ain't no way we're goin' to some big prison, and that means we'll just end up in juvie or somethin'... with a bunch of bad kids doin' bad things and tryin' to get us to do the same."

Mack's eyes wander. I wonder what he's thinkin' about. I spy a tiny heart drawn in black marker on his hamhock of a forearm and wonder if a little girl put it there. A little girl like me, whose Papa danced her around on his boot-tops so that her feet never touched the ground. He glances at me just then, maybe wonderin' the same. Then he spies our loaded bags and says to "get on home. I'll cut ya lose so long as you get on home." Don't neither of us budge, though, until he gets his growl back and roars, "Go on! Git!" which sends both me and Henry kickin' up gravel towards the fenceline. I glance back a time or two as I'm runnin', thinkin' he might change his mind and lasso me again, but he's just standin' there, watchin' us go, touchin' that little heart on his arm like a soft part that needs protectin'.

Meanwhile, Henry ferrets out the nearest exit, clears it, and then keeps on goin'. With me huffin' along behind him, he don't stop until four blocks, two street signs, and a spooked tomcat later. I think he's gonna be moonin' over our good fortune when I skid to a stop beside him, but instead he glares me down with a face as red as Mee-maw's "goin' out" rouge and spits sideways. "I told ya, Olive! I done told ya! We can't go hoppin' railcars. That's serious business. That's serious, illegal-type business!"

Course he's right. But I ain't about to say so. And I think Henry might like the sound of his big voice right about now, 'cuz he just keeps on with his "You coulda got hurt!" "We coulda got locked up!" "I coulda lost ya!" malarkey like a red-headed zit about to pop. Mama says there ain't no talkin' to a man like that. And hell, who'd want to? So, I let Henry keep on windin' his fiery self down until he quiets, and then I make like he ain't said nothin'at all. If thirteen years of livin' with a bunch of hotheaded Louisianans has taught me anythin', it's that pokin' at a fire is just gonna get ya burned.

I peek up at the lazy sun perched halfway up the sky in the lap of a cloud. It tries to sizzle my eyeballs, so I glance back down at Henry, who looks like he means to do the same. "So wadda we gonna do?" I asks him, scuffin' at the ground.

He's still got his big-boy voice on, and when he pops back with "We're gonna go home!" it feels like he just slapped my hand as it was creepin' towards the cookie jar.

"Go home?!" I wail back. "I ain't goin' home! Not now. Not ever!" Then I stalk off to who-the-hell-knows-where but circle right back, spittin' nails. I hammer him with every bit of my sad-sack life from gettin' carbon monoxide poisonin' in Papa's shit-can Wagoneer to bein' treated like some extra from The Land That Time Forgot, to Gramps croakin' on account of my dumb-ass mistake. I tell him,

"I ain't an Abernathy no more. I don't gotta answer to no one. I don't gotta do nothin' I don't wanna do. I'm as free as a damn bird. And I mean to stay that way." It gets real quiet after that. I think maybe I hear Mack's locomotive fire up again, and maybe the far-off bay of a wild critter who's probably callin' out a serenade to my freedom. But short of that, I just hear my heart tumblin' around in my chest. It takes a dip near my stomach as Henry leans down and scoops up the handle of his suitcase. That prim thing's a mess of railroad soot and gravel dust now. It probably wants to go home too. I just freeze there, starin' at a big dirt mark shaped like a Welcome mat near the handle, and wait for Henry to take it there. But he don't. He waddles on over to me, haulin' that banged-up thing along, and says, "So what kinda bird are ya?"

I shrug, and the corners of Henry's mouth turn up. Then he picks up my pack and slings it over his other shoulder so that he ain't so lopsided. He starts walkin' towards that half-baked sun, and his voice trails back to me still standin' there, dumbstruck on the sidewalk, and tickles at my earlobe: "I hope you ain't one of them parrot birds that just hollers out curse words all day long. 'Cuz if I was to guess, that's the kinda bird I think you'd be."

I try not to giggle, but I do anyhow. Then I scamper up beside him and ponder, "Could be I'm a butterfly. Mama said ain't nothin' got more promise than a grounded butterfly."

Henry stops hard on the pavement and gives me the once-over. He's got them too-big eyes that make it a quick operation. "Butterfly it is," he reckons, smilin' so wide that I can see his stubby little Chiclet teeth. Then he keeps on amblin' down the sidewalk like he knows where he's goin'. Of course he don't, so I skip up beside him again and peel my pack off'a his arm. It makes him good and crooked again, but at least he don't gotta lug two bags and pretend he ain't pantin' anymore. We walk on for another couple blocks that way, watchin' as the big metal buildin's shrink up into dull houses that look like the train done shook most of their shingles off. A few cars and a rusty ole pickup truck spewin' a nasty cloud of exhaust roll by and I reason, "We oughta just hitchhike."

"Ya know what kinda folks hitchhike, Olive?" Henry sputters back with his fat nose still pointed at the horizon. "Stupid folks, that's who. Stupid folks, and folks who got a death wish."

All the sudden, I don't feel like a butterfly no more. And I tell Henry just the same. I tell him, "Ya don't wanna ride the rails, ya don't wanna hitchhike. What'chya wanna do... have your drunk-ass momma cart us around in her Buick LeSabre until she drives us right off a cliff?" But oh, how I wanted to net them words right outta the sky as soon as they were spoken. Henry turned his face away and those words, they just hung heavy in front of the two of us. We kept on movin' forward though, maybe hopin' we could outrun them or maybe because neither one of us knew what else to do. We put ten-plus blocks of silence, ramshackle shacks, and mailboxes stuffed fulla unpaid bills between us and them words before it felt safe to trust new ones. I wanted to reach out... to grab up Henry's free hand. It looked so lonely, swingin' there at his side. So small. But instead I tickled his ear with a sad little whisper. It felt like confessional or Papa's eggshell talk at Mama when she had her panties in a twist. "Henry," I says, in a soft voice, "I'm sorry. Real sorry. I shouldn't'a said that."

I hear Henry sniff. He still ain't lookin' at me. That hand looks lonelier than ever now, so I snatch it up before he stops to face me. His glasses are kinda foggy, and his lips lay in a flat line. I tell him, "I'm sorry, *really* sorry" again, and I can feel it deep down in my bones.

"I know you are" comes back like one of his soft dodgeball throws that Coach Biggs always calls *"sissy shit,"* but then he smiles at me like he never done at the coach or anyone else in all the world. It's one of those smiles that's made just for me. He keeps holdin' on to my sweaty paw as he tells me that he just don't wanna go to prison or sit on a train all day just to ride ten feet. But he also don't wanna get snatched up by some psycho along the highway who makes wigs out of little kids' hair and wears their teeth on a string around his neck. But I know men. I know how to spot the bad ones. I know that good men have hard heads and soft voices; that they count their worth in callouses and sweat beads on their brows. And I know that the bad ones show up on your doorstep, all slickery from stem to stern, thumpin' Bibles and tryin' to sell ya salvation for $19.95. I promise Henry six ways from Sunday that Mama and Papa done taught me everything there is to know about good men and bad men, and that I ain't about to keep quiet about which is which. And I'll be...he believes me. Not sure if he should, but he believes me. So, we steer ourselves towards the I-49 under the settin' sun and manage to make it out there before lunchtime.

Henry plops his suitcase beside a river-blue sign that's tellin' us DON'T LITTER and fusses about bein' "famished" as he clicks his case open. I'm still not altogether sure how a twelve-year-ole boy packs a suitcase like a 40-year-ole math teaher, but Henry done it. He scoots this, and jiggles that, and piles one thing atop another until I see a silvery stash of granola bars packed up like neat little bricks beside his tighty-whities. He fishes four of them from the pot and tosses two my way. Man alive... didn't know how hungry I was until that thing went down my gullet. Number two weren't far behind, and my belly let out a happy grumble as the backfire from some passin' piece-of-crap car spooks Henry from his suitcase crouch up into a solider's salute. Probably a good thing that he brought so many changes of underwear. He looks around a little wily-eyed, and I wonder for a minute if he's searchin' for that no-good jalopy car or a toilet. Then he busies himself swallowin' down what had to be the best granola bar east of Texas as I size up an endless stretch of highway with possibilities as far as the eye can see. There's a half-dozen cars comin' up from either direction, and I mean-mug each one of 'em like Mama does the melons at the Piggly Wiggly, tryin' to figure which ones got rotten stuff inside. I ain't really sure what I'm lookin' for, but maybe if I squint hard enough like she does... 'til my eyes go a little crossed and the veins start to bulge outta my forehead... somethin' useful will pop in there. But the only thing that pops is Henry, right behind my shoulder, askin', "What the heck you doin', Olive?"

I shush him. After all, this is serious business. Then I squint harder. Harder still. I think I can feel somethin' formin' up in my head, but it's just a powerful ache. Plus, my eyes are so covered up in eyelid skin that I can only see the grill of a Volkswagen van with a bunny zip-tied to its grill. That gets my eyes curious enough to pop out again just as the van rolls up on us. It's goin' slow, real slow, and I can't figure if it's stoppin' or breakin' down. Gramps always said that those ugly-ass vans were made by foreigners who packed the engines all fulla gremlins who gnawed it to bits. But then again, Gramps also said that he invented the corn dog and women's roller derby.

But Henry reasons, "They're stoppin'!" He's soundin' half horrified, and half like someone just offered him cake. We both watch as the van slinks by us at slug-speed and then eases off onto the side of the road. I notice it's got frilly curtains in its windows like some ole biddy's house, and my guts sting a little as I think about sittin' beside Gran in her stuffy parlor as Gramps was snorin' not inches away. "He was a dreamboat back in the day," she always said. "Now he's more like a tugboat."

I can still see her little violet eyes twinklin' as she looked him over. I ain't seen Gramps light up like he did under those eyes since he laid her in the ground. Now I think about the two of 'em, up there together, steerin' through the heavens arm in arm in search of the Pearly Gates and probably lost as all get-out because Gramps won't ask for directions. I find myself smilin' at that, and it seems a good enough greetin' for this lanky fella who slides outta the drive's side of that frilly-curtained van and starts walkin' towards us. Cars are whizzin' by, flutterin' his loose trousers and his salt 'n' pepper hair, so he jogs quick over to our spot a few feet off the side of the highway. He's smilin' to match me, and his teeth are all gleamy and whiter than a fresh picket fence. Seems un-rotten enough.

"You okay?" he asks, cock-eyein' us through a pair of square glasses with lenses big enough for a T. Rex. A big rig streaks by as he's closin' in and throws up another gust of wind that near knocks him over. All of the sudden, Henry's planted in front of me, growlin'.

"We're fine," he barks out.

Now that fella freezes where he stands. Then he says, "You sure?" duckin' his head like a dog who's afraid of bein' walloped. He turns his wide eyes on me and says, "You were starin' me down pretty good."

Sounds dumb comin' out, but I answer back, "I was tryin' to figure if you was rotten or not," and I feel even dumber once it's said. But he looks me over, never mindin' my crazy-person talk, and warms his smile up so that it covers those gleamy teeth.

"Fair enough," he says back. Then he goes on to tell me

he ain't "been checked for an expiration date," but he's "pretty sure" he'd know if he'd gone bad.

The cars are still howlin' by, and it's hard to get a fix on Henry's mutterin's, but he's holdin' court not an inch from the tip of my nose, conversatin' with himself in as fierce a manner as he's ever done. If he weren't allergic to about anything mischievous, I'd think he had a devil on his shoulder talkin' to him too. But I know better. If anythin', he's got a shriveled ole man up there, probably tellin' him to do things like eat supper at 2 p.m. and trim his ear hair. I'm about to needle him when our new friend in the frilly-curtain van scooches closer and asks if we need a ride. I tell him we do, and all the sudden Henry's grumblin's to that little ole man get louder. He don't budge an inch from that spot right in front of me, but he zips his head around so that he's got one razor-slit eye starin' me down.

"I don't know about this, Olive," he hisses. Sounds like an ole man talkin' through his oxygen mask.

"That's what we're here for," I snap back. Then I give that skinny feller another once-over. He's tusslin' with a bug that's makin' figure eights around his head, and he keeps duckin' as it dives for his soft parts. His eyes are zippin' every-which-way like God's got a lightnin' bolt pointed right at him. I make a little snort and promise Henry, "He's a good'un. I can tell."

And he is, or at least he's still pretendin' to be by the time we make it about forty miles and halfway to Alexandria. He tells us that's his daughter's name—

Alexandria—and when he says it, his eyes get all soft around the edges. Problem is, he does the same thing every time he talks about any one of his other ten, or twelve, or however many kids this damn Fertile Freddie's got. I nickname him that and whisper it in Henry's ear, but man alive, Freddie yammers on so much that I don't even know if it gets heard. He's all about playin' license-plate bingo, and Beach Boys tracks, and "makin' the most of the journey" whereas travelin' with my family is usually about inventin' new curse words and makin' 4,000 stops to go pee. I ain't complainin' though. Freddie only spends five minutes pesterin' us about why we're hitchin' our way down I-49 before turnin' over like a timid puppy and barkin' out answers to Henry's shit-ton of questions. Half an hour in, I know that Freddie's a travelin' Fuller Brush salesman with a wallet fulla little kids that have his "wife's beauty and the milkman's brains." I know that he lives in a little four-square in Queens that smells of pastrami on rye and crayons, and that his favorite drink is Mr. Pibb. I know that his little girls sing long and loud enough to rattle the rafters and that he thinks they're gonna become fighter pilots, or judges, or police officers. Hell, after Henry gets done, I even know his blood type. That man gloats and chitter-chats about his girls so much that the little green monster who sometimes rides sidesaddle with the devil on my shoulder can't stand it no more.

"Most girls I know don't never do jobs like that," I tell him. "Fact is, they're mostly stuck up in the house, squeezin' out ungrateful little babies. They don't never go nowhere, or see nothin', or even leave their hometowns."

"That so?" says Freddie.

"Yup" pops outta my mouth easy-peasy 'cuz it's the God's truth. "My mama, she's so stuck on her spot that even when the mayor come up to our place carryin' a certified, one hundred percent official paper from City Hall that said we had to move, she couldn't get her fool ass outta town. I seen that thing with my own eyes—seen that fat, red stamp right in the middle. It was our ticket to see the world, but my mama, she's so rooted down in Louisiana soil and so scared of us gettin' out and growin' up, that she couldn't cash it in!"

Freddie asks, "So what'd she do?" like it ain't obvious. And I'm about to tell him too when Henry pipes in, eyes all a-gleam like he's watchin' the scene play out on a movie screen behind his peepers.

"She marched right down to City Hall," he busts. "I was there with my mama payin' a... errr... traffic fine, and in she marches, wearin' her best Sunday dress."

Freddie shoots an eye towards the rear-view, where Henry's cranin' forward in his seat, lookin' besotted. "She had her arms all loaded up with books from the library. Ole musty ones that must'a seen a million eyes. She hauled the whole mess of 'em up, dumped 'em right on Missus Calhoon's desk, and said she wanted to see the mayor." Now Freddie ain't even lookin' at the road. Henry's hooked him. I find myself wonderin' how well a body can drive if they're mostly hypnotized.

"And Olive's mama... well... she's got a yowl on her, and I expect that Mayor Rowdy knew that voice well enough to hear her a mile off. He popped outta his office right quick and asked what the fuss was about. And that's when she did it."

"Did what?"

Henry sprouts up a good inch or two in his seat, eyes beamin' bright as headlights out the windshield. "She just up and starts spoutin' city codes and narratives from property cases. She didn't even need to look at those books—knew 'em all by heart. She told ole Rowdy that he wasn't gonna push her and her family off'a their land and that it didn't matter how many papers and signatures he got—he had no right—and she'd fight him until they put her in a pine box or she put him in one."

I feel the van lurch as Freddie shoots eyes back at the road and sees he ain't even in his lane no more. Maybe it ain't a good day to die. "Wow," he says back. "Sounds like one tough woman."

Henry chirps back, "I'll say," but I do a good job of squishin' it. "Tough?" comes up outta me at a crow. "She ain't tough as she is stubborn. And all that stubbornness got her was stuck right where she's always been stuck."

There's a pause while Henry and Freddie study each other in the mirror. Then they're lookin' at me. Then they both get far-off stares, and Freddie says, "Sounds to me like she's right where she wants to be," and I find myself starin' off too. It's quiet after that for a mile or so before Freddie can't stand it no more and starts in about his marvelous kids again. He whips out a fat stack of photos and pushes 'em my way, but I don't wanna look at all those cross-eyed kids with their mouths fulla barbedwire braces no more. I wanna watch Big Boy, with his checkered-up short-pants and Elvis Presley updo, beamin' at me from the side of the expressway. I want to see the mulberry sky crawlin' over the Red River and the oak tree tunnels with creamy-white cotton plantations fifty stories high hugged between 'em.

I finally lug out my scrapbook and show Freddie my "Welcome to Alexandria" postcard as we come rollin' up on the city limits, but he just says how that reminds him of his little cherub-girl with her bulgy, buttercream cheeks and eyes wide and clear as a cornflower-blue sky. I've had about enough of them kids, so I plug the card back inside and try not to groan as I do it. If Freddie's gonna take us all the way to Denver like he'd promised, I ain't about to piss him off.

Henry don't seem against it though. He starts up with all his Columbo-style quizzin', just like he done for the past forty-five minutes. He gets to badgerin' and sly-eyein' our driver all about Alexandria. *How old is she? What color hair does she have? Does she like raisins in her oatmeal cookies? Does she pick her nose in church?* If that girl is just some made-up hooey that only lives in this fella's head, dammit, Henry's gonna find out. Unfortunately for me, that means another twenty minutes of Alexandria's Papa fawnin' on about how she eats her cherries jubilee like the Queen of England and likes to braid their dog's tail hair, and once made a diorama of *The Glass Menagerie* that "was so good, people cried." By the time he tuckers himself out with all of that showboatin', we're clear through town and I ain't seen much more than a few strings of twinkly lights and a four-faced clock that looks like it fell out of a Disney movie. And of course, he pipes up askin', "Should we make a pit stop?" right as Alexandria's come-hither lights are fadin' in the rearview.

I can't help it. I point back over my shoulder. "I reckon we could go back. Plenty of pits to stop at back there."

Freddie chuckles. It's a warm sort of sound, like an engine that just keeps hummin' because it never gets cooled down. But he don't even peek up at the rearview mirror. He just sets his sights on the lonely road ahead and says, "Aw, naw. Too crowded. Too spendy in town."

I make me a good *humph*, and don't even try to hide it, but he says he knows some truck stop a mile or two up that's got "the best burgers in all of Louisiana," and I find myself peerin' around the cabin to see if anyone noticed that *humph* get out. Maybe I can suck it back up again. Maybe with some French fries on the side. And oh lordy, then I'm dreamin' about juicy mesquite meat on a hot buttered bun with all the trimmin's. I start eyein' the cows as we roll through the pasturelands, picturin' them peppered in beefsteak tomatoes plucked fresh from Papa's tangle of vegetable vines, and crumbly cuts of homemade goat cheese big as truck beds. Mama aged that foul stuff down in the cellar for months at a time. She said it took her longer to make good cheese than it did a good baby. But hell, that stuff's only half as stinky as my brothers. And cheese never burnt off my left eyebrow like Pete and Wyatt did with their "bright ideas" involvin' a shitload of illegal Indian fireworks.

I get a little twinge in my guts right then. This must be what starvation feels like. An empty hollow foldin' itself over in your stomach and creepin' up on your heart. Feels like somethin's in there, eatin' me alive. I tell Henry, and he "don't think that's it," but what does he know? He just points his fool finger out the window at a mess of crows millin' around and tells me there's been a murder out there. This boy's got imagination for days. I think to tell him so, but I spy that truck stop up ahead and lose all train of thought. It's got a big, flickery neon sign standin' guard out by the highway that says Dottie's. There's a smilin' lady just under that name who looks like she just stepped off one of those pinup calendars that greasy men ogle in auto shops. But she's holdin' a plate with a hamburger bigger than Mee-maw's Shih Tzu on it, and so I'm oglin' her pretty good myself as we roll into the parkin' lot. "Well, here we are," says Freddie. He's grinnin' so big that those monster glasses of his put little dents in his cheek balls. Could be that I'm grinnin' even wider, still lookin' at that lady's big burger as I tumble outta the van behind Henry.

Good gravy, I ain't never seen so many big rigs all in one lot. I feel like some sleazy truck salesman might come creepin' up, tryin' to bamboozle us into buyin' an 18-wheeler. Mama said you could always tell used car salesmen from regular folk because whenever they spoke the truth, they got this look like it was givin' them indigestion. My gut gives another grumble at that thought and lets out a howl as I pile inside the diner behind Freddie. And all at once there ain't no Mama, no big rigs, no dime-sized callouses scrapin' my secondhand sneakers; there's just a grease-battered heaven scent twistin' up through my nostrils. I must'a looked a fool, snakin' right over to the cook's pass-through like some cartoon character floatin' after steam curls off 'a pie. But hell if I care. I'd eat a half-plucked hen at this point.

I s'pose Fertile Freddie's accustomed to wranglin' kids because he lassos me in a jiff and gets some waitress who looks like pinup Dottie's ugly older sister to poke us in a booth. Then he gives us a measly impression of *the look* and says to "stay put, and look over the menus" before he ambles off to pay John a visit.

Oh Dolly, it's a good thing those menus got plastic guards 'cuz I drown mine in enough drool to float the Ark. Henry's smackin' his lips too, and when I ask him what he wants, he just gives me big eyes and says "everythin'."

At this point, ten minutes feels like a hundred, and I peek over near the Men's for any sign of Freddie but don't spy him. I'm fixin' to dip that menu in ketchup and just eat the damn thing when Henry toots, "Oh, crap!" and points over my shoulder where Freddie and a grizzly-big deputy are stompin' our way.

CHAPTER SEVEN

Papa was smitten as a kitten with a yarn ball from the day he met Mama. He swore she had "legs for days, pluck enough to sell the Devil an icebox, and a quiet sorta strength... like she was holdin' all the world's secrets just under her tongue." And ever since I was ole enough to listen, he told me I was gonna be just like her. He said when the time came, I'd find myself swimmin' in oceans of moxie and cleverness enough to outwit any man you put in front of me. And dammit, it's about time.

I can't tell ya any better today than I could tomorrow how I manage it, but I get a busboy who don't speak a lick of English to sneak us through the kitchen, Underground Railroad style, and right out the back of the diner before Freddie and his deputy pal are any the wiser. After snakin' our bags from Freddie's granny-van, we even huddle in some little bushes by the dumpster for a few minutes, watchin' those stooges through the diner's plate-glass windows as they dash every-which-way and bump noggins a time or two. I could watch a whole episode of those two maroons bumblin' about, but Henry thinks we oughta beat feet before they come lookin' for us out in the parkin' lot. We don't stand much chance of skirtin' the law out on the open highway though, so I give

Mama's charms a second go and tell Henry, "There ain't a doubt in my mind that one of these here big rigs could save our bacon from that pig."

All I get back's a grumble that sounds like my name but rolled around in soot. Henry tells me he "don't think much" of kickin' in with a truck driver 'cuz "they know all the best places to hide the bodies."

I roll my eyes until they come back full circle to the diner, where Tweedle Dee and Tweedle Dumb are gettin' a little close to the exit for my tastes. "Well, you got any other bright ideas?" I bark back, pointin' hard in their direction. Henry gulps. You know he don't. He don't have a damn clue, so I pull myself up, and I pull him up too, and get us on over to that sea of trailers. A few of 'em are idlin', and I can see fellas perched up in the cabs... some all slumped and snoozin', others stick-straight, gummin' on jerky or sippin' out of thermoses that look like big silver bullets. Then I spy her. A *her*. Sure, she's got a buzz-cut shorter than the boys of summer and a wad of chew in her cheek, but it's a *her*. I'm sure of it. I point her out quick, and ask Henry, "That make ya feel any better? I can't recall the last time I heard of any lady killin' folks and hidin' their bodies."

Henry tilts his chin up and peeks in the cab. He squints. He wiggles his wooly little eyebrows. He squints some more. "Maybe that's just cuz they're really good and it. And besides, you sure... that's a lady?"

"Sure, I'm sure," I says. I peek up too. She's diggin' in her nose. All the sudden, I ain't so sure anymore. But I keep my mouth shut and stomp on over to her door. The rig's rumblin' and grumblin' and pipin' big, hot waves of air all around it. It stinks like Papa's farm rigs, but I reach up to give the candy-apple-red door a knock anyhow. It quakes under my knuckles right as Miss Nose-picker's face pops up in her driver's side window. She lowers the glass, damn slow though, with every crank of the handle squeakin' like a drownin' mouse. Then she hangs her fat head out and gives me a glare fit to spook the Devil.

It's about then that Mama's moxie drains right on outta me. I got my lips all puckered up to kiss my way inside that cab, but instead they just hang there. She squints one eye and spits a wad of chew out the window. "What'chya want?" comes out with it.

What do I want? Hell if I can remember. *A double-decker burger? Hair that doesn't kink up when it rains? World peace? Maybe an 18-wheeler fulla Twinkies?*

Nose-picker spits again, and tells me, "Well, pipe up!" but I just stare on as Henry zigzags up under her window. I see him tilt his head up like he's about to ask God to spare his dyin' runt kitty or somethin'. He's got those eyes that little Ethiopian kids give the camera when Sally Struthers says it only costs two pennies or some such bullshit to feed 'em.

"We're lookin' for a ride, ma'am," he mews.

Nose-picker stops her insufferable chawin', and her eyes get near big as Henry's. Then all at once, that lunchbox jaw of hers locks up, and I notice she's got pretty copper bits floatin' around in her eyes... almost like when the sweet gum trees drop their leaves into the limey bay-ou at autumn-time. Her mouth ticks up at the edges and she says, "Well, why didn't ya just say so?" sweet as you like it.

The driver's-side door yawns open, and she shoos us around to the passenger side. Climbin' up in there is like mountin' a draft horse, and I can't help but feel big once I get inside. She tells us her name is Paula, but every-body calls her Paul, and I make like that's funny to me and double over as we're pullin' out of the diner lot and onto the highway. Henry copies me by fiddlin' with his bag on the floorboard, and then gives me the all-clear nod when he don't spy the fuzz. I decide we'd make a good Bonnie and Clyde. I whittle a note into my brainpan to tell Henry later 'cuz I couldn't get a word in now if I wanted to. Paul says she ain't had company in a good, long while. Once she finds out we're headed anywhere but here, she says we can ride along all the way up to Charleston with her. She's been to West Virginia some-thin' like sixty-four times, and says they got all kinds of history there. She says the governor himself even lives in some fancy-nancy brick mansion that he lets people come and walk through, willy-nilly. She ain't never been though, and I reason I wouldn't want to either. What if he was drinkin' milk out of the carton in his underpants when we strolled through? Hell if I'm gonna pay to see that.

But Paul don't talk long about interestin' stuff like crusty ole politicians streakin' past folks in their skivvies before she starts askin' about our families. She says she ain't got no kids of her own, just a couple of nieces. Their photos are stuck to the dashboard, and she lays a kiss down on the tip of her finger and touches it to each of 'em. Her voice gets doughy as she says their names, "Samantha and Christine," and it takes shushin' my shoulder devil good to keep from tellin' her that they look more like Sam and Chris, a couple'a boys that live two farmsover and been hit with the ugly stick one too many times. "Sometimes I think those two little girls are the nearest God ever got to magic," she tells us, and boy howdy, that sets that lil' devil to spittin' in my ear.

I say, "*Oh jeez*, there ain't so such thing as magic," and she rubbernecks my way so fast that her eyes cross.

"There's no such thing as magic?!" she half-hollers, grippin' that tire-sized steerin' wheel good enough to bend it right off the dash. "No such thing as magic?! Lil' girl... women give birth in huts, squattin' over shallow holes in the earth. Women deliver babies on freeways, and airplanes are threadin' God's cloudy eye. Women weep, and scream, and rip, and spill souls from their bodies. So, don't you tell me that there's no such thing as magic!"

Oh Dolly, did the cab ever get quiet after that. Somethin' about those words had stayin' power, and they hung around for ages... wouldn't make no space for anythin' else. So I just sit there, listenin' to the road roll out behind us and watchin' the countryside spill across Paul's windshield in technicolor. I imagine bein' her... sittin' up in that big captain's chair, chasin' down the sun just so

171

that I could tuck it in my back pocket, and never lookin' in the rearview—not one single time. Once I can't stomach the silence no more, I run up my white flag and tell Paul about how cool her job is. I tell her how I'd love to be out on the open road, runnin' out the map lines until there ain't none left without my mark on 'em. I tell her that her life's "damn near perfect," but her eyes droop when I say it.

"Ain't perfect, kid. Ain't nowhere near it" slips outta her lips at a near whisper, and when she adds, "It's lonely is what it is," I near don't hear it.

Henry, the dirty traitor, says he thinks it seems "powerful lonesome too," but melts a little under my fiery glare. Then he tells Paul, "Well, at least we all got good company right now," and that makes her eyes glow with those hot penny flecks again. I reason she might use those as headlights at night because she keeps on drivin' as the sun sinks off the skyline and sends the moon up to take its place. I roll down my window and thread the wind with my fingers. Henry says it looks like I'm scoopin' up stars. Paul says he might be right. I think back to those hot August nights in Lafayette, when Papa and his woolly-faced hillbilly friends'd play their fiddles and moonshine jugs under a spill of stars until every critter under the salt 'n' pepper sky had bluegrass runnin' through its veins. I feel my guts twist up and get all grumbly again, and so I tell Henry that I'm hungry.

Paul pipes, "We can't have that!" and since she looks like she ain't missed a meal even once in all her years, I ain't at all surprised when she hauls out a mess of snack food that could probably put 7-Eleven outta business. Henry plucks a three-pack of Twinkies from the lot and hands it my way. I don't even got the heart to tell him they ain't my favorite nowadays. All that spongy stuff feels too soft for a woman of the world like me. But it don't matter much. Everythin' tastes like honey-drips from Heaven right about now, so me and Henry, we gobble up half of Paul's stash, and she don't even bat an eyelash. Matter of fact, I think she's pretty impressed. She looks at me the same way Mama does when I spin a yarn that ties Pete and Wyatt down to their chairs. She looks at me like I'm meant to be somethin'. Like I'm somethin' special.

For a minute, I think about Mama and her face lookin' at my face with that same look, and I wonder how she's lookin' right now. I think about them little chicken-feet scratches beside her eyes that bunch up like ribbon candy when she laughs. I think about the day I caught her tracin' those fine lines in the mirror. I asked her if she was ashamed of them, and she said, "Way I see it, there's two kinds of women... the ones who get all worn and wrinkly and the ones who die tryin'. I mean to laugh my lines in deep. Hell, I ain't ashamed. I'm survivin'."

I think about tellin' the story to Paul since she seems so stuck on her kin, but right about the time I work up the gumption, some fella on her radio starts squawkin' about a speed trap and hogs on the roadway. Paul shoots a "ten-four" into her mic like some kinda real-life covert spy or somethin', and then she catches me makin' googly eyes at her. She smiles sideways in my direction and then in Henry's. He's covered in pastry wrappers, and his gut's bulgin' out plumper than a fat tick's. The hummin' highway's done lulled him half to sleep, and his head keeps dippin' and perkin' and dippin' and perkin'. If he were a fishin' lure, I'd swear he had somethin' on the line. And it ain't long at all before he's slumped over and droolin' on my shoulder. Paul says I can "konk out too," that she's "got'er covered," but I weren't born yesterday. I ain't about to get my snoozin' ass hauled into some back-woods police station and wake up from sawin' logs only to find myself cuffed to one. No sir, I'm gonna keep my peepers peeled and my wits about me.

I tell Paul, "I ain't tired," and I sound sure enough that even *I* believe it. That seems to dill her pickles because she lights right up and starts yammerin' again like she ain't had no one to talk to since Jesus was in Pampers. She starts off with pressin' me about family again and then cuts herself short before I've got a mind to sass her back.

"Nevermind," she tells me, waggin' her chew-tin of a chin. "I think I've got the lay of the land here. And I'm here to tell you, you're not the only one."

I do a sideways look back, but she keeps her eyes on the road. I can see them pinchin' up at the edges though, like they're tryin' to hold somethin' in that wants to come out real bad. But she just sucks up a big breath and tells me how she and her sister "had it hard too." Then she goes on about her ole Pops, who "kept his knuckles rough, his belt undone, and his rage bottled in a flask." She says that she got to "hatin' the smell of him, the weight of him... the rough touches and sick-soft ones too."

Paul keeps herself fixed ahead. She don't look at me. She just lets that smooth pavement roll under her, roll behind her. She grips the wheel. She shifts that squawlin' engine. She tells that big rig where to go. She's mowin' down oceans of darkness as she keeps on, "He always wanted her—my sister, Julie. She was such a frail little thing... a little wisp of lemon curls and daisy skin. And a laugh. Oh Lord, a laugh that just tickled your bones until you couldn't help yourself from smilin' along. But I couldn't see him break her. I couldn't see the light go from her eyes. So I kept quiet. I was a good girl, and I kept quiet so that she didn't have to."

I keep quiet too. I ain't sure what to say back. I let the road do the talkin' as I expect it's the best friend Paul's got. It tells her *Mmmmm Mmmmm, Mmmmm Mmmmm*, and comes off soundin' like a lullaby. From the side, I see Paul's face slidin' down. I think maybe she's gettin' drowsy from the asphalt's sing-songin' to her, but then she up and starts talkin' about her momma. At first I think that crabby apple, with her "ashy fingertips" and her "porcelain skin," don't sound nothin' like a momma, and when Paul gets to the part where "she didn't ever touch me unless it was to hurt me," I know she don't. I can't even muster up a sad throat lump when Paul says that lady up and "vanished like a ghost that was never there in the first place." Paul says that after that, her and her sis lit out for the big city. I figure the story's about to get good, but Paul just talks about how they made camp in a soggy cardboard box 'neath the New Jersey Turnpike that sagged like their smiles whenever it rained. She says the pavement there wore their "soles down to the bone" and that if not for "takeout bags and crumpled dollar bills warmed by the hands of strangers," she'd have went tits-up, just like her momma. The way she talks feels like listenin' to Miss Beasley read poetry in English class, and I keep glancin' back at her big, mealy mug just to make sure it's really her talkin'.

After that story, I don't even got the heart to ask her if New Jersey's really just a big bunch of gardens, or if ladies really play volleyball on the beach in high heels there like they do on my Atlantic City postcard. And after hearin' about Paul and her sister scavengin' through the trash and fightin' rats as big as housecats for two bites of a leftover Whopper, I can't imagine ladies rompin' around on the beach like catwalk models just a few streets over. All the sudden, I wanna ask Paul why she didn't run away, and then I remember, she already did. But I s'pose I ain't good at hidin' my feelin' about fightin' slimy sewer rats for a half-dozen cold french fries because Paul glances my way and says, "It wasn't that bad, really."

I peer over Henry's fuzzy head and raise my right eyebrow up at her, and she giggles. It sounds like a little girl's giggle, and it makes me laugh too. Then she says,

"Well, it wasn't *great,* but at least no one was sluggin' us anymore, and at least Daddy wasn't…" and cuts out. Our giggles die away real quick, and even though she don't look back at me, it feels like her eyes are burnin' me up when she goes on. "It's worth just about anythin' to get away from that, right?"

I know she wants me to say *Right.* Maybe I oughta say *Right,* but I just can't, so I don't say nothin' at all. I just watch as a few fat skeeters splatter across the windshield. I watch their insides clump up and roll away to the edges. She watches me, watchin' them. She cuts the silence soft but strong with a little edge to her voice. She asks me if I know what she learned on the streets.

I shrug. I'm trackin' skeeter innards. I'm thinkin' I'd like to roll away too.

"I learned that I don't gotta be quiet no more," she says, growin' stiff in the stillness. "And you don't gotta either."

I nod. It's the best I can do. And through the cab's heavy air, I feel her ease back. I feel that body that's been pushed and pushed not wantin' to push back. And it lays on me easy as one of Mama's light quilts in summertime. I keep fixed on the windshield and count five more skeeter-cides in the next half hour as I'm listenin' to the highway slide out under Paul's eighteen wheels. It's got a rhythm to it, like shuckin' corn on the porch at eventide, and before I know it, I'm wound in the tether of a dream. But it ain't a dream so much as a memory put through a kaleidoscope.

I see Mama sittin' in the very last pew at church—all alone. She's got Gran's hand-me-down mint-green blazer on, and her hair's all pinned up like a bunch of wild wheat that God's wound around his windy fingertips. Her mouth is flat—almost sour, and she's got the Good Book clutched to her chest. I can see her tryin' not to see all those eyes on her... all those folks in the church pushin' on her with their quiet, screamin' eyes. All those silent voices yellin' for her to leave.

But then I snag her eye. I'm a half-dozen pews up, but I snag it good, and I feel it pullin' us together. I feel it pullin' and stretchin' until I can smell the little dollops of violet perfume that she puts behind her ears every Sunday. I can see her lips synch up the corners as she whispers in my ear, "You stay up there, girl. You stay in the light, where you belong. I'll keep quiet. I'll keep quiet, so that you don't have to."

And then all the sudden, I'm crackin' my eyes open to a blazin' sunrise the next mornin'. The truck's still as can be, and once I bolt up and get to lookin' around, it don't take long to see that I'm all by my lonesome. Outside the window, I spy Henry just a few feet off, millin' around the funkiest contraption I think I've ever seen. I stumble out of the cab, still gatherin' my sleepy head, and make my way towards him. About that time, I spy Paul traipsin' out of one of a half-dozen little buildin's scattered around this dusty ole parkin' lot of a roadside pit stop. She's got her arms loaded up with what Mama'd qualify as "God-awful junk food fit to tie your ass to the can," and she's comin' my way. "Ya like him?!" she hollers out. "Like who?"

Paul fumbles, near drops her cherry Icee, and swivels on around towards the curious mess of rust that Henry's got his eye on. "Him!" she bellows back. "That right, there's Rusty. One of *the* number-one roadside attractions in all of Tennessee."

I eye that big ole hunk of junk. "Number one?" I says, scratchin' at my head. "Looks more like a number two."

Paul snorts, near loses hold of that damn Icee again, and gives me a monster grin. She tells me it was "Henry's idea," and so I amble on over towards my friend, who's officially knee-high again, starin' at an ole Chevy hubcap that I s'pose is meant to be Rusty's kneecap.

"Says right here that's two tons of ole junk parts," Henry tells me as I join him beside a big plaque hangin' in Rusty's shadow. "Says he's the pride of Franklin."

I give Rusty's crab-hands a go-over and then make a flat face like the one he's makin' at me. "Hmph," I spits back, "them Franklin folks must not have much to be proud of. Looks like somethin' Papa'd haul off for scrap." "I s'pose," Henry says back, thumbin' his suspenders.

He copies me and squints against the big sun to watch Rusty's crabby face starin' down. Then he does like I'm doin' and snarls back. He hates everythin' I hate. He's a good egg. He even agrees that Paul's Icee makes her look a fool with that big, red tongue of hers. Looks like she ate some of that Christmas decoratin' icin' that Mee-maw keeps in her pantry. Wyatt ate a whole tube of that stuff once and then lied his little ass off, sayin' it was Pete who done it. Talk about gettin' yourself caught red-handed. What a numbskull. I wouldn't eat anythin' in Mee-maw's kitchen anyhow. She swears that expiration dates are "malarkey," and I'd wager that half of the leftovers in her fridge came from The Last Supper. Paul ambles over about that time, so I tell her all about that and she gives me a peculiar look, like my stories from down-home don't match hers, and that ain't right. So we all make our way back to her rig real quiet-like and hit the highway again with an eerie silence hangin' in the cab. I think Henry can tell it's makin' me squirmy, so a few miles down the road, he tells how he and Paul were cluckin' up a storm before I came to this mornin', and how she knows all about my postcards and my nonstop gabbin' about this, that, and the other place for the last zillion years or so. She says that she ain't "never paid 'em much mind before," but she starts pointin' out things that might "come off a postcard," like the Blue Ridge Mountains that ain't blue and the Bald Mountains that ain't bald. Lookin' at them, way off in the distance, they don't look so big. They don't look so fancy. They don't look no purdier than that ole whitewashed farmhouse out Indian River Highway with its sloppy strands of honeysuckle huggin' the foundation and Mama's wash dryin' on the line. I don't say so though. Wouldn't be polite. I just look on and smile one of Gramps' fake smiles like he used to make when Gran drug him to church for Sunday mass and Preacher Higgins asked if he was enjoyin' himself. "Best to just play dumb and let the women-folk handle things," he'd whisper my way with a wink. *Damn* I miss him. As we roll into Kentucky, I think about last June, when he bought me one of those extra-special glossy dollar postcards at Woolworth's with Churchill Downs on the face. It was all covered with racehorses: nostrils flarin', fleet feet flyin'. He'd pointed hard at them little fellas perched up on the saddles and told me, "Those jockeys ain't no bigger than a three-year-ole. I'd bet you a pecan pie and half my prune juice... you walk up to one of those jockeys, and they ain't even gonna hit your chin!"

I smile just then, thinkin' of his eyes sparklin' when he told me that. It still don't seem right, him bein' gone.

"What'chya grinnin' at?" is Henry's way of scoopin' me outta that memory just before it starts goin' grey.

I lie and tell him, "Nuthin'," even though I don't want to. I want to tell stories about Gramps, and I want Henry to tell 'em too. Maybe if we just kept tellin' 'em, Gramps'll be runnin' around in our brains so much, it'll be like he ain't gone. But after them stories that Paul told me about her kin, I ain't about to go on braggin' how Gramps was the cat's meow and how he'd make a gal laugh so much, she'd near wet her pants. Nope, I figure I'll acquaint her with the grizzly side of bein' an Abernathy. So... I own up to my grin and say I was thinkin' on Pete and Wyatt, and what little shits they are.

"Pete and Wyatt are Olive's brothers," Henry tells Paul, polite as the day is long.

I pipe in with, "But I wish they wasn't!" and tell Paul

all about Pete bein' so dumb that he thought a leprechaun lived in the couch because he saw me dig two quarters outta there. Then I tell her how Wyatt got caught playin' with his willie last summer and told everybody he'd "come down with a case of the hormones." Good gravy, did Gramps ever get a kick out of that! He told Wyatt, "Hormones ain't the flu, you rube. It's when all that stuff that fills out your tighy-whities heads up to fill in the space where you're brain's s'posed to be." Of course, Wyatt just gave Gramps his dumb-bunny look, but I recall Mee-maw hootin' up a storm in the room over. I reckon she did wet her pants. And just listenin' to me tell it over again, Paul laughs so hard that I think she might too.

"Crazy kids" makes its way outta Paul between the chuckles, and she's smilin' real big all the while, glancin' at the porky twins in that little photo stuck to her dashboard. A fat tear slips down her cheek as she stares on, and I can't tell if it's the happy kind or the sad kind. After the cab gets real still, she fesses up that it's the sad kind and tells me and Henry that she'd give "just about anythin'" for little shits of her own. She says she thinks "bein' a mother is just about the biggest adventure in the whole world." I'm about to ask why she didn't never pop out puppies of her own when she says she can't have no babies on account of what her Daddy done to her. Just hearin' that makes my insides quiver. I can't think about my Papa that way, even for a second. Papas string paper lanterns across the porch so you can find your way home after dark. Papas hang their prickly chins over the firelight and tell tales of Bumblewart the Roughneck Troll, who lives in fear of a brave bayou girl named Olive Abernathy. Papas don't hurt. Papas don't take. Not the papas I know.

I can't think what to say. I ain't never had use for no babies, but then again, Mama didn't either. She didn't want me... not until some nurse somewhere laid a screamy little pink thing on her chest and it grabbed up her finger and gave a squeeze. She said that after that, she couldn't go on livin' without me. Maybe that's why it felt like she was always tryin' to fold me up and stuff me in her pocket. I decide that knowin' how yowly, and messy, and sticky, and downright clingy little kids are might make Paul think twice about wantin' one, so I tell her my story. All through Kentucky and into West Virginia, I tell about how I grew up a wily weed in the bayou with buckets fulla bullfrogs and crawdads on the hook. I tell her all about what a fussy little twit I was... always muddy-kneed, and stained in blackberry seed, and just like Mama—tough and troublesome as a croc's eyetooth. I tell her how I pained my mama and made her forehead vein bulge so that it looked like a gut worm about to bust. Then I told her how Mama and Papa were always slow-dancin' to Billie Holiday in the purple twilight, holdin' on to each other so tight, and how I'd wiggle between 'em just to steal Papa away.

Rollin' fields of wheat, and dinged-up mailboxes, and shoddy storefronts, and whole towns fall in Paul's rearview as I go on about all my mischievous adventurin'. I tell Paul how Mama'd pin my hair up in curls for Sunday church, and how me and the Devil'd let 'em down while she wasn't lookin'. I tell her how I was always moanin' about this, that, or the other, and how Mama'd always pat my thigh and say, "Darlin', havin' hope's like havin' a stray cat. The thing'll desert ya the second ya stop feedin' it." And I told her how I never listened.

And good gravy, to top it all off, I tell the story of how Arthur Bixby from three farms over paid me a dollar to look at my underpants. I spent the money on a Mars bar and some lemonheads and felt pretty smart about it too. I figured it weren't no different than folks seein' me in my swimsuit, and hell, they never paid me a dime for that. But Mama about lost her head when I come home gummin' that Mars bar and told her what I done. I couldn't sit right for a week after that. And I can't imagine that Paul, Mama, or anyone with two brain cells to rub together would want a no-good kid after hearin' all about it. But Paul, she just leans across Henry's lap and says, "Girl, you don't know how good you've got it."

Someone coulda asked me for directions to Zimbabwe and I'd look less puzzled than I do right then. But Paul, she looks sure. Damn sure. Like she'd-bet-you-her-18-wheeler sure. So I let her simmer in her smugness for a few miles and then listen to the rig gear down as we float onto an off-ramp and slide into downtown Charleston. It's chock-fulla all those stodgy ole buildin's that the little ole man livin' on Henry's shoulder likes, so sure enough, he starts big-eyein' every barbershop, bakery, and market we pass like Papa lookin' at thick cornrows. The more crumbly-and-decorated-up with gargoyles and crooked awnin's, the better he likes 'em. I ain't heard so many "oohs" and "ahs" since Uncle Ern bought a mess of illegal fireworks at the Indian reservation and Gramps tossed his lit stogie into the bag, thinkin' it was the garbage. By the time we make it clear of Main Street, I think Henry's gonna have himself an asthma attack. Or maybe even one of those coronaries that ole folks have when they get themselves too excited over stuff like orthopedic inserts or grumpy little dogs that gotta get their hair done at beauty parlors. I'm almost relieved when Paul finally pulls off in a big lot fulla buses and there ain't much other than pavement and hunks of metal for Henry to look at.

Paul's rig lets out a powerful wheeze and eighteen good grumbles as each wheel stops its spinnin' and settles in for a well-earned rest. Paul herself gives a sigh too and then looks crossways at me and Henry with a mournful eye. She says, "This is it, kiddos. This is where we part ways," like she's recitin' a damn eulogy. She points at the ass-end of one of them buses and tells us, "Station's just on the other side. I want you to go in, and I want you to get on a bus back home." Then she shoves her hand deep down into her back pocket, scoots herself back and forth to a tune that sounds like toots, and plucks out a wad of money. I ain't seen such so much cash money since Mayor Rowdy turned up on our stoop come tax day, holdin' his bank pouch out like a trick-or-treater. Lordy, how

Mama hated that man. She always said he looked like a fat Cap'n Crunch, swanin' around in his Grandpappy's ole Navy blues. And when I told Mama that I thought those stanky ole cigars he was always gummin' coulda been dog turds, she told me they were, and said that's how you knew he was fulla shit.

Paul, on the contrary, looks earnest as ole Hemingway as she forks that cash over to Henry. He tells her there's "no need," that he's "already got some," but she pushes it on him, and pushes it on him, until he grabs it up and shoves it into some little pocket on his case. He gets bashful when he does it, turnin' his head down. He's proud, like his papa was. Sometimes I forget. Sometimes it's like Henry's papa never left. Sometimes it feels more like Henry did.

I ain't sure I'm ready to part ways with Paul just yet, but she's got a load to deliver down the road a piece and says it, "ain't a place for kids." Plus, she tells us she'll be "headed back to Lubbock after that with a load of hay." She says she's gonna visit her nieces on the way. I think maybe she oughta bring some pig slop to go with that hay. I *think* it, but I don't say it. My little shoulder devil hears it bouncin' around in my brain though. He thinks it's hilarious. He says I oughta do stand-up. He's peckin' at me good as Paul draws in close, smellin' like a pork sausage stick she had a few miles back. But then she says, "I'm glad to know you, Olive," and that shuts him right up.

Up comes, "Real glad to know you too," and I know it's true 'cuz I didn't think twice before I said it. Then, "I'm really sorry about what happened to you" comes up too because I feel it way deep down in my gut. I fess up, "I guess I didn't really know what *bad* kin was until I knew that mine wasn't," and Paul's eyes get somber. Those little leaf flecks floatin' around inside 'em get still like all the wind died away.

"I know, Olive."

"I ain't had it bad like you."

Paul smiles. I feel my bones warm. "I know, Olive."

I can't think of anythin' more to say than, "Thank you," and it feels so good, I say it again. "Thank you." Paul's smile scoops 'em both up, heaps Henry's on top, and tells us never to hitchhike again. She's Athena climbin' up into her chariot as she tucks inside the big rig's cab, and me, Henry, and the shoulder devil all three get sourfaced and flat miserable as we watch her roll out of the parkin' lot and get gobbled up by Henry's fancy buildin's. I feel like I've got a lonely coyote howl brewin' down in my belly, but I don't let it out. We're in the city now. Gotta be civilized. Gotta be everythin' I ain't.

So, I stiffen up my back and pull up my chin like I seen Mama do when prim folk in town was lookin' her over like slug meat crusted to the sidewalk, and I asks Henry, "So, where you wanna go, city boy?" and can you believe it, he points square at that bus station! I'm about to cuss him up one side and down the other for tryin' to send us straight back to where we come from again, but he cuts me short. "I ain't sayin' we go home, Olive. I ain't sayin' that at all. I'm sayin' we get us a bus ticket. Get us a *real* ride."

I peep an "Oh!" and swat away all them nasty words that were stewin' around in my head. Then I get a gander at the sky settled over this city. It ain't near as clear as back home... kinda gotta a haze to it, and a taste like diesel and Aunt Agnes' over-fried chitlins. I can see the sun good enough though. It's already inchin' off the sky like it means to slide right into God's pocket. Not much daylight left to be had. Sure would be nice to be curled up and inside when that dark settles in. And somethin' about the thought of a bus warms my insides. I can already see Huckleberry's big ole shit-eatin' grin starin' back at me from the driver's seat. I can near hear his thick drawl ticklin' at my ear, puzzlin', "Where you been all this while, Miss Olive? I thought maybe you done got ate up by a crocodile out there in the bayou!"

"Sure," I says. "Why not." And that sets Henry to beamin'. He scoops up his case, and my bag too, and trots off towards that sea of buses. They look sorta lonely, lined up out there, all empty... like big ships with no sailors. I get a hankerin' to crawl up inside one of 'em as we're snakin' through the rows. Maybe yell my name out and see if it echoes or not. But the first door I try is locked up tight as Mee-maw's mallomars, just like the second, and the third too. I'm fixin' to try a fourth when I spy Henry way off in the distance and hafta run to catch up. By the time I make it to him, he's already looped around the last bus and stopped at the back side of the station. He gives me his ole codger growl as I jog up and then mutters some business about tomfoolery and wastin' daylight.

"Okay, Grandpa" comes outta me with a snigger, and I rib him a little extra by askin' if he's worried that he might miss reruns of Lawrence Welk.

He waggles his head back at me and does a good stinkeye. Betchya about anythin' he *does* watch Lawrence Welk. But I can tell that all he cares about right now is gettin' to that cushy bus seat 'cuz he lobs my pack towards me and scoops his bag up before I've even caught mine. I'm hot on his heels as we whiz around the side of the station and thunder up a ramp towards the front door. It feels like the last leg of a marathon or somethin'. All the sudden I'm pretty keen on havin' that padded bench under my fanny too. I'm primed to launch through the door and scoop up a ticket to just about anywhere when Henry hits it and splats on the glass like a damn bug on a windshield. "It's locked!" he yowls, and stubborn shit that I am, I give it a yank too. Sure enough, locked up tight, along with them buses and Mee-maw's mallomars. Henry waves his booger-pickin' finger at an ugly blackand-white sign swingin' from inside the doorframe—CLOSED.

I no more than get a *"Shit!"* out before my shoulder devil starts eyein' a nice crop of fat rocks in a green area not far off. He whispers in my ear that *we're gonna get ourselves on a bus one way or another tonight,* and I like the way he's thinkin'. It's right about then we hear a fella hollerin' from a parkin' stall not twenty feet away. "It's closed!" he calls out, like that ain't just about as obvious as the nose on his face. It's a big nose too. Looks like he could sniff out folks trapped in the snow with that sucker. He's got his head popped out the driver's-side window of a real ole car, and between that monster St. Bernard schnoz and the way he's barkin' at us, I feel like offerin' him a Milk-Bone. He says again, "It's closed," this time softer, and I wonder if maybe he's waitin' for a "Good boy" before he'll go on to his next trick.

Henry's peeled himself off the door by now, and we're both eyein' this fella in his ole relic. Gramps'd call it *a classic*. I gotta wonder if it runs on Flintstone feet. I can't quite see underneath from our perch up on the steps, but when the fella crawls out and stands up, I'm kinda disappointed that he doesn't got a big set of naked Barney Rubble feet under him. He starts walkin' our way, and he's shakin' his head so that the wispy feathers on his comb-over catch wind. Halfway between us and his car, he starts in grumblin', "Yup, just closed down, not thirty minutes ago. I was meant to pick up my daughter on the last bus in, but it seems they had a bit of engine trouble and had to stop off just west of Sutton."

He clips up the steps in his dang borin' normal-size shoes and hangs a hand out in Henry's direction. "I'm Roger," he says, drawin' his mouth up into a little bow.

Them two slap palms like proper gentlemen, and Henry says his name. His whole, entire name, like it's a

G.D. job interview or somethin'. Then the fella turns my way, and real sweet-like he says, "And this is?" Henry answers back, "That's Olive," like I don't know my own stinkin' name. I think for a short spell about correctin' him and callin' myself somethin' fancy, like *Lady Olive of Lafayette: Scourge of the Bayou and Connoisseur of Gummy Worms*, but I don't. I just smile my Sunday school smile and nod. That seems to suit Roger just fine 'cuz his little bowtie smile cinches up all the tighter. Then he asks if we was aimin' to catch a bus, and Henry tells him we was. They trade a few ole-man grouses about how service done gone down the drain and how no one's ever there when you need 'em anymore.

Roger starts soapboxin' some business about "back in *my* day, we worked until we couldn't see the noses on our faces," and me and my shoulder devil have us a good snigger about that. Pretty sure ole Roger could see that monster nose of his even in the pitch black. Hell, Neil Armstrong could probably see it from space on a clear day. But Henry, he just nods and gives big-eyes back. Maybe 'cuz he agrees. Maybe 'cuz he's too damn polite. I'm watchin' those big eyes of his get shinier in the dull light, and I start thinkin' about how dusk is closin' in and we ain't got no bus and no smiley Huckleberry to keep us safe tonight. I'm only half-listenin' to this scudder talk, but I pick out the word "ride" and get real keen on the conversation in a jiff.

"Did you say *ride*, mister?" is the first thing to pop outta me since these two started yammerin', and Roger looks me over good when I say it. Maybe he thought I was mute. His eyes stay mighty hooked on mine as he answers back, "Sure did. Gotta go pick up my girl in Sutton anyhow. I can get'chya that far, at least."

Of course, I got no clue where Sutton is. I don't got but three postcards from West Virginia, and not a one of 'em says anythin' about Sutton, not even the one Gramps just bought me last month. Thinkin' about that puts a little dart in my chest. I wonder if it'll pin in those buttons that Mama says I get to bustin' whenever I talk about adventurin' and livin' the hobo life. She'd always say that the stars in my eyes were purdier than any of the ones I was aimin' to see. She said I probably wouldn't figure that out until I was lookin' at 'em all by my lonesome.

Damn Mama, needlin' me even from a zillion miles away. But I'd show her. I'd make it to Sutton, and New York City, and everywhere in between. And I'd see things she ain't never gonna see. And I'd do things she ain't never gonna do. And I wouldn't let Lafayette swallow me up like it done her.

I tell Roger, "I'm in!" and have my smart self piled into his ole rig before Mama would'a had a chance to spite me for doin' it. Bein's that the back's loaded to the gills, I even slide right to the middle of the front-row bench seat and let Henry have the window. I don't need it. I can see for miles.

Mind you, once Roger scoots in beside me, that window looks a whole lot better. He's got a kind of stale, sweaty smell to him, and his right leg keeps lollin' out so that it brushes mine. And every time that he shifts down at a stoplight, it feels like he's drawin' his hand back along my thigh on purpose. About the fourth or fifth time, I shoot eyes at Henry, but he's gapin' out the window at another one of them crusty buildin's—this one with a big, rounded entry that looks like an ole-man scowl. I elbow him, but by then we're rollin' down the street again and Roger's got both hands back on the wheel. He keeps 'em that way too, all out of town and into the countryside. We don't even see another stoplight, and all the busy buildin's and people left skitterin' about after dark sorta dry up as trees fill in to take their places. Rows and rows and rows of timber with their branches all twisted up together into an emerald fence narrow in on the road 'til I can't see nothin' but green. We go on that like for miles, just cuttin' through the sea of prickly pines as Roger's radio crackles out weak guitar strums and folksy cowboys singin' about girls on horses who rode away with their hearts. When one of those songs peters out he asks me, "You like country?" and gives me a side-eye.

I shrug. "I guess," I say back, thinkin' it sounds like a bunch of whinin' to me. Papa taught me that good music was ageless and sweet on the ear. This junk sounds like a mess of coon dogs gettin' run over by a tractor-trailer. But I still got my Sunday school smile on, so I s'pose it comes off believable enough that I kinda dig this crap.

Henry worms in his seat. "I like it," he pipes, beamin' his big white grin through the darkened cab. I'm pretty sure he's fibbin' too. That grin's a little too big not have some bullshit stuck up in it. Kinda gets me out of sorts. Reminds me of how Mama said that lies spoil your insides. So I fess up. I tell how Papa'd drop a hot needle down on Otis Rush, scoop Mama up slick as vanilla bean ice cream, and foxtrot her across our creaky ole floor-boards. Now *that* was music.

My story gets Roger swoony-eyed. "I bet your mama's *real* pretty," he says, lookin' me up and down. I get a funny, squirmy feelin' as he keeps on with the elevator eyes and adds, "but not as pretty as you, I'll bet."

I give another shrug and scoot closer to Henry as Roger gets to fiddlin' with his radio dial. "There isn't much signal out here in the boonies," he tells me as some Evangelical preacher fella starts spoutin' his *Oh Lordys* and *Halleluiahs* like we're about to be raptured right up through the speakers. Roger scans past that nonsense real quick and lands on Muddy Waters, who's leakin' his blue soul out across the airwaves just to be rid of it. "How's this?" he ask me.

"Good," I say back, true-blue as can be. Ole Mister Waters was one of my favorites. I can still hear Papa makin' soft little chick-clucks at that turntable as he laid Muddy under its needle to itch that man's lonely ole bones. I get a warm feelin' deep down in my gut as I think of Papa's head bobbin' along with Muddy and the rain splatter ticklin' our tin-top farmhouse. For a second, I wish I was there. But I ain't. I'm here. I'm here, with heeby-jeebies on one side and Henry half-way to Nod on the other. I make like I'm coughin', hopin' Henry'll keep awake, but he just sorta spooks and then plops his head back down in the window well again. Two minutes later, he's snorin' loud enough to drown out Muddy, and the plunkity-plunk of Roger's ole engine, and probably every other sound in a five-mile radius. Even Roger says, "Wow, that kid can snore!" and I think about givin' him a high-five until I realize I'd have to touch his clammy-ass hand.

Still, I all the sudden feel like a jerk for bein' cold to him and say back, "I been tellin' Henry that for ages! The turd keeps sayin' it's all in my head."

From there we work up a good plan, the two of us, on how once Henry wakes up, Roger's gonna make a big fuss about all them snores and how they rattled the cab and near shook off a couple of parts of that ole car of his. We giggle on that notion for a bit, but Henry keeps on snorin' his fool head off, and that makes us giggle a little more. When we're giggled out, my tired starts settin' in too. I keep watchin' them long, ashy rivers of road roll out between the trees, over and over again. My eyes get gummy and my head starts slippin' off over to the left. It plunks on Roger's shoulder, which shoots me back up, straight as an arrow.

"It's alright, Hon," he coos my way. I feel like scootin' back towards Henry, but I don't wanna be rude again. But then his hand comes down. Not a brush. Not a gear shift. It comes down like a lead clamp, right on my thigh. Then it starts kneadin' my jeans and creepin' towards my nethers. I freeze. I feel like them coons that get caught in the headlamps and can't figure which way's right and which one ain't. But Roger slides his fat, meaty hand another inch south, and I unfreeze right quick. I swat at him, but he don't budge. He tells me, "Shhh, good girl," and he tightens up that meat clamp 'til I can feel his long fingernails cuttin' down into my skin. "Shhh, good girl," he whispers. I smell somethin' foul bleedin' off his hot breath. Feels like it's curvin' up my spine and ticklin' at my ear like devilspeak. "Shhh, good girl." That hand comes loose and then dips hard down south.

I see red. I see Mama, stiff-backed and head high, tellin' them handsy fellas who flipped my Sunday skirt at Denny's, "Ain't no man ever gonna lay a hand on my girl," and I clock him. I clock him right in his fat head. And then all at once the car's skiddin', and spinnin', and barrel rollin'. Glittery glass is rainin' down in every direction, and I can't tell which inky scene flyin' past the windshield is road and which one's night sky. I go as black as the both of 'em and wake up what seems like a wink later to the feelin' of warm blood drippin' down my scalp like summer rain. I flutter my eyelids to find a nightmare playin' out past the passenger-side window, where Robert's draggin' Henry's limp body along the asphalt just as careless as a brat kid trailin' a ragdoll in his wake. They're all the way around to the trunk by the time I get my seatbelt unstuck and manage to wriggle outta that mangled-up car. As I'm creepin' up on 'em, I hear Henry's body hit the ground with a dead thud that makes my heart drop. With his hands free, Roger starts fiddlin' around the trunk lock. He spies me comin' up and snarls like he means to bite. "I see what you are," he sets out hissin'. "You're no good girl at all. You're a *bad* girl."

Roger smiles the kinda smile I've only ever seen on pictures of the Devil. Then he pops that trunk, leans down, and scoops up my only friend in the whole wide world. I no more than start rushin' towards him than he tosses Henry inside and slaps the thing shut. It makes the same sound the coffin lid did when they closed it on Henry's daddy, and I can't bear it. I just can't bear it. I start cryin' and bum-rush that son of a bitch with everythin' I've got. I'm yowlin', and punchin', and bitin', and usin' every one of my ninety-five pounds to put the hurt on this fella, but he just strings me up by the collar and lets me dangle there, flailin'. He glares at me good, eyes all lit up, crusty lips curled, 'til I wind myself down, and then he says, "You ready to be my good girl now?"

I spit right in his face. It feels good.

Roger smacks me back, and lordy, it stings. It ain't nothin' like Mama's paddle. Mama always said, "Never hit a child in the face. God made a better place," but this here don't feel much like the hand of God anyhow.

Next thing I know, Roger's droppin' me on the ground like I'm some sack of trash. He keeps one slivered eye on my hind-end as he scoops a few things out of his crumpled car. He tosses my pack at my feet. "Won't be comin' back here," he growls, watchin' as I scoop it up.

I pop up and inch towards the trunk. I let him know "I ain't leavin' without my friend" in a voice that's meant to sound like Mama's but comes off more like an eensy bug stuck up under her boot heel. And then all at once, Roger's ragin' at me again with his angry eyes bent and slit down to razors. His bald head catches the moonlight as he lunges my way, and I swear I see bone. I swear I

see somethin' undead reachin' out for me. I don't make it
a step before he's locked my arm again, and I can feel the
life squeezin' right out of me.

"You're gonna do whatever the fuck I tell you to do"
spits from Roger's mouth, black as tar. I can feel them
words stickin' to me... stickin' me on my spot... leachin'
into my bones and spoilin' my insides. He gives my arm a
twist. It's like the world's worst Indian burn, and I can't
help wincin'. Then his fingers relax, like they did on my
thigh, and his voice gets soft again. He asks if I'm gonna
be his "good girl," and them words make me wanna sick-
up all over his sweaty face.

I can't even manage a "yes" 'cuz I think I may blow
chunks out with it, so I just nod. I nod, and I feel like
a pile of shit for doin' it. That makes Roger smile. That
makes Roger tell me I'm a *good girl*. I ain't never wanted to be a good girl, and I sure as hell don't wanna be
his good girl. But I don't know what to do. I don't know
who to cry out to. There ain't no Papa here, scramblin'
to scoop me from my bent bicycle and blow the gravel
grits outta my knees. There ain't no Mama here to cast
her wide shadow over top of mine and blot out the whole
world. There ain't no Henry here to kick this behemoth
in the nads with his orthopedic shoes and slingshot a
couple of rocks right at his fat head. There ain't nobody
but me, and I can't do a damn thing. Roger keeps a soft
hold on my arm and leads me through a thicket of tall
pines bankin' the roadway. We get in there, and it's a
world apart. I keep glancin' back at the glint from Rog-

er's trunk catchin' the starlight, but beyond those trees, I feel invisible. I get gobbled up in the womb of the woods, listenin' to coyotes and hoot owls call out stranger-danger to their kin through the thick pitch as Roger tramples a path ahead. Before long, I can't see that mangled metal catchin' the light no more. It's nothin' but darkness. Darkness and the sound of Roger thrashin' at the brambles and the bushes as we push on. Then he adds some nasty curses in there. They get nastier when a low branch beans him but misses me by a mile. Part of me wants to laugh. The other part wants to cry.

Roger grumbles out somethin' about not bein' able to "see for shit," like he ain't just a flat-out idiot who don't know where he's goin', and then he stops dead. "We're gonna camp, girl. We're gonna camp here until it's light and I can see where the hell I'm headed."

I hear a peep. Maybe it's me. Maybe it's an owl. I can't be sure anymore. Either way, Roger don't care. He drags me on over to a big tree not a few feet off and throws his coat and some other crap down at the base. Then he leans over and spreads the coat out, wide as it'll go, so that it looks like the top half of one of those body outlines they trace around dead folks. He tells me, "We might as well have some fun while we're stuck out here," and pats at the coat with his free hand. "Right, good girl?" I don't move. I can't. He pats the coat again. He tells me to lay down. I don't.

Then he snarls so those yellow teeth of his catch the bare bit of light eekin' through the trees. He hisses out, "Nobody rides for free, buttercup," and then he collapses down onto that coat and pulls me along with him. I roll right up into his meaty claws. In a wink, I can smell that stale, rancid breath of his again. And his skin, it's like crusty sandpaper rakin' against mine. He's slippin' those clammy hands of his up under my t-shirt and down into my waistband, and I'm battin' at 'em and screechin' and flailin', but he just gets all the rougher. His breath gets all the nearer, all the hotter. He starts unbuttonin' my jeans and chantin', "Ahhh... good girl, good girl, good girl. Be my good girl," and I can't do nothin' to stop him. Not a goddamn thing.

CHAPTER EIGHT

I weren't no bigger than a prairie dog trailin' Mama's knee the first time I saw her moxie in action. Some grizzly fella at Bixby's Diner swatted her fanny as we were leavin' and called her a "knockout." Apparently, Mama took it as a request.

I always recall watchin' her palm her knuckles afterwards and thinkin' that she was the toughest creature in creation. I must'a had more stars in my eyes that day than the whole of the Milky Way, but tonight, I add a few more for Henry.

He's holdin' a shovel twice his size and shakin' somethin' fierce, but as he draws that ole spade back from Roger's bloody head, he's just as tough as Mama. Tougher.

He asks me, "You alright?" in a man's voice stuck inside a little boy, and suddenly, I am.

I don't answer. I just spring up from that dirty ole coat and launch myself into Henry's arms before he can even drop the shovel. As I lean hard in, a little blood trickle from his forehead spreads like salve over all of Roger's rough thumbprints. The shovel handle presses down my spine, its soft pine makin' a steady cradle that says I'm safe. I don't wanna let go. Not ever. I can feel my body quakin' under Henry's grip, and I think I'm afraid that it ain't ever gonna stop. But then he starts shakin' to match me, and when he says, "That fella probably ain't out for long," I know why.

I peek back at Roger layin' there in the dirt, right where he belongs. He's makin' groggy sounds like the sows do when they're fixin' to wake, and watchin' his fat, pale face twitch in blackness is the stuff of nightmares. I all the sudden don't feel so safe no more, so I slide outta Henry's tremblin' arms, scoop up my backpack, and follow my friend into the dark.

Me and Henry cut through the trees like wood nymphs, all quiet and swift. We know the wilds. Don't matter if they're West Virginian, Louisianan, or otherwise. Nature has a way of takin' care of forest children and keepin' 'em safe from the dark things that lurk in the night. I get to thinkin' that we oughta bed down somewhere... find us some safe spot to land and wait for daylight. But I just can't shake the feelin' of Roger coverin' our footsteps with his. I can't shake the scent of him from me. I think maybe if we get far enough away, I might not smell it anymore. But we both get winded before I can shake his brand from my bones, and poor Henry gets to wheezin' so that all the critters in our path are boltin' a few hundred feet out. He says, "Olive, I think we're safe now," clear and true as he can amid the scritchin' shadow talk eatin' up the night all around us, and I don't have the heart to press him no further. I don't notice until just then how deep in the wood we've gone, how soupy-thick the dark is... like

God done spilt his inkwell all over West Virginia. But a bare bit in the tree canopy is lettin' moonlight wiggle in enough to shine a spotlight on a fine bit of grassy earth, and so I stop there and set down cross-legged. I want to pat the green beside me and tell Henry I think we're safe too, but I don't wanna lie, so I just ask if he's okay as he plunks down at my side.

"I thought you was dead in that trunk," I tell him.

"Naw, just knocked cold. Good thing that fat ninny didn't figure on the trunk release."

I chuckle, but it sounds hollow. Thinkin' on it, I feel like my insides been scooped out, scrambled around, and only half of 'em put back where they came from. When Henry asks if *I'm* okay, nothin' but "no" feels like an honest answer.

Henry cracks his lips to say somethin' back, but nothin' comes out. I'm not sure what I want him to say, or need him to say, but the silence just leaves me fillin' in the blank spots all on my lonesome. I start thinkin' on all the things I'd said and done inside that rusty ole car. I'd smiled big at Roger dialin' up ole Muddy for me. I'd snickered about my best friend with him as Henry slept. I'd told him stuff. I'd showed my insides. I'd let him brush my thigh.

I feel my face flush in the blackness and wonder if Henry can see. I can't say if he does, but my squirmin' finally spooks an "I'm sorry" outta him.

"I'm sorry, Olive. Sorry I didn't get there sooner."

I'm all drawn in like a pill bug by then, but quiet words

bleed out between my hide chinks. I tell Henry, "It ain't your job to go pullin' me out of every pickle I get myself in."

A "Pickle?!" comes back sourer, louder. "You didn't get yourself in no pickle! You got yourself a ride with some sicko pervert who was probably lyin' up the wazoo about even havin' a daughter in the first place. Ain't no woman in her right mind ever gonna lay down with that piece of shit."

First time I heard Henry curse—ever. I think I kinda like it. And he lit off from there. He says, "Olive, there's nasty, bad men out there, and they do what they do— ain't got a damn thing to do with what ladies wear, or what they say, or how big they smile, or how little they fuss—those men do what they do 'cuz they're sick."

Maybe Henry's fiery eyes are lightin' up the night because all the sudden, it don't feel so dark no more. But they don't manage to burn away the dirty feelin' that's hangin' onto me tight. I keep drawin' my legs in closer to my chest and pullin' into myself tighter and tighter. I ain't sure if I'm doin' a shit job of squeezin' that filth out or just holdin' it in all the more. I can't get a word out anyhow. There ain't no room.

Henry's got plenty to say though. He keeps pressin' me—askin' to know what I'm thinkin'; what I'm feelin'. Finally, a notion creeps into my mind to tell him what I'm feelin' without sayin' it outright, since I ain't sure how to do that anyway.

"Remember that time we snuck up on the pilin's between Papa's grain silos, lookin' to pocket rotten egret eggs so I could hide 'em in Marcy Gibbons' locker?"

Henry nods, his eyes live cinders in the dim light. "And remember how I slipped on account of that slimy

bird crap and fell ass-first into the chicken manure pile so that I was all covered up to my neck with the stanky filth until it worked down into all my crevices?"

Another nod.

"Well, it took me somethin' like two months of showers to get all that dirty business worked out. That stuff was so rotten that it sunk down into me, under my skin, until I just couldn't shake it. Well, that's sorta how I feel now—dirty down to the insides. I s'pose I went out askin' for trouble, and it found me."

"Askin' for trouble?" came back to me double. I think a few hoot owls hangin' about spooked and took to wing. "You wasn't askin' for trouble, Olive. You wasn't askin' for it... not one little bit. This stuff happens all the time to girls who ain't askin' for it. Heck, do you think your mama was askin' for it?!"

I unfurl. "Waddaya mean, was Mama askin' for it?" I ain't sure if Henry had a mind to reply, but his hands had ideas of their own. Both clapped over his mouth like he'd done belched at the dinner table or somethin'. The echo shook a few more hoot owls from their branches.

"Waddaya mean, was Mama askin' for it?" This time with a bite.

Henry's hands slide down and down until they pool in his lap and start wringin' one another so fast that I can't tell the right one from the left. I watch 'em long enough to get dizzy and then set my eyes on his. The fire's died away, and the muddled ole man who's always lookin' like he's misplaced his teeth, or his marbles, or maybe both, comes floodin' back. "I ain't meant to tell you" makes its way out at a wheeze.

"Tell me what?"

"About your mama," Henry says back, eyes dartin' away from mine. "About what happened all them years ago, and why everybody started hatin' on her."

"Well, ya have to tell me now, don'tchya?" is as honest as it gets.

Henry says, "S'pose so," but he ain't happy about sayin' it. He just frowns into the woods—maybe searchin' all God's spilled ink for just the right words hidden somewhere between the thistle thickets. Then he says he only knows what his momma told him and fesses up that "half of it's probably hogwash."

I agree. Only thing his momma's fuller of than cheap wine and stale Cheerios is hogwash.

So, he tells me. He tells me that his momma and Mama was bosom buddies back in the day—until my mama up and blabbed to her, God, and everyone in town that the sittin' pastor at church had forced himself on her. "Mom said she hadn't been actin' right… hadn't been herself. Said she got real quiet, and stopped raisin' her hand in class. Stopped eatin' lunch with the other kids. Started dressin' real frumpy and not wantin' folks to touch her."

Henry pauses, maybe imaginin' my mama in a gunnysack with her head down, swattin' kids who tried to poke bubblegum in her hair. Or maybe not. Maybe that's just me.

"I guess she didn't say nothin' at first. She didn't say nothin' for a long time. Kept quiet. Got quieter. But then Mom said that one day, she just up and started shoutin' it from the rooftops to anyone who'd listen."

Now I picture Mama up on a rooftop, wild buckwheat curls twistin' in the wind, yellin' out to the whole town below that the pastor's a damn pervert who oughta have his willie lopped off. God help me, I smile.

"What's funny?"

I say, "Oh, nuthin'," but my smilin' twists a smile outta Henry too. So, there we is, beamin' at each other in the darkness—him all banged up to shit and me still with Roger's meaty fingerprints soilin' my skin—but beamin' none-the-less. Now I see Mama's buckwheat hair tangled with a superhero cape, but then she steps off that rooftop and sinks like stone. I feel my heart seize up as I'm watchin' her fall.

"So... Mama got..." is the most I get out before my throat chokes. I'm lettin' the rest of the words stack up in my windpipe, and I can feel 'em poisonin' me, so I swallow 'em back down. But then they start stewin' around and makin' my guts percolate. It ain't long before my head joins in, and I yowl out, "What the hell? So that's why everyone hates us? They hate us 'cuz Mama ratted out some perv-wad pastor back in the day?"

Henry ain't gotta say yes. His eyes say it all. But they

don't look anythin' but confused about it. He tells me, "My mom said that good girls keep quiet," and I give a hoot so loud that it calls all them owls back and then some.

"And what do you think?"

Henry pins his eyes to my torn collar, right above where my heart's busy heavin'. Then he whispers, "I think it ain't never good to keep quiet when you're screamin' on the inside."

CHAPTER NINE

There's a sorta light that comes over a body when they say somethin' profound. It shines so bright that folks can feel it through radio waves, and television sets, and across oceans so wide that you could bob around in 'em for a million years and never see the same fish twice. It echoes around a space and sticks there. It'll soak right into the walls and the floorboards—soak right down into your marrow if you're standin' there long enough. I expect it's the same kinda light cast by Mister Lincoln, givin' his Gettysburg Address, and Martin Luther King Jr, goin' on about all his dreams. I think I see that light lyin' in a soft halo around Henry just then. I think I feel the wind stop blowin' and the critters quiet to look his way. And I tell him so. Let him bust his buttons. He earned it. I let him lay out his whole story—how he come-to in the pitch of Roger's trunk with a whopper of a headache and no clue how he got there. How he jimmied the emergency pull and felt the cool night spillin' in as he crawled outta his grave. How he called and called for me, but I wouldn't answer. But once he gets to the part where he found some duct tape and that shovel in the trunk too, I get a sick feelin' that steals my breath away and I don't much feel like listenin' no more. All the sudden

I feel pretty preoccupied with gettin' out of them woods since they got a monster runnin' loose in 'em somewhere. Roger's gotta be up-and-at-'em by now, and I don't mean to see his pasty mug ever again in all my lifetime. So, I calls Henry, "Hendini," and asks if him and his lock-poppin', escape-hatchin' brain can find the main road. He's still doin' the cock walk right about then, so he fans his tail feathers and reasons he can. Once we get ourselves cleaned up enough that we don't look like we been workin' the kill floor at Big Ern's Slaughterhouse, he starts peekin' at tree moss, and angulatin' the moon, and talkin' gibberish to his self that sounds like Pete and Wyatt's crazy twin-speak. I'm about 99-percent certain he's puttin' on a show when he all the sudden points like a damn duck dog and takes off stalkin' through the underbrush. I can hear him sniffin' out the road gators and the oily asphalt puddles as he snakes through the trees with his nose tipped towards the sky. I ain't even sure how he can see two feet in front of him with all this blackness, but he just charges ahead, even though I hear him make a couple of milquetoast swears when a low branch or a sticker weed gives him a swat. We keep on like that for twenty, maybe thirty minutes, but all them woods start lookin' the same, which gets me to frettin' that we might be loopin' back around to where we started. Loopin' back around to Roger.

"You *sure* you know where we're goin'?" don't come outta my mouth until I been thinkin' it for a good ten minutes. Henry says he does, but he says it like he ain't payin' attention. He says it like when you ask Mee-maw somethin' while she's watchin' her midday 'stories.' You could harvest an organ from that ole bat, and she'd be none the wiser. I hope Henry ain't so powerful distracted as that. But I done asked, and I got answered, so I keep on followin' him through the woods, hopin' I don't end up in a gingerbread house with a witch cookin' me in her oven. Granted, I'd take that any day of the week over meetin' up with Roger again. I still ain't got his smell offa me, and just thinkin' of his pale face and his clammy skin makes it kick up like rotten meat in the July sun. I'm startin' to feel the grit of that filth still stuck way deep down in my crevices when Henry hoots up ahead.

"There it is! There's the road!" gotta be some of the finest words I ever heard. And Henry echoes 'em again as he bounces up and down a few times while pointin' at a bean-green sign that says we're at mile marker 56. I wrack my brain, tryin' to think where Roger's car went off the road, but I can't recall nothin' but heavy eyelids, and sweaty hands, and busted glass. When we make it down to the pavement, nothin' looks familiar, but that don't mean as much as it should. I should'a stayed awake. I should'a been wise. I should'a looked out for myself. Gramps always said he didn't trust folks because either a) he knew 'em, or b) he didn't know 'em. Strangers weren't to be trusted. Even babies know that. What a dumbshit I was.

So now here we was, roadside and hangin' our thumbs out again, waitin' for whatever serial killer decides to stop and pick us up. We have a row about it. Henry thinks we should keep to the woods. I think—well, I ain't sure what I think. I just don't wanna go back into that thick belt of green, where the shadows hide everythin' and all I can see under every tree trunk is a flattened-out coat with a hulkin' monster sprawled out on it. But I'm scared shitless too. Matter of fact, first car that comes up on us sends me divin' right into the thickets beside the road to hide. Henry follows behind, like a puzzled hound dog trailin' its master into a supermarket or somethin'. I s'pect the car would'a stopped outta sheer curiosity were it not too dark to see us divin' off the roadside. But maybe the night's lookin' out for us now. Maybe it owes us a favor.

Once those taillights shrink to Red Hots in the distance, Henry fishes me outta the brambles and gives me a good needlin'. "Thought you said you wanted to hitchhike, Olive. Thought you wanted a ride! What the heck was that?"

I wish I could answer. I want to. But I don't know any better than him why I'd done what I done, so I just shrug, pick some leafy bits outta my braid, and stalk back towards the fog line. When the second car comes, I get that urge to bolt again, but I keep to the road, knowin' I can't holdout my thumb without it shakin' anyhow. I think the night's throwin' me a bone this time too, 'cuz the car's headlamps miss me and Henry by a sliver, and then that rig keeps on down the road with the folks inside probably never knowin' we were there in the first place. I s'pect

Henry seen me slide a bit to the right as those high beams licked at my sneaker heels, but he don't say a word.

Sunrise brings a warm blanket on our backs and car number three. But it ain't a car so much as a big ole breadbox on wheels. It come rumblin' up from the north, and I'd wager you could hear it a mile off, maybe more. Sounds like a one-man band where the fella has emphysema and can't play none of his instruments for shit. We're already stopped on the side of the highway and starin' back into the yonder when it crests the hill behind us in all of its graffitied, backfirin', bull-nosed, school-bus splendor. I ain't never seen a bus done up like this one. It's like all the worst kids in school got together and decided they was gonna Mad Max their ride, even if it got 'em all expelled. And judgin' by the looks of them faces hangin' out the windows as it slows up alongside us, I'm probably right.

Me and Henry are both too flummoxed to answer back when the bus' door swings open mid-motion and a girl with too much eye makeup leans over from the driver's seat, callin' out, "You kids need a ride?!" Second time she hollers it, I get my wits about me and give a nod.

"Well, what are you waitin' for?" is all the reply I need. I can tell she ain't even gonna make a full stop, so I just scoop up Henry's hand like Mama done mine when I was scared of somethin' and pull us both towards the bus. It's kinda like train-hoppin'. I line up my target, leap, and then my guts do a little loop-dee-loop as I land. Henry's hand's tight on mine all the while and then falls away as we find our feet and the girl with the lined-up eyes snaps her gum at us. She asks, "Whatchya doin' way out here?" lookin' half at us, half at the road. Probably more at us... which makes me a little nervous.

My mouth hangs open like words mean to come out, but none do. Behind me, Henry pipes somethin' about "gettin' lost," and the girl just sorta sniggers.

"Yeah... well... you just boarded a bus fulla lost kids. Lost kids who don't wanna be found. So maybe you're in the right place."

I reckon that's pretty smart. I like this chick. I give her another nod—one like what Papa gives other farmers who got earth under their fingernails too.

She nods back, purrs "Welcome to the madhouse," and shoos us down the aisle. I tell you what, I ain't never come across such a mishmash of faces in all my days. There's street kids, and gypsy kids, and sassy-lookin' kids, and kids as black as night, and kids who look like they just fell off the turnip truck. There's every kinda misfit kid you could think of—most of 'em noisy and all of 'em one of a kind. And that makes 'em my kinda kids. Some of them kids say "hello," some of them glare, some of them beam, and some of them don't pay us no nevermind at all. I pick out a spot about halfway down the middle of the bus and pile in across from one of the beamers. My pack slides across that government-grade Naugahyde slick as a whistle, and it ain't until Henry slides in next to me that I realize his case is missin'.

I just blurt "your Papa's suitcase!" half in shock and

half outta bein' cross with myself that I didn't notice it gone earlier. Henry comes back with big eyes. Big, sadsack eyes that say everythin' he can't... that the one and only thing he had left in the world of his Papa's is gone now, and it's all my fault.

"I imagine it's still in that fella's car" comes outta him softly, gently... like it might hurt my feelin's less if I can barely hear. But I think it hurts worse. He lies and says he "didn't much like that ugly thing anyhow," but reminds me, "everythin' we had was in there. Everythin' short of some gummy worms and your crazy idea of what makes for a well-packed getaway bag."

I raise my finger to wag it at him, but there ain't no use. He's right. I packed like a fool four-year-ole goin' to space camp, and now we got zippidy-doo-dah to our names. I'm fixin' to bash my head into the window glass when the beamer across the aisle-way pipes up and says, "*Hi!* I'm Lori! What's y'alls names?"

One look at this perky twit and I wonder why the hell I sat us across from her. She's got these eager-beaver brown eyes that are battin' like they're fulla sand. She's leanin' on tenterhooks across her bench seat, waitin' to gobble up every word of my reply. It feels like I'm lookin' at a seagull that I just gave a french fry to and now it ain't never gonna leave my side again.

"That's Henry, I'm Olive," I answer back with a thumb crook'd at Henry's mop of locks. They're still all fulla forest gunk and I think I spy a spider crawlin' around in there, but I ain't about to tell him. That boy'd take on a full-grown bayou gator with his bare hands before he'd smoosh a spider. Up until age eight, he swore up and down that *Charlotte's Web* was a horror movie. I get distracted, watchin' to see if that shiny black bit is gonna move or not, and don't notice as Lori slides to the edge of her seat and plants her fancy Nike sneakers right in the aisle.

The bus is movin' good now, and as it starts whippin' through some gnarly S-curves, Lori grips her bench seat so as not to topple right out of it. She's got lacquered-up nails about as prim as can be, and I think about fussin' to Mama when I was no more than three or four about girls in school who had frilly getups and baubles that I didn't. I recall it, clear as can be, she said, "Child, you don't need all that fancy crap. Everythin' that's worth a damn is on the inside." So, I kinda snarl at Lori's shiny nails gripped over that bench seat, maybe meanin' to. Maybe not. But either way, she catches my eye doin' it.

"It's too red, isn't it?" she presses me, brown eyes battin' again. "The polish?"

I shrug. What the hell did I know about polish? Only polish we had in our house went on shoes, and Pete and Wyatt's cheeks when they was playin' Commando.

"It was the only bottle I could fit," she drolls on, takin' little peeks down at her hands and squishin' up her face every time she does it. By the fifth or sixth time, she reasons, "I should'a took the mauve. Mauve's always a safe bet," and I can't help but wonder if she's talkin' to me or some other girl who might actually give a hoot.

Henry tells her he thinks it "looks nice" like he knows what he's talkin' about. And damn, it's like he just tossed another french fry 'cuz ole Lori-bird scoots even closer to us, if such a thing is possible. She gives him this cheesy, spokesmodel kinda smile, and he sends it right back to her. Makes me sick. Then she asks him what his story is, and where we's headed, and fifty-thousand other questions before the poor kid can even spit out a word of reply. I sorta expect her to start spillin' her own tale before Henry makes a single peep, but after she finishes with the not-so-Spanish Inquisition, she just gets real still and quiet, and cradles her chin in her palms like she's settlin' in for a good, long yarn. And Henry, he gives her a few little threads that she tugs on and draws out until there's this whole patchwork quilt made up from the scraps of our travels. Reminds me of bein' stuck up under Mama's ole mint-green Singer and watchin' her Mary Janes pump on the pedal as she prattled on about mendin' baby blankets that smelled like soft spots and worn trousers that Papa done worked down to the bone. It's actually kinda nice how the Lori-bird perches while she's listenin' and makes like she's interested by cockin' her head every now and again. I wonder whether I oughta ask if she wants a cracker or if anybody taught her any good curse words to squawk out in prudish company. But instead, I just sorta watch her watchin' Henry as he finishes threadin' our adventure quilt. I feel a snag comin' on when he gets to the part in the story where we meet Roger. He starts talkin' of this friendly stranger with Elmer's-paste skin and eyes like those doors on a game show with mystery stuff hidden behind 'em. I start feelin' those eyes on me. I start feelin' those hands on me. My skin gets to twitchin', and the bus starts closin' up around me. I'm watchin' Henry's lips move in slow motion, but I don't hear no words anymore. I just hear the heave of Roger's girth above me. I hear him cooin' to me, "good girl, good girl" and I feel I'm gonna sick-up right then and there.

But then Lori chirps, "you two've had quite a time of it, haven't you?" and the quiet bit in my mind that made space for Roger fills up with her gummy smile. Then she looks square at me, not blinkin' a wink, and adds in, "Olive, you've gotta be the bravest girl I ever met!"

I think I might like this gal. She's aces. She keeps her eyes glued tight on me as I duck my head a bit and fumble with my pack. Henry says I'm "turnin' pink," and I'm just about to slug him when he reasons that Lori's "right about that," and tells her, "Olive's the bravest girl I ever met too."

Feels like these two are fixin' to start an Olive Abernathy fan club, so I press Lori to tell us all about her lonely bottle of nail polish and whatever place it used to live. And can you believe it, she starts out by fessin' up that she's a cheerleader! I s'pose I just figured all those gals was cut from the same snotty cloth, but the way she tells it, they don't seem so bad. They was like a family, her and her squad. They held each other up and caught each other when they fell. Kinda like Mama always told me, that "the right friend ain't the most popular one, or the one with the best toys... it's the one who holds you up when the world knocks ya down," and it sounds like Lori fell plenty, but she never hit the ground. Not 'til she up and got preggers and her folks flipped a lid 'cuz she wouldn't keep quiet and get the thing hoovered right outta her. Then it was goodbye cheerleadin', hello homeless. Lori says she ain't the only one on the bus with that kinda story. She says that most of the kids on this big breadbox either been knocked up, knocked out, or plain kicked outta wherever they was for bein' different. Some of 'em slept under overpasses and begged change offa folks with sappy signs sayin' stuff like, "Hungy, anything helps" or "I'll be your Queen for some Burger King," but Lori never done any of that. Lori got picked up not five miles from her house as she was racin' down the interstate all bleary-eyed, fixin' to throw herself in front of a big rig and flatten out that baby bump forever. She says the bus just rolled right up, "like a divine sign from God that looked like a giant pickle," and scooped her. She'd been ridin' since Kansas and says they stop every couple hours or so just to let her go pee. Then she pulls back the sides of her jean jacket and points at a little pooch pokin' out from under her t-shirt, tellin' us, "This little one keeps kickin' at my bladder."

I just stare at that lumpy belly of hers and think back to when Mama got big with Pete and Wyatt. Folk in town would give her the eye as she passed by with that round gut of hers. Men would point. Women would whisper.

Sometimes they even spat at the ground. I remember figurin' that all those folk were just cross at her for addin' another filthy Abernathy to their town. I even asked Mama once if she was ashamed of that big bulge, and she said, "Girl, this body's got the power to move mountains and birth babies. I won't never be ashamed of it."

And Lori ain't ashamed neither. Not no more. She says that when her folks tried to take that baby from her... tried to scoop it right out from her insides... she told 'em off six ways from Sunday. Called 'em curse names that she didn't even know she knew. And now, here she is, ridin' this crazy-pickle bus, "headed for *New York City!*" and clutchin' that baby belly of hers like it's the only thing that matters in the whole wide world. And when I look in those dopey brown eyes of hers, I can tell that it is.

Henry pipes up right about then and asks if she's havin' a boy or a girl. She don't know... says it doesn't matter. But then this gritty voice a few rows back says, "Sure as hell *does* matter. Last thing we need in this world is another boy!"

That's CeCe Meeks, the one and only. I know that 'cuz she tells us so. She tells us so just as Henry's oglin' her big ole bosoms. Mama'd have taken one look at that San Andreas fault line of cleavage and called it "the devil's ass crack." Course, I s'pect half of Mama's ever-lovin' wardrobe came from a defunct nunnery, and this gal here's wearin' a black V-neck that braves the fine line between Morticia and Elvira. Still, by now I've seen devils dressed up in plaid button-downs and cheerleaders wearin' baby bumps worth givin' your life for, so I ain't about to run CeCe off or ask if the devil really is moonin' us from her low-cut t-shirt. I keep quiet, but Henry gets his freckle-dy nose all outta joint and spits up, "What's wrong with boys?" as CeCe's hangin' her meaty, tattooed arms over Lori-bird's bench seat.

Don't take much ruminatin' on CeCe's part. She growls back, "How about everything!" before Henry can even get a blink in. "Let's see," she keeps on, "my dad was an as-shat. Every guy that I went to school with was either a bonehead toker, a man-whore, or a jock who had to get his girlfriend to do his remedial English homework be-tween blowjobs. So yeah, I'd say the world is totally fine without any more guys in it."

Boy howdy, that shuts Henry's trap right quick. Good thing, too. It kinda hides the drool that's been poolin' in-side there ever since he got an eye on CeCe's knockers. Plus, it gives her the floor, and lordy, she lambastes every inch of it. Once I tell her about our travels and the dirty SOB who landed us on this bus, she gets to philosophiz-in' about nasty ole men-folk, and folk who keep their se-crets, and folk who act all prim and perfect while they're doin' nasty stuff in the shadows. CeCe Meeks don't have time for none of those folks, no more than she's got time for her own folks. She gives a nod up towards the front of the bus, right at the driver's seat, and tells us that's her girlfriend, Mazie. Then she tells us how them two got turned out by their own kin once they copped to bein' lovebirds. I think right then that CeCe Meeks might be the first gay girl I ever met, but she says probably not. She says that they're all over the place, hidin' in the shadows of little backwards towns like mine with their mouths sewn shut, too scared shitless to come out. Her and Mazie bought this bus off'a ole hippy for $500 and a pack of Red Vines, and reckoned they'd hit the road and scoop up all the scared, misfit, tossed-out kids they could along the way. They've been glidin' down the highway in that great green monster for nearly a month now and added a baker's dozen to their crew. She tells us about Charlie, whose folks duct-taped him to a radiator 'cuz he can't sit still for more than five minutes without twitchin' for want of the vodka that him and his birth Mom shared in the womb. She tells us about Rhonda Hildebrand, the pride of the Davenport, Iowa pageant circuit, who's got more bejeweled tiaras than the Queen of England but couldn't never satisfy her mama's hunger for applause and shiny things. And she tells us about Beth Pendegrast, who kept quiet about her stepdaddy sneakin' in her room every night and touchin' her like no daddy oughta until she couldn't stand it no more. All them kids—left like trash scattered along the highway—but CeCe and Mazie scooped 'em up, dusted 'em off, and found the beautiful things underneath.

I pan up one row and down the other, catch CeCe's painted eyes and say, "Welp, I s'pose we fit right in since we don't seem to fit in nowhere else," and she grins. For the first time since I got on that bus, she grins. And I feel kinda special for it, like her smart mouth likes my smart mouth, and that somehow makes both our mouths wanna smile. Then she wanders off, quick as she come, and leaves us with Lori-bird, who's been holdin' her tongue for as long as her pee and starts fussin' about drinkin' too much Schweppes Ginger Ale that mornin'. She gets to squawkin' so good that Mazie hears her way up front and pulls off at a roadside diner somewhere near the Pennsylvania border. Me and Henry watch from the window as Lori skitters across the parkin' lot, holdin' tight to her downtown lady bits like they might fall right off. As she comes up on the diner's front door, a slimy lookin' feller holdin' an armload of Bibles comes traipsin' out and gives her a once-over. I see his steely eyes catch up on her baby bump and then flicker with somethin' like hate. Reminds me of that time late last fall when a slick snake-oil salesman showed up at our door tellin' Mama, "Don't be afeared, lady! The truth's gonna set you free!" I find myself smilin' now, recallin' Mama as she tapped the price tag on his dime-store Bible and said, "Truth don't make me nervous, sir. It's men sellin' it I got a problem with."

Mama'd have fixed that diner fella up good. She'd of told him that Lori was owed her mistakes, just like we all was, and that hate's a heavy cross to bear. She always said hate was "like swallowin' down poison, thinkin' it was gonna kill off your enemies," and what kinda dumbshit does that? I sit there, thinkin' on Mama slappin' her Mr. Yuck stickers all over the sacrament wine at church, as other kids spill off the bus and wander into the diner. In my mind's eye, I can feel folks eyein' those kids. I can hear their whispers. I don't wanna go in. And Henry... I think all these crazy stories, and big bosoms, and man-hatin' trash talk got him dumbstruck 'cuz he don't make a move to follow either. Soon as the clatter from that big herd of sneakers poundin' down the bus steps dies out, we're just sittin' there in this echoey hull. I elbow Henry, and he spooks like a bee stung him. "Hey," I says, "member that time you told Chet Gibbs to eat crow for callin' my boobies Raisinets, and he threatened to push us into his daddy's grain silo?"

Henry nods.

"I think we're in it."

Henry giggles, and it zings around the bus and bounces off all the cold corners until they get nice and warm. I even feel 'em hit me in the chest a time or two, and they make my insides heat right up too. I don't notice 'til then that Henry's been white-knucklin' the bottom lip of his bench seat so fierce that it's got little finger dents in it. But now they're fadin' away along with that pasty wash on his cheeks. I fix on that creamy freckled face of his and recall it lightin' up on the night when it came to my rescue. Next to the North Star, I ain't never seen anythin' brighten up the darkness like that. But I ain't about to tell Henry he looks like he could outshine the Milky Way. Boys don't wanna hear that sorta stuff. So I just tell him that I think that little baby inside Lori's belly *is* a boy baby. And I tell him I think that's pretty cool so long as it's a boy like Henry.

But Henry... he just makes a snorty sound and stares

at his loafers as a pair of returnin' footsteps start clompin' back up the bus steps. I see hair long before I see a kid under it—bushy, Brillo-Pad hair with a big ole pick stuck right smack-dab in the middle of it. It looks like this boy just got tired of combin' his rat's nest and gave up halfway through. He's comin' down the aisle at us, arms loaded up with chip bags and soda pops and candy made into necklaces as his hair's swingin' every which way. I don't realize 'til then just how damn hungry I am, so when he skids to a stop beside our bench and asks, "Hey, aren't you guys gonna get some food?" it takes all I got not to snatch them Fritos right out from under him. But Henry... Henry knows. Somehow he knows that I'm eyein' those chips. He knows that my insides are so empty they're eatin' away at themselves.

"Naw, we don't have any money," Henry fesses up, "but I'll trade you somethin' for those Fritos." Then he wiggles himself around, jammin' his hand deep down into his pants pocket and pulls out a Swiss Army Knife that his Daddy give him for his tenth birthday. He says, "This is all I got," and holds it straight out to the boy like it's some trifle he cares nothin' for.

I want to shout at him. I want to slap down his hand and tell him that only a fool trades a fancy pocket knife for a stupid bag of chips. But I can't. I can't speak a single word. My throat's just too choked up with a million other ones to let the right one out. But thank the Sweet Baby Jesus, this boy's got plenty of his own. His big, banana-shaped eyebrows flatten out as he puffs, "You serious man?" and then before Henry can answer back, he snorts like Mama does when she's cookin' with cayenne pepper. "I'm not gonna take your knife, kid," he tells Henry. "That ain't cool. I ain't about that."

And then it's like Preacher Higgins givin' alms to the poor. Well... Preacher Higgins with a rake stuck in his hair and braces that look like fresh barbed wire. That boy just uncurls his arms and hands down the Fritos along with two Snickers bars and a can of RC Cola. For a second I can swear I hear angel-song, and even the little devil on my shoulder leans hard into my ear and tells me that I'd better be nice to this fella for the duration. That boy says it "ain't no thing," but as he keeps on towards the back of the bus with Henry's humble *thank you*s trailin' behind him like lovestruck puppies, I know it is. It *is* a thing. A big thing. And I don't mean to forget it.

What I *could* happily forget is Lori turnin' up not a minute later, yowlin' about sittin' on somebody else's poo splatter in the ladies and then washin' her ass-end in the sink. I'm wolfin' down the Fritos, and even starvin' as I am, that put the brakes on the whole operation. And land's sakes, Lori's story made the Snickers bar look about as good as Mee-Maw in a bikini. Just thinkin' of that... thinkin' of Mee-maw and all her saggy bits and all her grousin' about how Grandpa Herb never did nothin' but knock her up... it gets me to thinkin' about Lori and her fella. When I mention him, her lips turn down as the bus engine roars up, and she spends the next couple of miles goin' on about how she thought them two'd be together forever. She says he was the most handsomest boy in all of Davenport, and I know damn well what handsome boys are all about. Mama told me that good-lookin' boys have fat-ass egos. She said, "A man's ego's like his gut. You feed it too much, it just becomes a bloated, insufferable source of bullshit." Hell, I wouldn't never trust no handsome boy who told me he was gonna marry me, and take care of me, and all that flimflam. But then again, I ain't been dropped on my head comin' down off some fancy cheerleader pyramid neither.

I tell Lori that if it makes her feel any better, bein' together 'til the wheels fall off ain't all it's cracked up to be. Mee-maw once told me that the crazy-ass romantical notion of growin' ole together was like the world's longest game of chicken. "Just two miserable ole farts glarin' at each other over cold soup and backgammon, waitin' to see which one of 'em croaks first." Mind you, Mee-maw'd been tellin' folks what's what and where they could shove it since circa 1938, but Papa said she hadn't made a lick of sense since Eisenhower was in office. I tell Lori that too, and maybe it makes her feel less stupid. But maybe it shouldn't. Either way, it sticks with me that Mee-maw's got her own sorta smarts, and I up and find myself missin' her caterwaulin' and the way she always called folks on their shit. I can see her clear as day in my head—teeth out, drawin' a gummy smile, and layin' a wink down on me. "Don't never hold your tongue, girl," she'd tell me. "It's bound to get dry and fall right off. Then how the hell you gonna eat an ice cream cone?" I smile at Lori, not really meanin' to, but it don't improve her sour face none, and she gets real quiet after that. I'da felt bad about it if I weren't so tired of her cluckin'. I want to talk about adventurin' and marks on the map, not some nincompoop jock who cares more about cradlin' a football than a baby. So, I leave Lori to her Mister Wrong pity-party along with Henry to coax her smile back while I head out to find me some hooligans with proper stories like I used to do on Huckleberry's bus.

I know what to look for. I know who has the juicy stuff. Them kids with clean shoes and Walkmans, they ain't seen nothin'. They ain't done nothin'. Nothin' worth tellin' anyhow. The best stories on Huckleberry's bus always came outta gnarled mouths and wrinkled-up faces that looked like they'd seen too much sun and braved too many storms. Those are the kinda kids I'm lookin' for. I pass a pair of twin girls with ugly perms who look me up one side and down the other with four doppelganger eyes, each one of 'em tellin' me to buzz off. Two seats up from them, the kid with the pick in his hair gives me a friendly nod, and his bushy mop sways with an S-curve. I near pile in beside him, thinkin' he might'a robbed a meaty gangster or a Wells Fargo to get all that junk food money, but then I see *her.* Just one more seat back—a girl with inky-black hair tied into two little knots on top of her head that look like rotten brussels sprouts and a sour grimace to match 'em. She's got a steel pin somethin' like pencil lead stuck through her right eyebrow and what looks to be a paperclip hangin' out from between her nostrils. Part of me wants to ask if she got herself in some freak accident at a stationery store. All of me's intrigued. But this ain't the kinda girl you can just waltz right up to and hold out your hand to shake. Hell, she'd probably lop it off with some paper cutter she'd stuck through another of her body parts. So I plop down in the empty seat across from hers and thank my lucky stars that I brought my pack along.

I ain't seen that postcard album in what seems like forever. As I lug it outta my bag, it feels heavier somehow. Different. Even a little cold as I spread it over my lap. But it still knows me. It's still mine. It falls right open to a double-page spread with every New York City postcard I've ever come across. Half them things got big ole Lady Liberty standin' watch over the cityscape and the other half's all peppered-up with little glowy dots that look to be a million souls lightin' up the high-rise buildin's. One card's got an ole man and a half-dozen ole ladies leanin' off the side of a cruise liner, pointin' their pruny fingers across the water at Liberty and her spiky crown. The man's eyes are waterin', but all the ladies just seem to be starin' at his backside. It reminds me of when Gramps first swaggered into Hubbard's Retirement Palace and all them ole biddies hit him with their saggy elevator eyes. Later on I overheard him tell my Papa, "You could'a cut the sexual tension with a dull spoon," and it must'a been funny because he laughed his crazy laugh that made the walls shake until sawdust fell out. I sorta choke-up and chuckle all at once, thinkin' of his wild eyes lit up. It's just the trick to snare me a side-eye from paperclip girl. "What's so funny?" she snips. She's got a fat book laid across her lap, and she's clutchin' it with gloved-up hands that don't move a muscle as she looks my way. If little Mazie had an overdose of eye makeup, this gal here's her dealer, 'cuz I can't barely tell if she's lookin' at me, the ceilin', or into outer space with those shifty raccoon eyes. I say "Nuthin'," but that don't seem to appease her.

Now I know she's lookin' at me. I can *feel* her lookin' at me... feel the weight of it. I ain't felt eyes burnin' a hole through me that fierce since Preacher Higgins stood up at the pulpit crowin' about "that little *someone* who drew a mustache on the Nativity Scene Baby Jesus."

She comes back at me with a "C'mon," and another "What's so funny?" that sounds even meaner than the first one. I can't quite reason why until she claps that book of hers shut and says, "Laughing at the weirdo girl, huh? Really funny, huh?"

I'm blubberin', and puzzled, and stumblin' all over myself, but I manage to squeak out that I was laughin' at somethin' else... somethin' my grandad did... and when I spill the story to her, she starts gigglin' so damn hard, I think she's gonna laugh that paperclip clean out of her nose hole. Seems she's had that clip in there since she was 15. She says her Mom even took her down the La Playa Mall and watched some yahoo with a mini-harpoon gun and curly red hair like the *Mad Magazine* fella poke it right in. I tell her my mama'd never go for a thing like that, although she *did* once offer to run my head through her Singer sewin' machine if I didn't stop naggin' her for pierced ears. That makes paperclip girl laugh too, and then we're both laughin', and it feels like her hardness is meltin' away. She starts askin' me where I come from, and what my kin's like, and what kinda sammiches we eat. She don't talk about crazy rail-ridin', or stealin' folks' cars, or hangin' out with tattooed-up bikers, or nothin' like that. Hell, she's done less stupid stuff than prim little Lori-bird. She don't even got a racy name or anythin'. "Sam, just Sam," she tells me. She even says, "Nice to meet you," and holds out that gloved-up paw of hers. I give it a reverent shake like the ones Papa gives those Indian trader fellas. A crow's cry north of November, when the maple leaves got all brittle and gold, those tawny men'd come to our farm tradin' pelts for wheat. Papa said they wouldn't take pay "'cuz it ain't right for a man to sell what was never his to begin with."

I even tell Sam that story as it floats through my brain, and she gets darts in her eyes. She says I "got a good Dad," and I reckon she's right, so I brag on Papa for a bit. I tell how in the summer of '74, our oldest ewe birthed a scrawny lamb that folks said was only good for stew meat. When I got to fussin' about it bein' my size, Papa started callin' it "the best damn lamb in all of Lafayette," and when people asked why, he'd give me a wink and say, "'cuz it's little... and all the best things are."

I ain't sure why, but that floods Sam's darted eyes with a rainstorm. She's spillin' tears everywhere like a cow pissin' on a flat rock, and I don't know if I oughta let her be or draw her up in my arms like Mama always done to me when I was blubberin'. I scooch to the end of the bench, not sure just yet if I'm gonna scamper on back to Henry or wrap her up in a bear hug, and right about then she tips her face up. She's got tire tracks of mascara plowin' down her lily-white cheeks and a whopper of a snot dollop hangin' from that nose paperclip thingy. My spot sandwiched between Henry and that chatterbox Lori don't look so bad right about now. I'm about fixin' to make a break for it when Sam squeezes out a "Sorry" between sniffles and fesses up that her daddy's six feet under with worms wigglin' through his eye sockets. I figure it can't get much worse than that, but then she up and tells me that her momma's down there too, all boarded up in a pine box right beside his. It seems they both bit the big one in some gnarly wreck on the interstate last Christmas and took Sam's kid brother with 'em. To look at her, I wouldn't figure Sam to be tight with her folks, but once she gets her tears good and dried up, she starts in tellin' me about all these ole memories followin' her like friendly ghosts or somethin'. She's got her momma's lullabies swimmin' through her brain, gentle as fingers through baby's bathwater, and crickets playin' their fiddle song to her Daddy pointin' out every constellation in the sky. She even remembers her rowdy brother perched still and silent on knobby elbows as her Daddy whipped up ginger sweet rolls in a cast-iron stove that looked like a dragon's belly.

I could see 'em... each and every one: her momma, with that long raven hair drawn up into a bun and eyes like the sea after a storm... her daddy, flour-dusted, starin' up at the salt and pepper sky... and even her wily-eyed brother, who was probably a little shit 364 days outta the year. Even he didn't seem so bad with a pair of angel wings slapped on his back. But Sam—poor, poor Sam—she said she loved 'em ten-thousand times more today than she did yesterday and that she'd go to her grave regretful for not havin' hung back to play Chutes and Ladders, or cut the grass, or watch ole reruns of *Three's Company* with 'em. She said she couldn't live with herself no more, passin' by that ole house of theirs as she made the trek to school from her Gran's apartment. She couldn't live with seein' all those happy memories wiltin' with the uncut grass. So she up and run. She run out to the woods west of her ole place, where her and her folks used to take campin' trips. She says she went out there to make a ghost of herself, and I ain't entirely sure what she means by that, but her eyes take on a cold look when she says so.

"But then there was this owl," she tells me. "This bigeyed owl. He just wouldn't leave me alone. I know it sounds kinda stupid, but I just kept feeling like I knew him. Like he knew me."

Right about this point, I'm givin' her my best big-owl eyes, and I shit you not, they swell up ten times bigger when she says she thinks that owl was her daddy. She says it's like that bird drug her right back from the edge of nowhere and wouldn't let her be until she promised to go on livin'. So, she hitched it back to ole Gran's, but still couldn't bear the thought of all them friendly ghosts followin' her from place to place, so she lit out on her own. CeCe and Mazie picked her up not long after, and as she says, "Now I'm here. Now I'm on my own."

For a minute, I just stare back at Sam and watch fence posts, and skinny trees, and telephone poles whiz by the window behind her. Reminds me of Mama sayin' that "we ain't got no control of this life. It's a runaway train from the second ya leave the station." I s'pose I never gave that much thought before now. It was just another wackadoo thing Mama come up with to annoy me. But backlit by that road spillin' out behind her, Sam and her sad face look like they don't know where they're headed. And I can tell it ain't any kind of thrillin' adventure. Somethin' about that sticks with me, even as Sam turns back to her book and escapes into its dog-eared pages. Somethin' about knowin' that she ain't got no home to go to—not now, not ever— that pains me. No Mama, waitin' on the porch with a broom and a dustpan, ready to sweep up her heart if it gets munched up into teensy little bits. No Papa, holdin' her ten-speed's hollow handlebars anytime they feel unsteady. Not even a pesky brother to play dominoes with when it's rainin' outside. Not like I have. Not like I *had*.

CHAPTER TEN

Mama's dead. Papa's dead. The whole lot of 'em... gone, gone, gone. I stand up there at the pulpit talkin' about how Mama come to that church every damn Sunday and kept quiet in the back row just so that me and my heathen brothers could know Jesus. I tell Pastor Higgins and a sea fulla frowny faces that she was right to speak up all those years ago and that no girl oughta carry the weight of a sick man's shame. But they call me a "stupid girl." A stupid girl for nevermindin' her pain. A stupid girl for up and leavin' her, for leavin' them all. Those folks holler out my name like it sizzles on their tongues. They holler it over and over and over like it's gonna pound me down into Hell. And then they swarm me, grabbin' at the folds of Gran's black hand-me-down dress. I feel like I'm swimmin' in that thing, and their clamorin' paws are doin' nothin' but pullin' me under the water. I can't breathe, but they just kept shakin' and pullin' and yellin' my name. "Olive, Olive, Olive!"

I think I'm gonna meet my end, right then and there. And maybe... I think... maybe I deserve it. Maybe just like Mack, and Fertile Freddie, and Sam had all said, we ain't nothin' without our families. But then I hear it, a familiar voice stuck in with the others. A voice that means

I ain't alone. "Olive, Olive, OLIVE!"

I spook awake right then to find Henry's little fists clenched around my shoulders and shakin' hard. He's just finished wailin' my name for what he says was "the zillionth time," and a couple of the bus kids chuckle as I pan around with crazy eyes and find them all starin' at me. "You was dreamin'," Henry puffs, eyes ablaze with the same sorta panic he got when Gramps told him that lil' kids who wipe their boogers under his car seats go straight to Hell. "You was dreamin' and thrashin' all around and cryin' out like someone was murderin' you."

I straighten up in my seat and roll eyes around the cabin. Then I start fussin' with my hair and listenin' to the thunder of my heartbeat ebb as a half-dozen faces turn away, one by one, until only Henry's is left. Those ninety years'd really caught up with him. His brow's all crinkled up in wavy fissures, and while I s'pect it's probably early-onset acne, I spy a couple of dots near his temple that could be liver spots. He tells me I had him "frightful worried" and that he "ain't never heard some-one throw such a fuss."

"What was you dreamin' about, Olive?" seems a fair question, but I ain't about to answer it in truth. I make up some malarkey about the Boogie Monster makin' me sit through one of Missus Waldrop's two-hour social stud-ies lectures with my eyes pinned open. That seems horri-ble enough, and Henry agrees it could cause a body to cry out even though we both know that little bookworm loves every bit of borin'-ass social studies class. He piles in beside me, pretendin' he ain't already daydreamin' about musty ole textbooks fulla fussy men in powdered wigs slammin' their gavels. Then he points past my lap, out yonder window, and says, "You see where we are?"

I must'a been asleep a spell. Dusk's crawlin' in across the heavens, and I peer out to find a cityscape all lit up right outside my window. The moon's already hangin' heavy in the sky, and it's slumped down between two giant skyscrapers like a dollop of sweat tricklin' down God's weary backbone. Just over my shoulder, I hear Sam croon, "New York City, baby," like a real fancy actress I think I seen once in one of Mee-maw's ole blackand-white movies.

I can't take my eyes off of it. I never seen so many lights. I never seen so many buildin's. It's like a kingdom in one of Papa's storybooks. And all them lit-up, sky-scrapin' towers are glazin' their colors off a big watery pool of blue about like paint leakin' down a canvas. I crack my window to let the night air seep in and lordy... I wish I hadn't. In all my days, I ain't never heard such a mess of clatter. Well, maybe that one time when Gramps gave Pete and Wyatt a drum set for their birthday. Maybe that was a close second. But this ain't just drums. This is hollerin', and buses chuggin', and bells and sirens and the chitter-chatter of hungry pigeons cooin' for seed. And it's too much. It's all just too much. I clap the window shut, but I can still hear it bleedin' in. And it gets worse, too. CeCe says, "We gotta head to the Bronx." She says we'll "know it when we smell it," and after half an hour spent rollin' through a mess of cars that all seem cross with one another, I find myself nose-deep in oceans of piss and roasted garbage as we roll into an alleyway that somebody near the back of the bus calls *Decatur*. Mazie stops us cold there in the alley, and that ole bus lets out a sigh like it's gone to the grave.

"We're campin' here tonight" comes trailin' back to us from the driver's seat, and I hear a groan roll through the cabin. A few kids pop up and skitter off the bus while some others start pullin' out bags and blankets and hunkerin' down in their seats. I got a mean growl buildin' in my tummy, but lookin' out on that shadow-socked alleyway, I ain't so sure I wanna venture out to quiet it. Lucky for me, Sam pipes up right about then, askin' if we wanna share of some trail mix and beef jerky she's got stashed in her bag.

Henry says, "That'd be great," and I see his eyes fixin' on the same spooky, shadowy holes in that alley that mine are. A man wearin' at least fifteen coats and drivin' a rusty shoppin' cart pops out of one of them dark spots like a damn specter and, I shit you not, he just whips out his pecker right then and there and starts pissin' on a dumpster not ten feet from the bus! I pretend not to notice and, thank the Sweet Baby Jesus, Henry pretends right along with me.

We busy ourselves pokin' through Sam's snack stash and get all filled-in on the big N-Y-C. It seems Mazie and CeCe got some work lined up here that's gonna give 'em grub and gas money enough to motor across the nation ten times over. Sam says they been talkin' it up since Arizona and coasted into The Bronx on fumes. I see those girls up there, near the head of the bus, all hunched over and gabbin'. Could be they're talkin' tactics. Could be they're whisperin' sweet nothin's and fixin' to smooch. I figure that oughta give me the heebie-jeebies, but it don't. I like that they get to do as they please. I like that they can hold each other so close, you can't see a shadow in between 'em.

I'm thinkin' on what folks back at home would say about those two girls when Lori pops into the aisle and blocks 'em from view with her big, fat belly. Since I'm already lookin' that way, she catches my eye and lights right up. "Hey!" bounces outta her like some kinda cheer, and I feel like I just threw her another french fry. No ifs, ands, or buts about it... she just rolls right on down that aisle and then piles in beside Sam. Sam gives her a side-eye, and we two snag each other's pestered looks like me and Gramps used to do when flirty-Gerties at his retirement home tried to horn in on us watchin' *Good Times*. I can tell that Lori and Sam ain't friendly just yet, and those two couldn't look more out of place next to one another if they tried. I figure for sure they ain't even gonna speak the same language, but it's like that don't matter. Lori's near enough to be rubbin' thighs with Sam when she just reaches her ruby-red nails over, scoops Sam's hand up, and squeezes it real tight. "I heard some of what you were sayin' about your family," she whispers. "And I'm just real, real sorry." Sam don't budge an inch.

I think she might snatch her hand away, but she don't. Matter of fact, I see her skin turn a whiter shade of pale as she squeezes Lori's hand back. Her eyes get big. Big and wet. She says, "Thank you," and I can feel the weight of it drawin' them two together as good as magnets.

"The way you talked about Mom. The way she was. That's the kinda mom I wanna be," Lori adds in, cradlin' her lumpy belly.

Sam don't say nothin' this time, but her eye makeup starts bleedin' down again. She bites onto the meaty part of her lower lip and rocks her head a time or two. Between sputters, "She was the best" finally makes its way out. Then she sniffles up some of that sadness and tells us a story about gettin' hassled at school on account of dressin' so funny and even gettin' pulled into the principal's office. It seems that some of the other parents made a scuttlebutt about her bein' some kinda devil worshiper on account of all them dark clothes and pointy jewelry she had. And you know what her mom done? Her mom marched right down there to school, dressed tip-to-toe in black and wearin' more mascara than Tammy Faye Bakker, and told 'em all to eat crow. She told the principal, all them uppity parents, and every soul who'd listen that her daughter was gonna be what she was gonna be, and even if that was the Devil's henchman, that was her business and no one else's. Of course, Sam weren't nothin' of the sort, but her mom said that so long as she wasn't doin' no one no harm, she could be whatever the G.D. hell she wanted to be. And guess what she done next? Welp,

Sam's mom, all in her shady getup... she made like she was puttin' a hex on the whole school and swore up and down that if anyone hassled Sam again, they was gonna blow up in smoke or somethin'.

Oh, how Lori giggled at that. And me too. It was pretty damn funny. I could see Mama doin' the very same thing, and thinkin' on that flooded me with pride. I couldn't recollect a time when she'd shushed me for speakin' my truth so long as it didn't hurt no one. Sometimes she stayed quiet, and my voice boomed all the louder. Now I found myself wonderin' if I hadn't been hurtin' someone after all.

Lori says her momma would'a done none of that. "I think my mom liked the *idea* of me" is how she puts it. "I think she liked having a cheerleader for a daughter. She liked telling her friends that I was top in the squad and might get myself a scholarship. She liked putting my cheer pictures on her desk. But they always faced out to the people watching from the other side—never towards her."

Sam says, "Oh, Lori," soft and heavy, and those girls squeeze hands again. I see a fat tear rollin' itself bigger in the far corner of Lori's eye.

"She loved hearing me cheer, though" comes out with a slow shake of Lori's head. "Boy, did she. It's kinda funny, really... 'cuz once I found out I was pregnant, all she wanted me to do was shut up and get rid of it so that I wouldn't get booted from the squad." Now that tear gets itself mixed up with a few others and bails down Lori's cheek. She tells me and Sam that she ain't never "felt so ashamed," but when Sam says she knows that feelin' of hatin' on yourself all too good and well, Lori says, "I wasn't ashamed of me. I was ashamed of her."

That strikes me dumb silent, and so I sit there lettin' my brain chew it up while the gals fix on Lori's baby bump and start talkin' of happier things like newborn names and little pajamas with feet sewn into them. Lori piddles out around eleven, and since I'm too restless to sleep and don't wanna hear no more about Sam's sad life, I reckon I'll pipe up and start retellin' some of Papa's tales to keep us all warm through the night.

Kids come, and kids go, and some even perch on laps and hang over seatbacks listenin' to me tell Papa's stories. I tell the one about the rogue band of Ozark hobos who made ends meet by thievin' and livin' offa the land. I can near see Papa's wild eyes sparklin' over the firelight as I talk of those still November nights when frost hung on the moon like a silvery rouge. That's when the hobos would spill pistol-smoke breath and tales of begotten billfolds fat as fresh-fed piglets, rubber-knuckled coppers, and hot huckleberry pies coolin' on every lonely windowsill.

Them kids is swoonin'. Papa has 'em in the palm of my hand. I feel like a million bucks. The way Sam and Lori are beamin' at me, maybe it's two million. I can see stars shootin' through their eyes, and so I go on and tell one of Papa's all-time favorites about him and Mama's late-enight ride to Louisville. Papa'd borrowed the Olds and said he took the top down on the ride back. He said the pale moonlight spilled in and lit Mama all up like Doris Day at the MGM Grand. She hadn't a stitch of makeup on, and her hair was done up in one of those silly handkerchiefs with a gingham print like Dorothy's dress from *The Wizard of Oz*. Papa said he just stared at her. Just stared... thinkin' about how quiet beauty is sometimes the loudest kind.

The whole mess of 'em are straight-up googly-eyed after that one, and even CeCe and Mazie drift on back to take a listen. One kid, a ginger with a mohawk and ears as big as flapjacks...he asks if these stories is made up. I fudge a little and say that they're "the God's honest truth," and figurin' I oughta ease up on the whoppers, I haul out one of Gramps' jim-dandies.

Ginger leans in with his emerald eyes all a-sparkle as I croak out, "Picture this... I skitter down the steps of my shit-shack of a school, General Lee Junior High, and there sits my Gramps in his big ole boat of a Olds. He's sippin' a flask that I'm pretty sure he paid the Devil a wooden nickel for and is lookin' down-right cantankerous. Now Gramps, he ain't a-skeer'd of any soul, livin' or dead, so he just tootles around town milkin' that scotch like a baby sippin' its bottle. Hell, he'd drive right past the police chief holdin' a Budweiser and just give that fella the finger. And me, I got fearless runnin' through my veins, so I just pile in next to Gramps and figure I'll give every flatfoot in Lafayette the bird right alongside him." I can feel my head swellin' up about like an over-ripe watermelon. I can see Henry drift in and start givin' me cross eyes not an inch away. But all the other kids are hangin' on tenterhooks, so I just keep on. Maybe my voice even booms a little louder as I tell 'em, "But my friend Henry, he's a real wet blanket. He marches down the steps waggin' his finger at ole Gramps so good that I think he might'a broke it, and he says 'Ain't drinkin' and drivin' illegal?'"

"And you know what Gramps does?"

Ginger spooks like a sunbeam just hit him. "What?"

"I tell you what he does," I goad. "My Gramps, he just smiles like the Devil watchin' Jesus shoot craps and tells fussy ole Henry,*"Only if they catch ya, kid!"*

And lordy, they clap. Them kids *actually* clap. I don't think I ever heard a clap meant for me aside from the one when Mama's paddle hit my ass. Even CeCe and Mazie clap. CeCe even smiles. And here I thought that girl was allergic to smiles. She tells me I'm now the "Official Storyteller" like she's Runaway Royalty handin' down a title. If such a thing is possible, my head swells up a little bigger. I'm tryin' to think of a melon bigger than a watermelon as all the other kids are *ooh-in'*, and *ah-in'*, and eatin' up every bit of me. Feels good. Feels damn good. And when CeCe wrangles me by the arm and says, "Let's you and me chat," I feel about as important as I ever have in all my days. Finally, for once, *I'm* the cool one. *I'm* the one the kids are lookin' up to. It ain't *'Olive, that's dumb!'* or *'Olive, you're weird!'* or *'There goes that stupid Abernathy girl, lyin' like her redneck kin again!'*

It's claps, and back-pats, and the Queen of Misfits herself haulin' me off for a private convo. I'm over the moon. I trot off to the head of the bus on CeCe's coattails with Mazie bringin' up the rear. I don't notice 'til CeCe plops down in the driver's seat and Mazie perches on her lap that Henry's trailed behind us and is kinda skulkin' in the shadows a couple of rows back. CeCe eyes him with those nightshade peepers of hers all whittled down.

"You cool, kid?"

Henry? Cool? I nearly laugh out loud. Henry don't make a peep either though... just nods and keeps to the dark, which seems to suit CeCe just fine. She taps an ole clock on the dash that looks like somethin' outta Gramps' war locker and tells me, "We got a job we gotta do right around twelve o'clock. We could use someone like you. Ya know... someone who's bent the rules before. Someone sharp, quick... clever. Someone who's ready to make a life of it out here. Someone who's ready to join our little family."

She thinks I'm sharp? Clever, even? Somehow... after that... I ain't got wits enough to say much more than, "Job?" back at her. *Damn, I sound like a stupid parrot.* I guess I look featherbrained too because Mazie giggles. CeCe smiles again. It's like the sun just come out.

"It's not like a bank heist or anything, kid," she ribs. Then she fidgets so that Mazie bounces around on her lap as she's goin' on, "Matter of fact, if you ask me, it's some straight-up Robin Hood shit. Makin' it so the rich assholes feed the poor. That kinda thing."

I bob my head. Much more of this and she's gonna offer me birdseed. Then I get quiet for a minute. I can hear Henry's ole-man shoes pawin' at the hollow bus floor from the shadows. They get a little louder, and a little louder, and then clomp towards me. I feel him grab up my hand before I see him. I feel his soft little whisper hit my cheek as he clucks, "This don't sound right, Olive. Nothin' good ever happens after midnight."

Now CeCe's lookin' the pair of us over the same way Mama does my math homework. Then she says it's "no big deal," they can "find somebody else," and it feels like she's stickin' that red feather meant for my Robin Hood cap right up my ass. Maybe I ain't a parrot after all. Maybe I'm just a chicken.

I blurt, "No!" without realizin' it and shake Henry's hand off. I'm a woman of the world now. I'm a train-hoppin', adventurin', hoboin', perv-thwartin' Amazon, and I mean to prove myself. I mean to make my mark, and if that means outwittin' some fancy-pants rich folks, I'm gonna do it, and nobody's gonna stop me. Besides, Henry told me himself that rich folk just spend their days sittin' in stank, steamy mud baths like pigs in a lagoon and swimmin' through big oceans of pocket money. What does it matter if we snake a dollar or two?

"I'm in!" I says, not knowin' exactly what that means, and there's that smile of CeCe's again. It lights up the whole damn bus. Before I know it, she's grabbed up the same hand I stole from Henry and called me *Sista*. But Henry, he don't shake so easy. He trails me all the way

back to our seat and reads me the riot act as I'm strap-
pin' on my backpack. He starts tossin' around words like
jail and *murderers* and *gutter gremlins* meant to spook
me, but it don't do a lick of good. I got my mind made
up. I ain't even listenin' no more. I feel like Mee-maw
when she turns down her hearin' aids until all the fussy
chatter just bounces right offa her. I let him prattle on
through, right until I'm fixin' to de-board the bus and join
CeCe and Mazie in that shady alleyway. Then I spin to
face him, and I give him a shush. "I'm goin', Henry. I'm
goin', and that's that."

His mouth looks fulla tobacco chew. I can tell he's
about to spit up a bunch more cockamamie sass that I
ain't gonna listen to anyhow, so I shush him again. Then
I do my meanest impression of *the look* and tell him to
quit his belly-achin'. I can see now that I gotta get rough.
I gotta White Fang him, or he ain't gonna stay put. "I
don't need you" feels cold, even as I say it, and when I
walk away, I feel just like that fella leavin' his poor be-
loved dog behind in the snow. Henry even gives me the
damn puppy eyes, and I can feel 'em hauntin' my footsteps as me and the gals round the corner out of the alley
and hit the sidewalk.

It's cool for summer. I s'pose I ain't accustomed to these
East Coast seasons. I get me a chill right away and hafta
fish a sweatshirt outta my pack. Even once I've got it on,
my insides don't wanna warm, and I wonder how much
of that's the weather and how much is from what I just
done to Henry. I think CeCe can see my eyes tuggin' back

towards the alleyway, and she grumbles like she don't like it. We're tough women. Tough women gotta look out for *numero uno*. Tough women gotta walk on. I all the sudden feel like Mama stompin' up to the pulpit to say what needs to be said and do what needs to be done. I'm takin' care of business. So I tip my head back in the direction we're goin' and leave my sad-eyed puppy behind to freeze in the cold.

We don't get two blocks before I spy other folks lurkin' about. Aunt Agnes always said that only harlots and hoodlums skulk about in town after dark, so I keep my eye on those strangers like they mean to shank me, or maybe offer me a date. Then I get to thinkin' about how *I'm* skulkin' about in town after dark, reason that Aunt Agnes is a nut bar, and stop eyein' 'em so fierce.

CeCe says we "just got a few more streets to go" 'til we get to where we're headed, and that girl may be streetsmart, but I figure out real quick that her momma didn't make her read the dictionary front to back 'cuz she don't have an ever-lovin' clue what "a few" means. As the crow flies, I'd say we were a good quarter-mile from that dirty corner lot fulla garbage where we ended up. I ain't never seen so much trash, short of the city dump... and folks, they're pawin' through it! Grimy folks with knotted-up hair, and folks with rusty shoppin' carts fulla Pepsi cans, and even little kids holdin' smushed-up dolls that look like they got rescued from the jaws of a trash compactor... all of 'em just rootin' through the trash like pigs at the trough. They don't hang about for long though.

Once they get eyes on us, most of them street folk skitter on outta the lot. There's two or three who don't pay us no mind, but once a troupe of boys dressed in red as wicked as the blood moon roll in a few minutes later, they skedaddle too. The tallest of them kids, a boy with long, girly hair that's done up in braids enough to make him look like Medusa, he even kicks his ice-white sneaker at the last bum who makes her way out. I swear I hear that lady squeal. I'm sandwiched in between Mazie and CeCe, and I feel both them girls shrink beside me as they look on. Maybe it's them that squealed. Then that biggest kid, he comes slidin' up like hot butter off a rye roll with all his crew sluggin' along behind him. He gives us all cool eyes and tells CeCe, "Wassup, girl!"

Couldn't tell ya if that was a question or not, but if it were, CeCe don't answer. She just locks arms with ole Braidy-boy and them two pull together for some kinda awkward hug that I reason neither one of 'em enjoy 'cuz they kick out of it real quick. Close-up, that boy's pretty rough around the edges. He's got those empty sorta eyes that tell ya a body's insides are cold, and every move he makes is a spook... like some sketchy dog that's been beat and is forever lookin' out for the next blow. Watchin' him search the shadows all nervous-like, I wonder if he's lookin' for a bigger, icier white sneaker to pop out and kick at him. I imagine him for a minute: smaller, younger, eyes still bright with wonder, clutched quiet in the shadows as a man with eyes as empty as his are now is loomin' over him. But then I blink, and it's the man lookin' back at me from where the boy used to be.

Mazie whispers, "He's cool," but I wonder if that means the same thing to her as it does to me. Meanwhile, him and CeCe stick their heads together and get to conversatin' at a hush while his cronies idle on their heels. The Man in the Moon has his eye on the lot of us. Funny, he looks the same here as he did back in Lafayette, and for a minute I figure that I do too. But I sure don't feel like it. And lookin' around me, I'm pretty sure that he don't think so either.

A growl comes trollin' up the street just then, and a black van built like a toaster follows just behind it. It turns in on our gravel lot and swallows us up in its high beams as the braided boy pipes up, "That's Tony." Then he shuffles his little minions towards the light, and CeCe hangs back with her hand held out to wave me and Mazie over. It's like watchin' a clown load his car, seein' Braids pile those red-suited boys into that van, and when CeCe says that we're gettin' in too, I feel like I'm about to join the world's dodgiest circus.

Somethin' in me don't wanna step towards that van. Some little voice says it ain't right. I check my shoulder, but that little Devil of mine has his trap clapped shut. He just gimme a shrug and points at my noggin. And there it goes again. *Don't do it, Olive. Don't do it, Olive.* Easier to tell the second time around... sure as shit, it's Mama. There she goes again, bossin' me. Tryin' to keep me all hole up in that museum of hers. Tryin' to make me her dumb little Abernathy doll forever. Well, I ain't an Abernathy anymore. I'm a card-carryin' misfit wonder woman, just like CeCe and Mazie, and I'm gettin' in that stupid van even if it kills me.

It's like a troll belly in there. Or at least what Papa said one was like. Half those stories he told us about Bumble-wart the Roughneck Troll ended with some ornery little kid gettin' swallowed down into Bumble's tummy and rollin' around in a big, dark pool fulla leftover brussels sprouts and all the other crap kids hid under the dinner table. And judgin' by the smell in this van, cabbage and maybe liverwurst was on the menu too. I don't say so though. Ain't nobody else talkin' anyhow. Whoever's driv-in' this beast backs out onto the road and fills its gut with some street noise, but other than that, I feel like all I can hear is the sound of big eyes blinkin' at each other. That don't last long though, and I'm glad for it 'cuz curiosity's gnawin' up my insides.

Braids points square at me and says, "So this little scrub's goin' in?" and when CeCe nods back, I can't help myself no more. I spit out about sixty questions in a sin-gle breath, like I'm some jazzed-up three-year-ole:

"Where we goin'? What we doin'? I gotta go in? In what? In where? How far? How long's it gonna take? Is it ille-gal? Are we gonna get in trouble? Didn't you say we was Robin Hoods? Are we stealin'? Are we gonna use bows and arrows? Who's the bad guy? Sure he ain't gonna miss his stuff? Is it gold? Are we stealin' gold?" By the time I've asked every question under the sun except maybe what color underwear everybody's wearin', the whole

mess of them are lookin' me over like I oughta be fitted for a straitjacket. Then them boys start laughin'. They laugh and point, and one of the little ones even squeezes out a tear or two. And dammit, that makes me mad. It feels just like bein' back at school with all them stuck-up whoop-de-doo's makin' fun of my thrift store clothes, or my stupid Uncle Ern sittin' in his yard with a fishnet, waitin' for Bigfoot to wander by. I've got half a mind to clock one of them boys. I can feel my fists clenchin'. I can feel Mama's hand-me-down vein poppin' outta my forehead. It's right about then that I feel CeCe's eyes on me. She and me are sharin' a bench seat stuck to that troll van's insides, and she pushes her big bosoms out and scoots so that she's blockin' me from those fellas.

"Look guys, give her a break," she tells 'em. Then she glances back my way with soft eyes and says, "She's just a kid" while tossin' a wink my way.

Braids quits his laughin', and his boys shut up right then. Now I can feel his eyes on me too. They've got a heaviness to them that I ain't keen on. He tells CeCe, "This ain't a job for kids," and then snarls and adds in, "Thought you were bringin' one of your crew."

I ain't expectin' it, but just then CeCe wraps her arm around me and gives a squeeze. "She *is* one'a my crew," she says. "One'a my family. She's one of us now," and while that don't seem to impress Braids much, it busts my buttons. Then she tells me it's "all gonna be alright," and "we aren't doing nothing that bad."

CeCe says we're just takin' somethin' from her mean

ole Daddy's shop. Seems he owns jewelry stores all up and down the coast and everywhere in between. This one here in New York City is where Braids' older brother Jerome works. Jerome knows the combo to the safe where CeCe's no-goodnick Dad puts all the jewelry that folks bring in for repairs. But that dodgy ole papa of CeCe's, he don't trust his help to do much more than send dumb folks back home with some different, fixed-up jewelry that's just as fake as CeCe's stepmomma's boobs. He has 'em put all the real stuff in a drop box with a combination that he don't give to a one of 'em. But CeCe, she knows that combo frontways and backways 'cuz it's her silicone stepmomma's birthdate. Now she says we just need to shimmy up the air vent into the shop, swipe the drop box, and we'll all be speedin' down easy street with her rotten, homophobe Dad eatin' our dust. She says he deserves it. She says he put her out right in the middle of the night with nothin' more than the jammies she was wearin' and a knife in her back. He don't deserve them jewels. They don't belong to him anyhow, and I reckon she's right. By the time we make it across town to Meeks' Jewel Emporium, I'm hot-to-trot and feelin' like I oughta have a bow and arrow clenched in my fist.

The troll van tosses us up into an alleyway that ain't near as nasty as the one in Queens. Mind you, it don't smell like roses, but it ain't got filthy folks scurryin' through the shadows alongside the cockroaches. Braids is the first one out, and he does some sorta Mission Impossible creep that makes him look like a sand crab with a big clump of seaweed stuck to its head. I choke on a giggle, but Mazie hushes me right quick. Then she follows, low-like, behind CeCe, and coaxes me along with a curled-up finger. Both of Braids' boys stay back, I s'pose as lookouts, while we girls slink along the buildin'-backs trailin' Braids' mop-top. I start feelin' like a proper hooligan as we all four stop below a barred-up window that's just a stone's throw into the alleyway. CeCe holds one finger over her big lips and points the other one at a dumpster not far off. She gets her voice down to a hush and then cranes towards my ear to ask me, "You see that?"

I nod, wonderin' if she dropped her marbles somewhere in the van. Unless her Daddy's jewels are polished rat turds and day-ole taters, they sure as hell ain't in that garbage bin. But it don't take a minute before we slink closer and I get her meanin'. She ain't pointin' at the dumpster, she's pointin' at the vent cover up above it. One by one, Braids hoists us up on top of that stanky metal box and then leaps up there his self. He fishes a Phillips-head outta his back pocket and starts goin' to town on the cover. There's wiggle-worms o' moonlight creepin' through that vent grate, and as he's workin' away, they jitter across the tin tunnel on the other side. It looks like the gymnasium floor at my third-grade Daddy-daughter dance, when Papa taught me how to do The Hustle and told me I was "hell on the toes, but worth every step." Braids though, I don't think he's worth the brain God gave him 'cuz he gets to cussin' up a storm at that grate, and it ain't until five minutes in that he figures out he needs a flat-head. Of course, he don't have nothin' of the kind, but CeCe has a dime in her pocket that does just as good. She says that lesbians know how to make do with what they got to get the job done. Then her and Mazie share a snicker and point me at the tunnel where that grate used to be.

I can't argue. Don't make a lick of sense for anyone but me to go in. After all, they're all twice my size, and like CeCe says, I'm *clever.* I'm good at thinkin' on my toes. I make some smart-aleck remark about how my toes ain't gonna be much help since I'm crawlin' through that teensy tunnel and not walkin', but Braids don't have no time for that. He points at that open hole like it's a doghouse and tells me to *"Git!"*

Maybe I ought'a told him to piss off right then and there. After all, I don't have to take sass from no one, no more. I'm Olive. Not Olive Abernathy. Just Olive. One name, like Prince, or Madonna, or Oprah. All them folks have moxie up the wazoo, and hell, I do too. But I get the sense that Braids ain't fond of girls who speak up, and I don't wanna upset his rotten apple cart, so I inch up to that big ole echoey hole and let it swallow me up. No sooner am I inside than I hear Braids clap the damn grate back on and start pushin' the screws in. "What you doin?!" comes outta me so loud, it sends cockroaches and alley cats burstin' out from the shadows. CeCe yowls good too... starts battin' at Braids' backside... but he moves so quick, I nearly don't see that gun come out of his waistband. He levels it up sideways, right at CeCe's head, just as Mazie cries out. He tells both them girls to "shut the hell up!" and says that he'll let me out "when the job's done." But I don't trust no man that holds a gun that way. Papa said only gangsters and stupid fellas who don't line up their sights hold a gun that way. He said never trust a man that don't take care with his weapon because that man's a fool, and fools kill decent folk. So... I just watch Braids grippin' that gun with his sweaty paw and dime-screwin' me into my early grave. I just watch him, and I wonder who's the bigger fool—him or me?

Just as he finishes with the last screw, a hoot comes shootin' up the alleyway. Braids spooks on the spot and then this high sound, like Lafayette's storm siren, spills in and rattles us all. All the sudden I'm tucked up in our drafty ole root cellar back in Louisiana, huddled between Mama and Papa as the cannin' jars are clankin' and booms of thunder like the Devil's footsteps are closin' in. Funny how safe I felt, sandwiched between them two, even with the storm clawin' at our back door. But now, here I am, caged in this tunnel with strangers watchin' me from the other side like I'm a damn zoo animal, and I feel anythin' but safe. And once the red and blue lights spill in, I ain't only adrift in a storm, I'm alone. Alone with the law and all the wrongs I done.

CHAPTER ELEVEN

As a little girl still in curls, I'd sit up behind Mama's battered ole butcher block, gummin' Georgia peaches and watchin' her whip up sweet tater pies. I remember her kneadin' a stubborn lump of dough while holdin' baby Pete on one hip and Wyatt on the other. She fixed clear eyes right on me and said, "Honey, they'll tell ya strength comes in numbers, but it don't matter a lick until that number's one."

I never thought I had it in me. I never thought I was that strong. But after six of the longest hours in my short life, I felt like I coulda dug my way out of Alcatraz with a sugar spoon. For a while, bein' trapped in that vent was just the ticket. I stayed all safe and hid as CeCe, and Mazie, and Braids all got shackled-up and hauled off in screamin' cop cars to the tune of their own wailin'. But then, when the alley got quiet again, and I could hear the cockroaches skritchin' and the tomcats flossin' their teeth with crackly mice bones, I didn't wanna be hole up in that hole no more. Damn trick of it was, Braids'd done a halfway decent job of screwin' that cover back on, and even after a few good kicks with my high-tops, I couldn't budge it an inch. But Mama's words, they keep ringin' in my ears, and for once, it didn't bother me. Every time they boom, I feel a little stronger. Every time I fix on her face hangin' over that butcher block, all peppered-up with sweat beads and determination, my kicks get a little harder. And it may have took a hundred kicks. Maybe a hundred-and-one. But somewhere around the time that bike bells and people chatter started sunnin' up the sidewalk, I bust myself loose.

* * *

Grey, and stanky, and filth-splattered as I am, I still skip my way outta that alley beamin' brighter than Dorothy did down her yellow brick road. I'd been all curled up in a ball for most of the night, so just stretchin' out my limbs feels goddamn glorious. Once I hit the sidewalk, I can't help smilin' at folk, and I s'pose half of 'em probably think I'm crazy. I can't get over it, just how many there are! Men in fancy suits glancin' at their wristwatches, ladies that look like they crawled right offa a magazine cover. Hell, I see me an ole biddy who looks like she pinned her wrinkles back with a few yards of Scotch tape. I can't help sniggerin' once she passes, thinkin' about Mama scowlin' at those *Cosmopolitan* magazines by the checkstand at Piggly Wiggly. She told me, "Them fool women chasin' youth are 'bout like your Papa's dumb hound dogs goin' after pickup trucks. They're either gonna run themselves to death or end up with a face that looks like a tailgate."

And good gravy, Mama's eyes'd swell up fat as sassy ticks if she saw some of the getups these gals have on.

Here it is, cold as a witch's teat, and their lady-bits are hangin' out for all creation to see. Mama called the underwear models in the Sears catalog "godless hussies." Lord knows what she'd say lookin' these gals over. My best guesses involve holy water and crucifixes, but who's to say.

I amble on for a good few blocks that way, soakin' in all the different faces, and strange noises, and peculiar smells. Every now and again, I catch hold of somethin' I like... somethin' like the hint of a smile or a whiff of baked bread, but then the next dozen faces are glowers, and that bread gets overtook by some garbage stank or bum pee. Before I know it, my mug's just as screwed up as all these folks'. It's no wonder either— all the bright lights, and taxi horns, and people screechin' at one another, it's enough to drive a body mad. Don't take me long to figure out I'm not keen on The Big Apple. It ain't nothin' like my glossy postcards, fulla smilin' faces and folks wavin' flags. It's grey here. Grey, and hard, and cold, and lonely. It ain't nothin' like back home. Back home is street chefs roastin' sweet mesquite bayou meat, battered okra, and fried hushpuppies by the glisten of gas lantern light. Back home is trailin' Mama and Papa down Main Street as they tangle up in the Spanish moss 'til I think it's gonna take an act of God to part 'em. Folks here, they don't look at each other that way. Watchin' their sour faces, I'm not sure they know how. And all the sudden, I feel like a puzzle piece stuck in the wrong box. Worse yet, I get to glancin' around and realize that I don't got one ghost of a clue where I am, or where Henry and that bus are, or any means to get any kind of anywhere on my own. I'm alone. Alone like I ain't never been.

My heart starts pumpin' fierce-fast, and I feel the kinda machine-gun breath comin' on that Henry used to get right before he'd grab for his inhaler. And then I'm runnin'. I don't know why, but I'm runnin'. First I think I'm runnin' away from somethin', but as my lungs get to stingin' and my head floods with pictures of Mama, and Papa, and the twins, and that hodgepodge farmhouse fulla soft edges and hard lessons, I feel like I'm runnin' *towards* somethin'... for the first time in a long time. I spy green a couple blocks up and steer that way, thinkin' Ma Nature must be callin' me home, offerin' to scoop me up in her woodsy womb and keep me safe from all these grey faces. I think I can near hear bullfrogs bayin' through the tangled cattails, but when I get there, it's just some fancy-pants park fulla cut grass and trash cans every five feet. I don't think a bullfrog'd even be caught dead in this place, but from the smell of it, there may be a few dead ones here already. At least they got benches though... hard, smelly, uncomfortable benches. I grab me one that ain't already fully loaded and try to get myself calmed down. Mama says that fear, and panic, and all that nonsense is just like a mangy dog clawin' at the back door. You let him in, and he's just gonna tear up the insides. So, I watch Mama in my mind's eye, hollerin' at that pesky dog, tellin' him to go off and bother some other girl... and it helps. My heart stops boomin' in my head, and my breathin' quiets just enough to let my tummy growls creep on through. I can't figure when I ate last, and a quick fish through my pack don't get me nothin' but my scrapbook and some lint that I gotta admit I gave a thought to eatin'. I start noodlin' just how far up the creek I really am, and that mangy dog gets to trollin' around the back door again, so I pop open my scrapbook and try to get distracted. A few little licks of sunlight pop out from the clouds and lay down on a postcard for Delaware that's got big, burnt-orange letters across the face reading, "You haven't lived if you haven't been to Delaware!"

I snort. What a load of hooey. Some smiley fella in a canoe is paddlin' right beneath the 'e' in Delaware, and I look him square in his brain-dead eyes and tell him, "You're fulla shit."

"Who's fulla shit?" ain't a question I expect to hear, and it takes me a hot second to figure out that it ain't smiley canoe-guy askin' it. I peek up, and that lone ray of sunshine hits me square in the eye just as I see him. "GRAMPS!" is about the loudest I've shouted in recent recollection. I pop up and that scrapbook goes flyin', but the ole man catches it on the downslide.

I'm near ready to throw my fool self into his arms when he comes back, "Welp, I've been called worse," and looks me over with the eyes of a stranger. I get to lookin' back, puzzlin'. The fuzzy inchworm eyebrows are there. The shiny eyes that look like they got turned over in an agate smoother—they're there too. And dammit if that ain't Gramps' cockeyed smile crookin' its left side up at me. But it ain't Gramps. It can't be Gramps. Can it?

The ole man plops his self down on my bench and says, "Hope ya don't mind. All the others are full." Then he sets my scrapbook beside his skinny thigh and asks me again, "So who's fulla shit?" but I just give back a dumb stare. He waits a minute or two, those shiny eyes narrowin' by the second, and then he asks, "You slow, kid?"

I don't reckon I've ever been called that. I once heard Uncle Ern get called slow nine times in a single day when he found Mayor Rowdy's lost toupee on Main Street and thought it was a Sasquatch pelt. But me, slow? Not ever. So I tell un-Gramps, "No, I ain't slow. It's those fellas who make postcards who got a screw loose."

"That so?"

I say, "It's so!" and set myself down beside him. The book's wedged between my dirty jeans and his tweed trousers at that point, and I scoop it up and splay it open on my lap. "Look here," I tells him, tappin' hard on a Kentucky postcard. "You see that big, fancy Capitol Buildin' and that purdy horse all shinin' in the sweet Southern sunlight?"

He nods, and I can already feel words chuggin' up my throat. "Well, that's top-grade, alfalfa-fed, hot-out-thepoop-chute bullshit! Don't none of them places look like they do on the postcards. And there ain't no fancy horses or red carpets rollin' out the Capital Buildin' to meet ya when ya get there. Hell, that horse is probably an overgrown coon hound in a pony suit that's got rabies and is fixin' to bite ya the second ya cross the state line!" Now it's un-Gramps who's struck silent, so my blabbermouth just keeps on, "But I tell you one thing, every postcard I ever seen for Louisiana don't do it justice. I've got mountains of 'em," I say, flippin' through the book until one with a big, ugly pelican comes up, "and look there... not a single sycamore stretchin' up to the heavens, or one—not even one—fresh lily-pad bud skimmin' the limey bayou. Nope, just this bird with the dumbest bullfrog on planet earth sittin' in his beak like it's a damn Jacuzzi!"

Un-Gramps sniggers. I *know* I heard that snigger before, and I eye him good. He eyes me back. "You're weird, kid," he tells me, inchin' up his woollies so that his cheaters slide down. "Why do you keep looking at me like that?"

I fess up, "You remind me of someone" without really meanin' to, and now his woollies arch their backs even higher. Those familiar glasses slide another half-inch down his liver-spotted nose.

He comes back at me with, "Pray tell," which is somethin' that Aunt Agnes started sayin' right about the time she decided that God was puttin' baby-Jesus shapes into her cornflakes. I'm pretty sure she didn't know what it meant, and I ain't sure either, but un-Gramps seems to be urgin' me on, so I give it to him straight. I tell him he looks like my grandpa, who used to let me drive his Olds when no one was lookin'. My Grandpa, who took me skeet shootin' and let me eat Whoppers until I couldn't see straight because I was "invincible anyhow." My grandpa, who once faked Alzheimer's when a lady at Woolworth's caught him peepin' in the women's dressin' room. My grandpa, who was the funnest, orneriest, smartest grandpa on all planet earth. My grandpa, who I killed.

I reason he wasn't expectin' that… expectin' to meet a girl who's turned cold-blooded killer at the tender age of thirteen. But that's what I am. I know it, Gramps knows it, Mama knows it… hell, even Gran is probably givin' me the stink-eye from her cloud-perch in Heaven.

Of course, he wants to know. He wants to know how I done it. With a gun? With a hay thrasher? With a candlestick in the parlor? But nope, it ain't nothin' so entertainin' as that. "I got into trouble, and he had to pick me up. He had to pick me up, and then we was drivin', and then we got hit. And after that… well, it all went to shit." Un-Gramps' agate eyes get a kind tint to 'em. It looks like the first soft light comin' through my bedroom curtains. "You know that isn't your fault, right?"

Hmph ain't the thing to do, but I do it anyway. "My Mama'd tell ya different."

He says, "Would she?" more like an answer than a question, but I bark back anyway. I tell him, "*She would. She done said it. I heard her.*" I tell him all about leanin' my guilty face through those banister spindles and listenin' to Mama curse me like I was the worst girl ever to wear pigtails. I say how she's gotta hate me near as much as I hate me if such a thing's possible. But that ole coot, he's waggin' his wrinkly mug the whole time I'm tellin' that story. Before I even get to the part where I lit out into the milky moonshine never to be heard from again, he clucks, "No mothers hate their children." But this fake Gramps, he don't know Mama. He don't know how stubborn and sassy she can be. He don't know how she had to suffer all them cruel words and icy stares just so that I could go to church, and school, and even to the damn bathroom in the stockroom at Piggly Wiggly. He don't know how much I pained her, how much I done every little thing under the sun to turn her hair grey. He don't know how I always felt like I was some sorta dream of hers that never quite came true.

I crack my lips to give him the business, but he plants a finger right in front of 'em. His hand smells like peppermint gum and pomade—just like Gramps'. "Mothers don't always get the time to tell you they love you," he says to me. "They're too busy racing around... kissing your boo-boos, and packing your lunches, and hemming your jumpers. Meanwhile, their hearts get put away in little boxes along with bits of undone lace and other things yet to be mended. But if you look close, it's there. It's probably sewn right into your shirt cuff."

This fella's peculiar. But I like peculiar. Plus, I still got my suspicions about him bein' Gramps' East Coast twin or maybe some spiffed-up, strait-laced angel-Gramps that got sent down to lecture me. He draws his hand away, but that peppermint smell sticks with me. For a second, I'm back in the Olds on a thick, sticky August night... one of them nights when it was so damn hot that you'd-a thought Lafayette got stuck on a rotisserie. Gramps'd sneak me and Henry into Lambert's Drive-in with our pockets stuffed fulla gobstoppers and pumpkin seeds. I remember watchin' that picture show sandwiched between him and Henry like a happy clam with my eyes so starry, they outshone the heavens.

I peek over at un-Gramps now and find tender eyes lookin' me back. "I'll bet that mama of yours is missing you even more than you're missing your grandpa," he reasons.

Not possible. Not even close. This fella may look like Gramps, but he ain't got half the smarts. He fingers the cover of my scrapbook as I'm hittin' him with my best you're-a-certified-nut-bar look, and then he pipes, "So, you been to all the places in this book?"

Of course I ain't, but that don't sound very excitin', so I lie and say, "Almost." Hell, at this point it feels like I done run all the way from one end of the map to the other, so it's as good as true.

"You wanna see the rest?" seems a reasonable enough question, but before I get a chance to think it over, my mouth pops open and says *no*, which don't seem to puzzle him near as much as it does me. He goes on to say how he's been all around the globe and back again durin' wartime, and even between the belly dancin' beauties in Cairo and the velveteen moors off England's ruddy coastline, he ain't never seen nothin' finer than the orange glow spillin' out his own parlor windows. Now he lives in New York, where he "can't even afford a parlor," but that don't give him no nevermind. He says that so long as he's got his wits about him and grandkids down the block, the Prince of Siam ain't got nothin' on him. Of course, then he gets on to fussin' about how I oughta be with my kin and not sittin' on a park bench talkin' to some borin' ole blowhard with his pockets fulla pigeon seed.

"I got friends here," I say, which is such a white lie that my shoulder devil don't even perk. Far as I can see, I only got one, and I all the sudden feel like a mushy dog turd for not thinkin' of him sooner. That seems to settle un-Gramps, who tells me that friends gotta look out for one another here in the big city.

"I'd say it isn't the best idea for you to even be out here in the park on your own, young as you are," he goes on. Then he shoots eyes past me at a couple of other benches slung with dirty fellers, and clean fellas, and ladies too. His lips pinch up like an orange peel's butt and "It's not always safe for young girls" squeezes out at a whisper.

I say, "I know" in a voice that don't really sound like my own. Meantime, I'm lookin' over bodies scattered across the park benches sittin' to his back. They got clean ladies, and dirty ladies, and men fit to match too. I search the faces for a while, lookin' for a pasty one wearin' big glasses and a greasy comb-over. My heart gets to thrumpin' a little faster with every one that I pass. When I don't see Roger's, it quiets itself, but then a feller wearin' a holy-man collar plops his self down beside a lady who could pass for a young mama, and I feel it racin' again. I look un-Gramps square in the eye.

"It ain't always safe for girls just about anywhere." He

says I'm right. He says it kinda surprised. He says, "You may just be a little older than I thought," and I feel like I just grew an inch. But then a little buzzer on his wristwatch gets to chirpin', and he tells me he's gotta go and cart his grandkids off to daycare. "You gonna be alright?" he asks. "You gonna get back to that friend of yours?"

"Couldn't stop me if you tried" sounds like somethin' a girl older than this girl would say, so I say it. Then I watch the un-Gramps toddle away after a partin' handshake and hope he don't see me sniff my palm to get one last whiff of that peppermint. When I look back up again, he done vanished—*poof*—like he weren't never there to begin with. It feels like the man upstairs is playin' tricks on me, so I *humph* up at the sky, and it thunders back. Then that little split in the clouds where the sun had come through closes up, quick as a wink. So there I am, moody blue sky gloomin' down on me like a sadness that I just can't shake... still stuck, still starvin', still titsup broke, and still got not a clue where I am. I'm eyein' that preacher-man sat across from teenaged-mama and thinkin' I should'a asked un-Gramps for directions back to Louisiana when a racket catches my left ear. I turn just in time to see a horde of ratty-lookin' kids speedin' up on skateboards.

Now, after what I just been through with Braids, and CeCe, and Mazie, and that van fulla ragtag rotters, I ain't so keen on befriendin' anyone who looks like they might live in a school bus, so I keep my head low to let those kids cruise on by. The first couple are older boys, and they got those distant kinda eyes that say they're too cool for school. They don't even give me a sideways glance. Then up come a girl and two boys, about nine or ten years ole. They look curious enough, but not too curious. They keep on too. There's a few stragglers after that. Mostly slow, bored-lookin' kids... like the ones who follow along at the end of Lafayette's Easter parade pickin' up the horse pucky. They ain't about to get any further behind, so they zip by just before two teenage girls finish out the pack. Now these two girls, they ain't the poop-scoopers. They look like they're in the rear 'cuz they're guardin' the pack's ass-end. They both got snarls tuggin' up their painted petunia lips and eyes made up like coons. There's a fierceness about 'em that makes even my shoulder devil shrink.

The first one comes rollin' up on me and gives me this look like I just said somethin' stupid. I give it back and track her sourpuss as she passes. The second girl ain't far behind, but I feel her slowin' as she gets nearer. I'm still givin' her twin's backside the evil eye as she goes from near flattenin' my toes to swipin' my pack right up off the bench.

I holler, *"Hey!"* and spring up cricket-quick, which only gets both them girls to chuggin' all the faster. I bolt to chase 'em but realize only a stride or two in that my scrapbook's still layin' on the bench, so I gotta juke back and grab it. By the time I do and then get myself all turned back around and revved up to runnin' speed, that whole crew of skateboardin' vagabonds is just a little cluster of thumb-sized dots in the distance. I still keep poundin' through that Brady Bunch park for a good half-mile or so, yowlin' out for them to stop every couple of minutes, but no one seems to pay much mind to crazy girls around these parts. I s'pose we're a dime a dozen.

I run myself out of gumption just as the green dries up and the city bleeds back to endless grey asphalt and traffic lights. It feels like the gloom's soakin' down into my bones, so I raise my finger up to give God the bird just as another clap of thunder booms through the heavens and rain starts spillin' down on me. From there, I skitter into the nearest alleyway I can find and hunker down beside a graffitied dumpster that smells like moldy cheese and cat piddle. Some street kids painted a gnarly monster on the side, and I get this feelin' like I'm stuck in a nightmare that there ain't no wakin' up from.

God's pissin' mad. I gave Him the *humph* AND the finger, and He means to drown me. Them sheets of rain in the alleyway aren't nothin' like the fat dollops at home. These are cuttin', icy things, and I start scattin' eyes around the alleyway, lookin' for somethin' to cover me. Then I look in my lap. My scrapbook—the one and only thing I have left to my name. I raise it up over my head and fan out the cover until it's done a proper job of playin' umbrella. It ain't much shelter, but it's some. I can feel raindrops rattlin' the vinyl and sendin' quivers up my fingertips. I suck up a cold breath and pray for it to stop, but the rain just seems to rail all the harder then, like I deserve to get drenched. It pounds that book cover. Beats it, really… until postcards start spillin' out from the pages and into my lap.

I ain't sure if it's the raindrops or the tears that done it, but when I peek down at those half-dozen cards that fell out, they get splattered up good. All the sudden, there's ink runnin' every which way, and I notice writin' that I hadn't never seen before. It's bleedin' away with every drip-drop, so I lower the book down and do my Scouts-best to scoop those muddy cards inside. The rain lets up a pinch just then, so I gather up the whole drippy mess and skitter deeper into the alley in search of better cover. A back-door divot on some crusty ole brick buildin' that Henry probably would've loved did just the trick, and I dive into it pretendin' it doesn't smell like a musty, dead ferret.

It ain't nothin' like a toasty-warm farmhouse, but I'm glad for the roof over my head. I set myself down, Injun-style, on a week-ole copy of the *New Yorker* and let my book fall back open. Right on top there's a California postcard that Gramps'd bought me two summers back. It's got a bottle-blonde surfin' a curly wave on the front. The big sun's turned her as orange as a Cheeto puff, and she's grinnin' so big that astronauts could probably see her pearly whites from space. I remember when I got this one. I pretended I was her for a solid week. I tried six ways from Sunday to get Mama to bleach my hair and buy me a bikini, but in the end she just handed me some of Papa's ole briefs and a tube sock and had me lookin' a fool. But now I don't want nothin' to do with that smiley surfer gal or the shark that's probably lurkin' on the other side, just under the spot where a postage stamp goes. I flip the card to check for Jaws' kid brother and there it is, plain as day—Mama's chicken scrawl. Sunny as it was, California dodged most of those raindrops, so her words are still readable. *Darlin' girl* is in the address line, and underneath it reads, *I want you to always be true to yourself because it don't matter how much sun a fake flower gets, it ain't never gonna grow.*

I look on that card for a spell until I get this feelin' like it's warmed my bones. Then I set it gentle on my right knee and pick up the next. This one's from the great state of Virginia, and it shows two folks tangled up in one another with a big heart betwixt 'em. *Virginia is for Lovers,* it says.

I snort at that and roll my eyes before flippin' to the back side, where Mama's put it attention to *My Little Olive.* The words beneath are near drippin' off the cardstock, but they're still clear as day—*A heart's like a book, baby. The story's gonna get better every time you open it up.*

For a second, I could swear that a clean whiff of Ivory soap curled through the alley filth and up into my nostrils. I smile, without knowin' it, and look down to find that there's another card from Virginia waitin' right underneath the first. Some sad-sack on the Greyhound gave me this one at the start of school last year. It's got a mushy couple beneath an umbrella swappin' spit on the front, and the feller who gave it to me said he couldn't bear to look at it no more after his ole lady up and left him. He said he bought it at the dime store, thinkin' it'd remind her of the time they got caught up in the warm rain on their honeymoon. Turns out, it just made her miss all the kissin' they used to do. I guess she went lookin' for somebody who could remember how to smooch like that, and accordin' to ole sad-sack, "someone who could remember to pick up the stupid milk on the way home."

A quick flip and I can see that Mama's worked her magic on this'un too. It says, *Never forget, my girl, that love— good, strong love—is like one of those big umbrellas in a rainstorm. You huddle up under there, hold each other tight, and everything that life throws at you is just gonna slide right off. I don't want you settling for nothing less, because even though I've tried and failed to give it to you, you deserve the world curled up right in your soft little palm.*

It ain't a thing I think on often, but after readin' that, I get a picture up in my head of Mama and Papa lovin' on each other. I remember once askin' Papa as he was makin' woo-woo eyes, just how him and Mama met. He'd tease this, and giggle that... sayin' they might'a met huckin' horse pucky at some backwoods ranch. They might'a met at a malt shop with Patsy Cline croonin' from the jukebox. But then he said that it didn't much matter where they met because they held on tight, and they never let go.

That makes my cheeks flush pink as I pile them West Virginian lover postcards on top of one other, supposin' that's the way they'd wanna be. Then I spy one of my all-time favorite cards stuck underneath. It's one that Huckleberry got me from Las Vegas, and there's a big ole pyramid buildin' on the front. It looks so much like the ones they got over there in Egypt that the folks in Vegas even stuck two furry, stuffed camels right out front. On the flip side, Mama's words are near wore off, and I gotta pull it up real close to my face to read it like Mee-maw does with the *TV Guide*. Mama's drawn one of her silly hearts over where the stamp oughta go, and just south-east of that, she says, *Baby Girl… your Gramps drug me all over this world when I was no bigger than an inchbug. I felt silks in Morocco, furry old camel humps in Giza, and saw sand so white, you'd have thought it was angel dust. But I ain't never felt nothing so fine as your little heartbeat in my belly.* That card don't let go so easy. I find myself hangin' on to it and readin' those words over and over as the rain goes *plunk, plunk, plunk* in the alley potholes. In my mind's eye, I see Mama, years younger, draggin' her pruny fingers across my bathwater and gig-glin' herself silly as I'm slappin' my fat little hands in the milky-warm suds. I smile to myself. I feel even warmer.

I tuck that card in my shirt pocket, near to my heart, and see that it's the last of the loose ones. Then I start thumbin' through my album, thinkin' back about that big kerfuffle me and Mama had when she took down all my postcards. I think I called her "selfish," and a flash of hurt cut through her eyes that was so deep, I could feel it. Knowin' now that she'd skirted them cards all away to leave me her secret messages, I felt that hurt all over again. But it was deeper this time. It stuck to me this time.

I set myself to distraction by peelin' back the film on the first page of my album and pullin' out a card from Montana. As I slide it off the page, a little scrap of somethin' tumbles out, and I snap that thing up quick before the rain gets it. Don't take a minute to tell it's a newspaper clippin', folded down to matchbook-size. There's an ad for frozen peas on the face side, and I think maybe Mama's so hellbent on me eatin' my vegetables that she's taken guilt trips to a whole other level, but as I crack it open, I find an ole article on the inside.

Local girl booted from Lafayette Primary School's football field

Parish County resident Olive Abernathy (age 10) was removed from Adler Field on May 10 after unsuccessfully insinuating herself into the Lafayette Primary School's Junior Football League. Abernathy, who attends the school as a third grader, had recently made a plea to join the historically all-boys football team, much to the chagrin of coach and players alike. According to school officials, while there is no standing rule which would disallow a female player, it is strongly discouraged. Principal Ronald Langston, who says that Ms. Abernathy is "the first girl who's ever expressed interest in joining the team," has concerns that "she may become injured by the larger and more skilled boys."

Cheers from parents, onlookers, and fellow students

alike erupted as Abernathy, clad in a homemade jersey and a non-regulation helmet, was removed from the field after attempting to participate in the game without authorization.

"I just hope it's over," Coach Joe Sharp remarked. "Little girls should do little girl things and leave these rough-and-tumble sports to the boys."

Just under some grubby picture of Coach Sharp holdin' a football and grinnin' from ear-to-ear, Mama'd drawn what I can only s'pose is a mule's ass, complete with toothy grin and wide derriere. Beside that she wrote, *I've never been prouder to be your Mama than I was on that day.*

It's funny; she never said so at the time. Or maybe she did, and I didn't hear it between all my bellyachin' after stormin' home from the field. Then again, maybe it had somethin' to do with me tearin' that jersey she'd made into teensy little bits, figurin' it was the closest thing to victory confetti I was ever liable to see. Maybe it was all those things and more... but here she was, sayin' it now, from worlds away. She weren't done though.

I grab up the postcard that hid my clippin' and give the hill-climbin' girl on the front a good gander before flippin' to the back. There, Mama tells me, *Girls ain't gotta be prim and fancy no more than boys gotta shoot guns and chew tobacco. To be happy, a girl's just gotta be true to herself. You make your own path, baby. Let everyone else ask for directions.*

That one goes in my shirt pocket too. I start pullin'

those cards out by the fistful after that and eatin' up every one. Some have baby teeth, or scraps of my ole blue ribbons, or silly little drawin's of mine tucked behind 'em. Some smell like her—like Ivory soap and pie crust—like she held them as close to her chest as I was to mine now. One, about halfway in—a postcard from Maine with a pea-pod lighthouse on the front and a mailbox set in its front yard—even has a bit of flour dust on it. I can see Mama leanin' across her butcher block, halo of white pepperin' her brow, as she scrawls across its back, *Child, life's like a big mailbox stuffed full of invitations. Starts out with birthday parties and proms, then weddings and baby showers. By the time the funerals start rollin' in, I just hope you been to all the parties.* I whip the flour dust off that one and stack it on my fat pile, beamin'. By the time I reach the end of the book, that leanin' heap looks like one of Gramps' triple-decker dill-pickle and Spam sandwiches. And it's near as edible too. As I'm comin' up on the last page, I feel like it's Christmas Day, and I've only got one present left. Half of me just wants to leave it under the tree so that it'll never end. The other half of me's foamin' like a rabid coon. As usual, the coon wins.

I slide out that final card, but I don't recognize it. Somethin' slips from behind as I read *Lafayette* in big, curly-Q letters bridged right over the top of the cardstock. I set my mystery scrap to the side while noticin' that Mama's taped a picture over the top of whatever borin' business the card came printed with. The photo's old and faded at the edges, but I can tell our farmhouse anywhere—

the long, leanin' porch tangled in wisteria, the half-slung shades lit up like lazy eyes. It makes a thud bloom in my chest and beats my insides warm. I even notch up another degree when I see a young Mama standin' on the porch, beamin' and holdin' a swaddled baby in her arms. Photo's too ole for it to be Pete or Wyatt. It's gotta be me. A smile tugs my mouth up as I run my thumb soft over Mama's face and then see what she's got to tell me.

I must'a read that card a thousand times. Maybe a thousand-and-one. *I didn't want no babies,* it said. *I never had any use for them. But here God give me one, and every time I looked at you and felt the warm weight of that little Olive lain down on my chest, I couldn't imagine that my heart'd go on beatin' without it.*

I didn't think I had any tears left in me. I was wrong. But then again, I was wrong about damn near everythin'. As I cram that last card in my chest pocket, the seam splits, but I don't care. I take up Mama's final secret scrap and unfold and unfold until I've got two big sheets of faded confusion facin' me. The first is printed on fancy parchment paper that looks like it got rolled around in clay-dirt and then left to dry in the sun. It's got long, pretty letters scrawled across it, but the first thing I see is two baby feet stamped square in the middle. Then I see my full name—Olive June Aber... but wait. It don't say Abernathy. It says Barton. Mama's maiden name. And under that, it lists Mama as my mama and Fr. Michael Reid under father. I hold that birth certificate in my hand and just stare. And stare. And then I stare some more. I don't see my hands tremblin'. I don't see the rain muddyin' up that fancy clay-dried paper. I don't see none of that. I just fix on that name—Fr. Michael Reid—and I hold my breath, waitin' for it to change to James Abernathy. But it don't. It starts to wilt. It even runs a little bit. But the name don't change. I think I might hold onto that paper forever, just starin' it down, but a homeless feller comes rumblin' down the alley with his shoppin' cart and spooks me into breakin' my gaze. He glances at me as he passes. I see somethin' like sad in his eyes, but it ain't sad on his account, it's sad on mine—like he thinks I probably got it worse than he does. And maybe he's right. I don't know anymore. I don't even know my own name no more. But once his rickety-racket dies down, I lay that paper off to the side and pick up the second. I don't lay it on my postcards. I don't want it touchin' those.

I feel a bit of my own self floodin' back to me when I see Mama's handwritin' coverin' that second paper from edge to edge and front to back. *Dear Baby Olive*, it reads. *I'm writing you this on your birthday. Two days after I turned sixteen. I couldn't resist naming you Olive—teeny little thing that you are. I hope you don't hate me for it. I couldn't bear if you hated me, since I never loved a thing more than I do you. I never thought I could love this much. I never thought I could love someone I just met. But here I am, throwing everything away because my heart tells me to. I was supposed to give you up. I promised to give you up. They said that if I just kept quiet and gave you up, it was best for everyone. But I can't do it, Olive. I just can't do it. They set you on my chest, right on top of my heart, and I knew right then and there that I couldn't do it. I couldn't let you go—ever. I knew that I was going to have to make them all hate me, just so that I could love you.*

Even your Grandma and Grandpa wanted me to keep quiet at first. They didn't want to hear that Father Reid kept me after choir practice. They didn't want to know that he said I was doing "God's will" as he ran his hands up my skirt. They didn't want to see his cross swinging at my bare chest like a guillotine. No one wanted to hear none of that, much less that it put a baby in my belly. Not even my best friend. I told Ida first. After all, she's been lead solo in that choir since we were knee-high, and she knows Father Reid as well as anyone. But when I told her, she just shushed me. Olive—she put her hand right over my mouth, right when I told her how his breath smelled of sacrament wine and stale bread. I could see it in her eyes then. I knew. He done it to her too. But she kept her tongue. She knew what would happen if she tattled.

So I was gonna keep quiet. I really was. I was gonna give you up—quiet in the night—just pass you off for some good folks to raise. A baby with no father. No one would ask questions. No crying in the night. No hushed talk around town. Clean as a whistle.

But then you came. You came with your one little buckwheat curl right on top of your perfect head, that soft head that smelled like home. You twisted your tiny hand around my thumb. You looked in my eyes and my heart was done. And I knew I had to protect you. I had to pro-tect you from all those Father Reids and Ida Mae Blevins' who hush up good little girls and hide dirty secrets be-tween the church pews.

So, I spilled the beans all over this hospital. I yelled it loud enough to wake people up down in the morgue. I said what he did to me. I said how it hurt, and how I bled, and how I felt something drain out of me that was even more precious than blood. I got every eye on me, knowing that they'd never take you from me then.

Now here we are—you and me—alone in this cold hos-pital room with nurses and doctors traipsing by every now and again, and glaring inside at the blasphemous pair of us. I know I've made a mess of things. I know I have. I know that people around town are going to say my name like a curse word from this day on and spit at me when I cross the street. I know the church is going to call me a liar, because it's easier for everybody. And who'll people believe? Some teenaged hussy, or a man of God with roots so deep in this town that they probably tangle all the way down to Hades?

And I'll probably lose Jim. How could he love someone so broken? How could he make a life with pieces of what could've been a woman?

I may be all the things that people are whispering about me. I may be a filthy, disgusting, God-defying girl with no morals and no sense. But I don't care what I am anymore, so long as I'm your Mama.

At the close, she put one of her silly little hearts, the

same ones she's been drawin' on my lunch sacks and birthday cards for all my years. I get to gatherin' those little hearts up in my head—tryin' to string 'em together and make sense of things. But it don't work. Then I just go numb and start pluggin' cards back in my scrapbook, gentle as can be—each one with the address side out so that all her little messages show. I reread each one as they find their way inside, maybe tryin' to untangle all the yarns of my lifetime, but it don't do no good. I can't feel nothin' other than the cold of that New York rain settlin' in my bones. I sit for a long spell, just seepin' in it. I let time tick by on its own accord. I listen to the street chatter echo down the alleyway and mix in with the drip of dyin' rain. But somewhere in there, I start hearin' Mama hummin' to the drippity-drop of bathwater slidin' off my spine. I start feelin' her warm hands rubbin' circles in my back. I start smellin' them Ivory soap bubbles bloomin' from the faucet water and inchin' up to tickle my nose. Then I hear Papa rumblin' down the hall, talkin' sweet of Mama's singin' and of his baby girl, who's turnin' into a tiny pink prune in the bathtub. I find myself smilin' a little smile. I find myself feelin' a little more like Olive Abernathy.

The clouds peel back, and a little peep of sun touches down in that alleyway. It ain't much, but it's enough to set me to rights and get my attention. I start stuffin' the last few cards into my scrapbook and find my birth certificate still cupped on my free knee. I read that name again—Fr. Michael Reid—and I see red. I rock back on my haunches and get to my feet. There's a sting of soreness in my bones from lazin' so long, but I shake it off and stomp out of that dark alleyway feelin' ready to howl at the heavens until it brings a storm down on Lafeyette. Out on the sidewalk, the folks are so thick that I near gotta wait for a traffic signal before I can cut in. I set my nose on the skyline and start searchin' for somethin', anythin' familiar. If I can make my way through the Louisiana bayou in the thick of night with nothin' but my wits to guide me, I can find Henry in this rat-nest of a city.

Fired up as I was, there's a few things I didn't account for: 1) people... *so* many people, 2) borin' ole buildin's and rivers of grey road that all look the same, and 3) a powerful hunger growin' in my gut and eatin' up my energy with every thud of my sneaker on the pavement.

I must'a walked ten country miles that day, and I kept seein' Mama's eyes in the faces of strangers—in soft little girls cringin' under the thumbs of ole men, in pepper-haired ladies peepin' up from their rosary beads, and in young, sad-eyed women carryin' heavy loads and a look about them that said they were scared to let go of yesterday.

At first, that seems every kind of peculiar, but after muddlin' all that strangeness while the hazy sun inches from one end of the sky to the other, it doesn't seem so strange after all. I ain't really sure I knew Mama until I read that letter of hers. And around dusk, when my soles are worn-down to the heel bone and I feel like I've officially walked from one end of that God-awful city to the other, a lady with tangled buckwheat hair catches my eye. She's lain out by the streetside, cradlin' an infant baby and pokin' spare bits of food in its mouth. She's dreadful thin, and I can see her lips quiverin' as the last of a soggy rye roll vanishes in her child's mouth. I can see her growin' weak to make that little thing strong. And it's there that I see Mama most of all.

Come sundown, I'm right tired of bein' a city mouse and no further along than when I started. The night's closin' in, and the people are thinnin' out, and I'm startin' to spook at shadows glancin' past the lemon moon. I get to thinkin' serious about what my tombstone oughta say and if Henry'd wear his papa's same suit to the funeral. But then I see it—a mile-high sign as bedazzled as one of Mee-maw's denim jackets—that reads *Meeks' Jewel Emporium*. It's CeCe's papa's shop—the same one where I got stuck up in the air vent and spent last night. I ain't sure why, but I snake on back to the alleyway. Maybe because it's the only thing in this whole loud, miserable city that's familiar to me. Maybe it's somethin' else. Maybe that obnoxious neon sign was a beamin' beacon put there just for me, 'cuz right when I round the corner, I see Henry. And he sees me too.

Good gravy, I didn't know that boy could run so fast. Or maybe me runnin' off the rails right at him made him look like he was goin' faster. All I know is, when we hit, I think we might'a created a black hole or somethin'. It near knocks the wind outta me, and it must'a him too 'cuz I could barely make out his gushin' about how CeCe'd bailed out, and fessed up, and told him where they'd left me. He says he'd shimmied his little ass way up into that vent, callin' my name 'til he couldn't wail no more. He said he'd checked in the dumpster, and in the corner coffee shop, and even peeked down in the sewer grates, lookin' for any sign of his "Little Olive," like I might'a rolled right down there and got myself stuck somehow.

And me, I am so damn happy, I can't wrangle a word to save my life. But once Henry simmers down and my gutted heart gets itself settled, the words come easy and clear... like they was the realest ones I ever said in all my livin' life. "Henry, I wanna go home."

CHAPTER TWELVE

There's exactly 1,417 miles separatin' New York City from Lafayette, Louisiana. I can tell ya that for a fact 'cuz I counted every one of 'em. Miles 1,417 to 1,023 I spent watchin' the grey skies of New York fade to Pennsylvania's cornflower blue from the lap of a cushy Greyhound bus seat. Thanks to CeCe's guilty conscience and her Papa's fat pocketbook, me and Henry got us a one-way ticket home. So, as them two Meeks' were mendin' fences, I was speedin' towards the whitewashed one that hugged my Louisiana farmhouse. Sittin' there next to Henry on that seat that smelled of a thousand different lives, I felt mine was forever changed, but all at once the same. Henry said I'd gone back to bein' my "loud, fierce Abernathy self," but somethin' about that self was different. Maybe I was fiercer now. Henry said I was definitely louder.

"I figure I'll be quiet sometimes," I tells him. "Maybe just for Mama and God on church Sundays 'cuz I don't want folks whisperin' their prayers to go unheard." Then I wink.

Henry ain't much for my winks. He says they "mean mischief," but this time, he winks back. I can see his eye stick a bit though because he ain't full-on with bein' cheeky just yet. Once I told him all about the scrapbook messages, and about my birth certificate, and about Mama's long-winded letter of givin' birth to a little bastard me, he couldn't seem to shake the sad from his face. It just hung there, all through New York, and now it's draggin' through Pennsylvania and Virginia too.

Miles 1,022 to 654 see us right down through Tennessee's tangles, past heavy-headed willows and red oaks scrapin' at the waterline. I watch little eaglets light on the wing ridin' in their mommas' tailwind just past Henry's window as I tell him about how Father Reid done treated my mama like a ragdoll and made a mess of her. I tell him how his momma and my mama was the best of friends back in the day and how Henry's momma kept quiet like folks said she oughta when Father Reid made a gutted doll of her too.

"It's okay," I says. "My mama was gonna keep her tongue too." Then, since I know Mama backwards and frontwards now, I add in, "I don't think she hated on your momma for doin' it. I think she understood. She was just disappointed is all."

This settles Henry in his deep blueberry seat. But he's still wearin' his ole-man frowny lines and suspenders stretched to saggin', so he looks a little bit like a dead fella layin' in his coffin as he melts back into the velveteen. "I always felt bad for your mama—knowin' what happened. And I always felt like knowin' without her knowin' I knew was sourin' me. Keepin' that dirty little secret tucked up under my tongue probably tasted just about as bad as my momma keepin' hers." His eyes get dark just then. I can tell he's thinkin' on her—seein' his momma like I saw my mama with that cold cross swingin' up on her, and her with no way to stop it. "I wish she'd said somethin'," he whispers. "I wish she'd told too."

I say, "Me too," and keep on starin' out the window. One of them eaglets got left behind and is strugglin' to catch up to its family. It's still got that soft whisper-fuzz like dandelion peeps framin' its face. I wonder if it's still too young to fly. I wonder if its holdin' onto that fuzz outta comfort. Maybe outta fear? After all, once that baby fuzz is gone, the whole big world's gonna open up and maybe swallow it whole.

"Ya know," I says, "maybe your momma had it right to just let go and get on with it, 'cuz I think some part'a my mama never moved on from that day. I think some part'a that sixteen-year-ole girl's still stuck up in our farmhouse, listenin' to ole-timey records and radio shows, and dreamin' about a time when the world weren't so dark."

I just get a "maybe" back, but it's one of those *maybes* Papa gives when I ask him for a dirt bike for the zillionth time. He's just sayin' it to appease me. Ain't no truth to it. I see then that Henry's eyes are still dark, and when I press them with mine, he tells me, "Things like that just don't go away, Olive. And there's a lot worse things folks do to quiet their demons than listenin' to Bing Crosby every time it rains."

I chew on that a bit. I listen to "Pennies from Heaven" playin' on repeat in my head. I heard it so many times, I know the lyrics by heart. It ain't a bad song. It kinda grows on a body. But I ain't about to let on that I think so. Instead, I watch miles 653 to 489 glide by on the cool spill of the mighty Mississippi River. Meantime, Henry gets his eyes cleared up and stops murderin' Father Reid a million times over in his head. When he turns and pokes my arm chub, he don't look so much homicidal as suicidal, and I reason that I like him better the first way. "I'm real sorry about your Papa," he sputters. He's knottin' his hands and glancin' here and there about the cab. We picked a seat in the way back, so he fixes on the Emergency Exit sign likes it's news to him and does a banner job of not lookin' me in the eye.

But I thought this one out as clear as a bell while I was poundin' down that New York City pavement in the Big Rotten Apple. So I smile big and say back, "Ain't nothin' to be sorry about. I got my Papa, and he's a good Papa. He raised me up strong, and he raised me up right, and he wouldn't never harm one hair on my fool head no matter how much I backtalk him, or snigger at church, or leave the fridge door open and send half his paycheck to the power company."

Henry ain't got nothin' to say to that. Every now and again, I shock him good, and dammit if that ain't one of the great pleasures in life—just to see him lookin' me over like a shootin' star with his little wishin'-well eyes. I smile bigger. I figure I'm on a roll, so I rails on, "Blood is blood, but I can tell ya true that I remember the very first time Papa showed me how to shoot a whiskey bottle to bits from a zillion miles away. Dammit if I didn't think he could do magic. Twelve years, 109 bottles, and four Daddy-daughter dances later, I knew he could. And that's as good as blood to me."

Henry says, "Damn straight!" and sass-wags his head good enough to shake off any little angels sittin' on his shoulder. I make a quick check only to find my shoulder devil missin' and reason I musta left him on CeCe's bus. I guess he felt at home with all them misfit kids who was as good as blood to one another. Now that whole lot is bustin' their pickle-shaped bus through all the square-shaped houses fulla bad folks who try to pin 'em in. I hope he's yuckin' it up with those kids—hootin' and hollerin' and fillin' that whole bus up with enough noise to keep it warm as it cuts through the cold of the wild blue yonder. I tell Henry so, and he agrees. He's still chewin' on that cus though, so he flashes mischievous eyes out the seat-side window and hoots us up some heat. "Hot damn! Look, Olive—*Welcome to Lousiana!*"

Them last 281 miles are the worst. Or maybe they're the best. I can't say for sure. We play Slug Bug 'til my arm gets numb and watch sputterin' beetles of every color in the rainbow chase the sugar-maple shadows that tickle the asphalt. We talk about drownin' ourselves in frosted malts and two-fist cheeseburgers from Mott's Diner until our buttons burst. We count scissor-tailed flycatchers scoopin' up the wind until one of 'em poops midair and it ain't fun no more. By the time we get ourselves down to the 100-mile mark, I can't think straight about nothin' but rollin' up on that farmhouse off Indian River Highway—smack dab in the middle of nowhere and everywhere I wanna be. But once we get there, nothin' about that place looks the same anymore. Papa's fat tomatoes— them seedy, God-awful tart creations that it seemed a sin to call a fruit—now they hang off the driveway vines like ruby-red jewels. Pete and Wyatt's hand-me-down trikes are propped up beside the Abernathy mailbox like kingpins. And it seems Papa painted that ole box a warm Harlow gold while I was away because it looks somethin' like a shrine now…a shrine fit for simple, good folks who do the best they can with what they have and don't have no need for finery.

But damn, it looks fine anyway—every bit of it. I'd swear that crooked ole porch arches up into a smile as I come tootlin' down the drive, and when Mama pops out the screen door and gets eyes on me, I'm sure of it.

Henry just stands back and lets me run to her. And I run like I never done before. Faster than in track. Faster than to catch a hobo-in' train. Probably faster than Superwoman. And she comes at me the same way so that we hit somewhere around the middle. We hit so hard that I think we might mush into one person. I'm already sobbin' from the joy of it all as I sputter out, "I read your letter from my scrapbook."

"You read my letter?" comes back to me, streaked in tears.

I tell her, "I did," just then spyin' Papa watchin' us two from the front porch. He's gleamin', absolutely gleamin', lookin' us over and holdin' Pete and Wyatt back from bum-rushin' the pair of us.

I push away from Mama in that second, but I keep hold of her by the forearms. Her hair's a mess, and I can see it hasn't been tended to for ages. She's lookin' me over with bloodshot eyes, muddied with worry and wonder. "I did, Mama," I says. "And I ain't ashamed of what you done—not one little bit. And you shouldn't be either. You don't need to hide. You don't need to hold your tongue on my account."

Then I look out over that beautiful farm with bayou warmin' all its edges and that beautiful family standin' on the porch, just over Mama's shoulder. I take her eye again and smile. "After all, Mama, we ain't quiet little girls. We're Abernathy women. We were born to roar."

ABOUT THE AUTHOR

K. (Kristine) Kibbee is a Pacific Northwestern writer with rain on her Duck boots and stars in her eyes. A storyteller from the womb, Kristine's inescapable passion for creative writing led her to the doors of Washington State University, where she studied in the Professional Writing program. Kristine, followed her scholarly pursuit of the written word by publishing works in *The Vancougar, The Salal Review Literary Review, Just Frenchies* magazine, and *S/Tick Literary Review*. She is presently a regular columnist for *Terrier Group* magazine.

Kristine's novella, *The Mischievous Misadventures of Dewey the Daring*, was her first and only self-published release, and is still currently available online. Since then, she's had several mainstream books published, including the YA *Forests of the Fae* trilogy, three chapter books in the *Theodore and the Enchanted Bookstore* series, and the re-tooled and released, *Whole in the Clouds*.

Kristine regularly engages on a variety of social media platforms and can be followed:

On Twitter @K_Kibbee

On Facebook @ facebook.com/KKibbeewrites

ACKNOWLEDGEMENTS

It's with equal parts pleasure and pain that I confess I needed help... so much help ... to bring this book into being. I cannot in good faith press forth with autographing a single copy or a potato sack full (hey, it could happen!) before acknowledging that both of my publishing partners: Michael Conant and Janice Bini, were instrumental in producing the tale that lays before you. Likewise, my most magnanimous appreciation goes out to editor Matthew Bucemi, whose ability to see my works in an entirely new light proved transformative for Olive and her journey.

But perhaps most of all, I wish to acknowledge the contributions of fellow author and dear friend, Skip Schmidt. A literary genius in his own right, Skip showered me with encouragement, support, and even some late-night beta reading and editing sessions that no sane person would've signed on for. My dear Mr. Schmidt, these characters are just as much yours as mine.

CREDITS

This book is a work of art produced by
Incorgnito Publishing Press.

Matthew Bucemi
Editor

K. Kibbee
Author

Star Foos
Designer

Janice Bini
Chief Reader

Robert Cooper
Proof Editor

Michael Conant
Publisher

Daria Lacy
Graphic Production

September 2020
Incorgnito Publishing Press